This is a work of fiction. Names, characters, places, and incidents either are the product of the author's imagination or are used fictitiously, and any resemblance to actual persons, living or dead, business establishments, events, or locales are entirely coincidental.

Wahida Clark Presents Publishing
60 Evergreen Place
Suite 904A
East Orange, New Jersey 07018
973-678-9982
www.wclarkpublishing.com

DISCARD

Library of Congress Cataloging-In-Publication Data:
Game of Gwop/ by Trae Macklin
ISBN 13-digit   978-1936649-12-9 (paper)
ISBN 10-digit   1936649128 (paper)
ISBN 978-1-936649-54-9 (e-book)
LCCN 2014916391

Fiction- 2. Newark, NJ- 3. Drug Trafficking- 4. African American-Fiction- 5. Urban Fiction   6.thug life
Cover design and layout by Nuance Art, LLC
 Book design by Nuance Art, LLC –
 NuanceArt@aCreativeNuance.com
Edited by Linda Wilson
Proofreader Rosalind Hamilton
Printed in USA

TRAE MACKLIN

GAME OF GWOP

A Novel by

Trae Macklin

TRAE MACKLIN

CHAPTER 1
- The Lick -

"Yo Crook, you make a pretty ass bitch!"
Charisma cracked as she turned in the passenger seat and passed him the blunt. Even in the dark, she could see the vexation in his evil ass eyes, but she didn't care because they were family. They all were family. Besides, she had a reason to clown with him—he was dressed like a woman.

"Ay yo, 'Riz, watch your fuckin' mouth!" Crook growled, inhaling the blunt.

"Chill, Crook, she ain't lyin'. Ay yo, after this, leave the wig on, ai'ight?" GQ laughed.

Crook lunged across Shamar, who sat in the middle, and tried to swing on GQ. He easily weaved the wild blow.

"Yo Crook, get the fuck off me!" Shamar shouldered Crook hard. "You see me loading this shit!"

Shamar squinted an eye as smoke rose from his Newport while he loaded the Mac-11 extended clip with hollow point explosions.

"I don't know what you laughin' at, G, wit' yo' pretty self. You sure you ain't a bitch?" Charisma cracked.

GQ gave her the finger. He was already a light-skinned, green eyed, curly headed nigguh. Now with the makeup, his eyebrows arched, a black, bone-straight wig, and all his facial hair shaved, he looked like a girl.

5

All three of them did. Crook, with his wide 5-feet 5-inches tall frame squeezed into some black, stilettos and coochie cutter shorts. Shamar was brown-skinned and 5-feet 10-inches tall, wearing a red miniskirt with butt pads. GQ looked like a broke ass Beyoncé. The only dude not dressed as a woman was Black, the driver. There was no way he would pass as a female. He was too ugly, looking like a shiny, ashy-lipped Biggie Smalls.

"Yo 'Riz, kill the jokes. Black, turn the music down," Shamar ordered, and the ruckus in the car quieted down.

Shamar may've been the youngest at twenty-four, but his brains and cold heart made him stand out as the most vicious of these cold-blooded killers.

"Run it down to us again, 'Riz," he said.

"The shit is sweet, yo. The club keeps like at least fifty stacks of singles in the back room, plus work. It's always a nigguh on the door and one inside the room with the money," she explained.

"And you said they both strapped, right?" GQ questioned, now deadly serious.

She nodded.

"No doubt, but the pussy . . ." She chuckled. "I don't know what Infinite was thinkin', but the one at the door, Big Mike, nigguh look like the Incredible Hulk. But he just come home from doin' four years as a nigguh's bitch on the yard!"

"Yeah, but that don't mean his gun don't bust just 'cause he a bitch."

"You a bitch and your gun bust," Crook reminded her, getting his crack back from earlier.

"And you suck my bitch, nigguh. Anyway, trust me
. . . he won't bust."

"And we good on getting the door open?" Shamar
questioned.

"No doubt. I'm the one who takes the money from
the bar to the back," she replied.

"Then let's eat!" Black barked with a cold chuckle.

"Nigguh, shut the fuck up!" Crook spat. "You just
the fuckin' driver."

"Naw, son. Fuck wit' me," Black shot back.

The two of them eye-boxed through the rearview
mirror. The tension spread like a mist through the
already tense air.

"Yo, y'all nigguhs let that shit go. We 'bout to
come up!" GQ cracked, trying to lighten the mood.

"Ay, Crook," Charisma said.

"What?"

"How much for a lap dance?"

He mushed her in the back of the head.

∞

When they got to the club, Charisma, Crook, GQ
and Shamar got out. Black pulled off like he was
leaving, but parked around back, as they had planned.

Charisma strutted across the parking lot with the
little suitcase on wheels. As soon as nigguhs saw her
face, every eyeball was hers. She was definitely worth
the look, standing 5-feet 10-inches tall in heels, bow
legged, and thick-thighed, ass plump and juicy—but not
too big. And pert titties that needed no bra. She seemed
to have permanent dimples, even when she wasn't
smiling. With her butter-smooth complexion, gray eyes,
and short, sassy cut, she looked like a young Lisa Raye.

"Goddamn, Charisma! Whateva the price, I'm buying," the bouncer at the door commented, looking her up and down lustfully.

"Nigguh, don't let your wife hear you say that." She chuckled, referring to his wedding ring.

"You worth the risk, ma."

The girl at the window sucked her teeth, hating. "You got your tip out?" she sassed, hand out and rolling her eyes.

"Don't I always?" Charisma shot back, dropping a fifty in her hand.

She had been working at the strip club for a month, just so her team could get the inside scoop. Now that they had it, it was on.

"And who is them?" the girl asked, looking the three 'girls' up and down, tone dripping with contempt.

"This fam'. They came to make a few dollars," Charisma answered, smirking at the term, "few dollars."

In the dark, the girl couldn't really see their faces, but their outfits screamed "stripper trash!" The three of them each gave the girl fifty dollars then followed Charisma inside.

As they passed the bouncer, he patted Crook on his ass.

"Oh, and it's soft, too." The bouncer winked.

Crook tottered on his high heels and started to double back, but GQ pushed him inside.

"Yo chill! He think you a bitch. So, good!" GQ hoarse whispered.

As they walked in, the butt pads had all three nigguhs looking like they had phat asses. They eyed all the ballers inside, jewels dripping and looking like new money.

"Goddamn, yo! Look at the nigguhs! We should rob the whole club!" Crook exclaimed.

"Stay focused," Shamar told him, looking straight ahead.

They entered the dressing room, then waited for two chicks to leave, while they gathered around Charisma's locker. As soon as the two chicks left, Charisma opened her suitcase and handed out two Mac-11's and two Techs.

"I don't want the Tech," GQ protested.

"Why?" she asked.

"They jam."

"Not these, yo. I oiled 'em," Shamar assured him.

"Then you take it," GQ reasoned.

Shamar gave him the Mac and took the Tech. GQ kissed it with a chuckle.

"Ai'ight, I'm headed to the bar. Wait here. When you see me come back through, it's on!" Charisma explained, then walked out.

The three men/girls gathered around the door, peeping out periodically. GQ took a step and damn near twisted his ankle on the stiletto. He kicked them off with disgust.

"Man, I can't walk in these shits! We shoulda brought sneakers!" he said.

"This is how I used to rob nigguhs on the slave ship," Crook joked.

GQ and Shamar cracked up.

Shamar peeped out the door. "Yo, it's a stripper comin'!" he announced.

They all put their guns behind their backs. The stripper walked in, looking thick and delicious, red-boned and juicy titties bouncing.

"Who y'all?" she asked, eyeing her competition.

None of them spoke, scared to give themselves away.

"Hello! Is you bitches deaf!" she sassed, neck rolling and hand on her hip.

"We new," GQ replied, voice squeaky and artificially high-pitched.

Shamar had to stifle a snicker.

She narrowed her eyes and focused on GQ's too-prominent Adam's apple.

"Wait . . . you ain't no girl," she huffed, then quickly turned on her heels and started for the door.

She didn't take another step.

Shamar caught her with a vicious left hook that broke her jaw and dropped her to the floor, unconscious.

Charisma stuck her head in the door. "What the fuck y'all waitin'—" she started to say, then looked down and saw the stripper sprawled out. "Oh, come on before that dumb bitch wake up."

They dipped out of the dressing room and followed Charisma down an L-shaped hallway. Charisma stopped before the bend and held up her finger. Her Mac-11 was tucked under the large canvas sack full of money that she was carrying. Shamar nodded. She stepped around the corner and plastered her face with a false, seductive smile for the guard.

"Hey, Teddy. How you, baby?" she asked, getting on her tippy toes to kiss his cheek.

"Better now," he answered, eyeing her lustfully.

"Well, I'll be better when I get this inside. Too much money makes me nervous." She giggled.

"I know that's right," he replied, giving the special knock. Three knocks on the door were heard from the inside, and he replied with two more. As soon as the door opened, Charisma kicked the guard in the nuts with all her might, while sliding the Mac from under the bag.

"Surprise!" she bellowed, taking aim and letting loose.

As soon as they heard the door open, Shamar, Crook, and GQ burst around the corner, guns blazing. Whether the guard would have shot was irrelevant, because he never had a chance to. Shamar *Boc! Boc! Boc'd!* him in the chest and face, sending blood flying one way, but his brains another. His body slumped and slid down the wall.

Charisma took cover on the side of the door, because automatic rounds were exploding out the door in rapid-fire bursts. Instead of one dude, two were inside.

"It's coming from the money room!"

They all heard the cackle of voices coming around the bend. Shamar doubled back and went to the corner of the bend and saw four dudes, guns in hand. He pointed the Tech around the corner without looking and let loose.

Boc! Boc! Boc! Boc!

"Oh fuck!

"Assrrggh!"

He peeped around the corner. He had hit two, while the other two back peddled, letting off shots to provide cover.

"Make it happen!" he barked at his team, snatching the wig off his head and adding, "I can't keep them off all night!"

Thinking quickly, Crook and GQ grabbed the guard's dead body under each arm and struggled to stand him up against the wall. With their adrenaline pumping and shots ricocheting, they got the body up quickly. They used the dead man as a shield, holding him up in the doorway, while Charisma aimed over his shoulder and sprayed the two gunners like roaches.

"Move, yo, move!" she barked, squeezing past the body and entering the room.

One dude wasn't dead. He tried to raise his gun but caught two in his forehead that emptied his brains into a red halo around his head.

"Come on!" GQ barked, stuffing money in the bags lying out on the table.

The table was stacked with piles of rubber-banded one dollar bills. Charisma and GQ stuffed their pockets with as many as they could, while Crook grabbed a duffle bag lying next to one of the dead men. He opened it and saw bricks of cocaine inside.

"Bingo! Jackpot!" he cracked.

Crook put the duffle bag over his shoulder and looked at Charisma and GQ gathering money.

"Fuck that short ass shit! Let's go!"

They both got one last stuff, maybe two, inside their pockets, then headed out behind Crook. Shamar was still holding them down at the bend. He stood from his half crouched position and followed them out.

Crook was first to exit the back door, only to find Black using the driver door for cover as he sprayed rounds at several dudes on the other end of the building. Having heard the gunfire, they figured the stick-up team would have to go out the back, so they hoped to trap them off. But what they found was Black and an AK-47 with diarrhea bbbrrapppping out round after round. He had dropped two men and had the rest pinned behind cars and the edge of the building.

For a precious few seconds, Crook and Black were the only two of the team outside. Crook had been waiting for such an opportunity, so he didn't plan to lose it. He raised his gun just as Black turned to look at him. The look on his face read like he always expected it.

"Bitch ass nigguh," Crook spat.

"Fuck you!" Black retorted gruffly.

Then Crook pulled the trigger and blew the whole left side of Black's face out of the right side, sending his brains skittering in red streaks across the top of the car. Just as Black's body slumped, Charisma, followed by GQ and Shamar came barreling out of the door, sending shots back in the building.

Everything had happened so fast, but in Crook's mind, shit was slow motion. "They got Black!" he burbled, as the team looked at Black's body twitching on the ground.

There was no time to mourn as the barrage of gunfire shattered the windshield. GQ and Shamar busted back. Charisma threw the duffle bags in the car with one hand, firing with the other, and then jumped into the passenger seat. Crook snatched Black's body out of the driver's door and got behind the wheel.

"Come on!" he barked.

Shamar wanted to grab Black's body, but the intensity of the shots were exploding all around.

"Fuck! I'm hit!" GQ agonized from the gunshot tearing through his shoulder. His whole left arm went numb, and he dropped his gun, sending it clanging to the pavement.

"I got you, fam'!" Shamar vowed, pushing him into the backseat and busting shots wildly at the same time.

"Go nigguh! Drive!" Charisma yelled, aiming her Mac out of the broken windshield and spraying shots in a sweeping motion, clearing a path.

Crook mashed on the gas and barreled through. Charisma's shots found home in two nigguhs' flesh, lifting one off his feet and spinning the other's body into a fatal oblivion. Crook drove like the expert car thief he was, hopping the curb and screeching off down the street, the sound of gunfire fading in the background.

"Yeah! Hell yeah! We did it!" Crook said with venomous adrenaline.

The rest of the team was happy and sad. Happy because the lick was a success, but sad because it had cost them Black.

"Fuck yeah!" Crook exclaimed.

The whole time Charisma was looking at him out the corner of her eye . . .

CHAPTER 2
- Justice Must Be Served -

Lompoc, California
Maximum Security Federal Penitentiary

Finesse stepped inside the law library and walked around until he spotted his man. He walked with the confidence of a man who was at home in the jungle called the penitentiary, but with the bounce of a man who knew it would be over soon. He had only been down three years on a Federal life sentence, and he still "smelled like the streets," as convicts liked to say about people just getting started on their sentence. If it wasn't for the khakis, he looked like the streets, too. He kept the fresh shape-up with ice pick sideburns and 360-degree-waves. His Egyptian brown skin and thick eyebrows made him hard to forget when it came to the ladies, who kept his letter count up and account on swoll. He was 5-feet 10-inches tall and on the slim side, even though his regular routine of push-ups and dips were giving him a nice prison physique.

Finesse walked across the room toward the tables and typewriters, which were partitioned with glass partials and doors. Inside, Gray Melvin was banging away at a typewriter.

"What up, unc?" Finesse greeted as he walked in and shook Melvin's hand. Then he propped himself up on the corner of the table.

"Ain't nothin', youngblood. Just gettin' my Johnny Cochran on." Melvin chuckled.

They called him Gray Melvin because he had all gray hair, gray eyebrows, and even flecks of gray in his eyelashes. He was only forty-eight and had been down fifteen years, but he had been born with gray hair.

"Yeah, well, Johnny Cochran should be gettin' at you! I got my letter back from the courts," Finesse exclaimed happily, handing him the official-looking envelope.

Melvin took it, extracted the letter, and then read it. As he read, the concentrated expression on his face turned into a smile. "That's all right there, youngblood. You won your appeal," Melvin remarked.

"No, unc, you won my appeal! If it wasn't for you, I'd be fucked up!" Finesse replied, shaking his head. "Believe me, that little thousand books of stamps I paid you to do my case ain't shit! The God gonna bless you when I touch, that's my word."

Melvin shook his head. "Youngblood, God has already blessed me. I helped you because you deserved it. Them crackers tried to railroad you. You don't owe me—no, I take that back—you do owe me. You owe me to go out there and make something of your life. You gettin' a second chance, and not to do the same thing that got you in here," he lectured.

Finesse nodded solemnly. "Yo, I hear you, unc. I'm definitely gonna hold it down and stay out them streets. But yo, I just came to thank you and let you know you won't be forgotten."

Finesse gave him dap, then walked out, leaving all of Melvin's good advice behind as well. He respected Melvin too much to tell him all that square shit was for the birds, because the only thing on Finesse's wild, young mind was mo' money, mo' murder!

He walked through the smoke area where a gaggle of inmates were all smoking and discussing the law. Finesse slipped through the smoke like it was a curtain, and on the other side was a dice game. The smell of cigarette smoke turned to weed, and all eyes were focused on the dice at the center of the circle of gamblers.

"Point five!"

"Yo yo. I bet he don't five!"

"Who fadin' me?"

"I'm ridin' with the shooter! Ten books!"

Finesse stepped in ready to place his bet, when he spotted Lil' Uptown in the midst of the circle. "Yo, Up! Up!" Finesse called out, making his way over to him.

Lil' Uptown glanced back, but then turned his attention back to the dice game.

"Yo, Up. What's good? I know you heard me," Finesse remarked with a deceiving smile.

"What up? I'm tryin' to get this paper," Lil' Uptown replied in a tone that sounded like a brush off.

"That's what up, yo. My paper. Let me get those fifty books you owe me," Finesse requested.

"I ain't got it." Lil' Uptown had his hands full of books of stamps.

"What?"

"I said I ain't got it!" He mumbled audibly, "Jersey ass nigguh."

Blah!

Blood flew from Lil' Uptown's mouth as Finesse followed up the vicious left hook with a 1-2 combination. Blood was everywhere, not only from the punch, but also from the fact that Lil' Uptown had a razor in his mouth, so when Finesse hit him, it cut the inside of his jaw and tongue. Convicts rushed to get out of the way of the blood, as Finesse stomped Lil' Uptown comatose.

"Bitch-ass, Harlem-ass nigguh," Finesse growled while he went in Lil' Uptown's pockets, taking all his books of stamps, including the ones in his hands.

"Yo, Finesse, what up? You good, ock?" somebody with a Jersey accent called out.

"I am now." Finesse chuckled as he walked off counting over a hundred books of stamps.

∞

On the next ten minute movement, Finesse headed for the recreation yard, a large area close to the size of a football field. Encircling the yard was a wide track used for jogging or simply walking and talking. In different parts of the yard were different activities, including weights, pull up and dip bars, as well as a handball, tennis, and Bocce ball court, a full and two half basketball courts and even a mini golf course.

As soon as he came out, he heard, "Finesse! Hold up, God!"

He turned and saw his man, Everlast, coming over to him from the shed area where convicts played cards. Everlast was a cock diesel dude and as wide as a door, cut up like a bag of dope. He looked and sounded like Ray Lewis.

When he caught up to Finesse, he gave him dap and a gangsta hug. "Peace, God, how you?" Everlast greeted. "Lap with me."

Finesse and Everlast turned toward the track and began lapping. "Yo, Fin, when the last time you hollered at the God, Infinite?" Everlast questioned.

"Like a week ago. I had to flush my phone. Why? What up?"

"I don't know, God. He wanna know the same thing."

"What you mean?"

Everlast glanced around, then pulled out his flip phone.

"How you get that shit past the metal detectors?" Finesse wanted to know.

"The God move in mysterious ways." Everlast chuckled. "But yo, Inf wanted me to give you this message." He showed Finesse the text. Finesse frowned. It read:

YOU FUCKED UP

Finesse never saw it coming. While he was looking at the phone, Everlast pulled out a long, thin blade. It looked like an ice pick, but it was made of plastic and had been sharpened to a menacing point. Everlast hugged Finesse to him and sank the blade into his stomach several times in lightning quick succession.

"I'm sorry, fam', but justice must be served." Everlast gritted his teeth.

Finesse couldn't speak. He felt paralyzed. The searing pain in his gut seemed to screech through his brain, until everything short circuited and went blank.

When Everlast released him from the deadly embrace, he slumped to the ground. Then Everlast walked off, leaving Finesse for dead . . .

CHAPTER 3
- Cold-Blooded Killer -

"Yo, Tarik, what are you doin'! Tuck the ball into your body! You're carrying it like a loaf of bread!" Infinite scolded his nine-year-old son from the sidelines.

Infinite never missed his son's football practice if he could help it. He loved his son, and he loved Pop Warner football. He furnished the whole team with uniforms and the best equipment. To the other parents, he was just a good father. They just didn't know he was a cold-blooded killer who ran a heroin operation and controlled major parts of Newark.

Even looking at him, you didn't see it. He was barely 5-feet 9-inches tall, chubby and wore designer Cartier frames, not for looks but for need. His receding hairline made him rock a baldhead, and he matched it with a full beard that he kept trimmed and close cut.

"Peace," Supreme said as he approached. Supreme was Infinite's right hand man. Short and stocky, he favored Mike Tyson.

"Peace."

"Yo, that's done. It's a wrap."

Infinite looked at him. "What you mean 'a wrap'?"

"I mean it's a wrap, it's done. Everlast served justice."

Infinite pinched the bridge of his nose. "Naw yo, I ain't want him to kill the God. Just chastise him."

"Well, yo God, you gotta be more specific," Supreme shot back defensively. "You said to touch him up."

"Yeah, but that don't mean kill him."

"Since when?" Supreme shot back.

Infinite shook his head and changed the subject. "Any word on where those nigguhs at?" Infinite asked, referring to the guys who robbed his club.

"Naw, yo, but nigguhs on it. It goes without sayin' they probably left town. Question is, where?" Supreme surmised.

Infinite nodded. His phone rang. He looked at the caller-ID.

"Yo, I gotta take this. Stay on it," he instructed.

Supreme nodded and walked away. Infinite answered his phone.

"How you, ma?"

"You tell me," she purred in the sexiest voice he had ever heard, but at times like this, it also sounded like the deadliest.

"Believe me, shit is a little hectic but I got you. I just need a couple more days to get that. I took a major hit," he explained.

"So I heard. But like you said, you took a major hit, not me. You already know: rain, sleet, hail, snow. Are we clear?"

Infinite flexed his jaw muscle and felt his temperature rise. He hated to be dictated to, especially by a woman, but this wasn't your average woman, so he held his tongue.

"Yeah . . . we clear."

"Good. Oh, and Inf . . . I love those new uniforms," she said, then hung up.

He knew what she was trying to say:

1. She was close. Today was the first day the team wore the new uniforms, so she had to be seeing shit in real time.

2. It was an oh-so subtle threat to his family. Infinite commanded a small army, but he knew it was no match for hers. He may have been God, but she was the devil.

Casually, he glanced around and felt a cold sensation creep up his spine, feeling like he was in her cross hairs . . . literally.

∞

It's always the ones that act tough. He had been belligerent during his arrest, cursing the police out.

"Punk ass, pig muthafuckas! Take the cuffs off and you'll see what it is!" he huffed.

But once they got him downtown, booked and charged him with murder, his whole tone changed and his voice hit a Mariah Carey octave.

"Murder! Yo, I ain't fuckin' kill nobody!" he protested.

"Yeah, well, somebody did. And once we run the ballistics on this gun, we'll know, won't we?"

He knew he was fucked. The pistol definitely had bodies on it, just not the bodies they were investigating. But if he waited too long, they might charge him with those bodies, when all they wanted to know was about this body.

Which do you think he chose?

"Yo man . . . the fuck? I ain't had shit to do with this shit!" he huffed.

"Then tell us who did!" Detective Simmons threw back, straddling the chair opposite him, positioned backward.

The dude looked around the small interrogation room and at the other two detectives standing around.

"I don't know, but I'll tell you what I do know, and that's that I ain't do it!"

"Fuck this shit, take this maggot to booking," Simmons retorted, then started to get up.

"Ai'ight, ai'ight, look . . ." he said, shaking his head, not wanting to snitch but seeing no choice. "It was four chicks."

"Chicks?" Simmons echoed incredulously.

"Yeah man, chicks, bitches, whateva! It was four of them. One of them is a stripper called Champagne or Charisma, some shit; she just started working there."

"So you're tellin' me four broads robbed the club? What about the other three? What's their names?" Simmons questioned.

"I don't know. I never seen 'em before. They wasn't too hot, but they had fat asses," he remembered.

"Helluva description. You think if they bent over, you'd recognize 'em?" Simmons quipped sarcastically.

"Man, I'm tellin' you all I know!"

"Yeah, yeah, you're a model fuckin' citizen. You say Champagne?"

He thought for a moment and said, "Naw, it's Charisma."

"You sure?"

"Positive."

Simmons nodded.

"Okay . . . one other thing. What's your name?"

"Man, I already gave you my name," he replied, unable to look Simmons in the eyes.

"Bullshit. You're not fuckin' Dennis Mitchell, that's a fuckin' alias! Now, if you wanna play ball with me, give me your real name, or murder one is—"

"Tyrone Jefferson," he blurted.

Simmons eyed him then, satisfied with his response. He said, "Okay, Ty, you listen—"

An officer stuck his head in the door. "Detective Simmons, can I see you a moment?"

Simmons got up and walked out, holding the door closed behind him. "Talk to me."

"The prints on that Mac-11 came back," the officer informed him.

"And?"

"They belong to a Gregory Quincy aka GQ—mile long rap sheet and all around asshole."

"Trust me, I know already. Put it on the wire. Find 'im."

The officer nodded.

"Done."

Simmons went back and eyed Tyrone.

"Tyrone, you lied to me, you fuckin' maggot! Tell me about GQ!"

CHAPTER 4
- Thug Club -

PHWOKK!

The cork of the Moet came out with a bubbly kiss cascading down the neck of the bottle as GQ hurried to fill all four champagne glasses.

"Yo, fill my shit up. Why the fuck you stop?" Crook gruffed, holding up his three-fourths filled glass.

"'Cause, you ghetto ass nigguh, you ain't 'posed to fill it up," GQ shot back, then swigged straight from the bottle.

Crook snatched the bottle and filled his glass to the rim. "Fuck that bougie shit. We celebrating!" he exclaimed.

Contrary to Supreme's assumption, the team was still in Newark. They were in the Key Club in downtown Newark, a small hole-in-the-wall thug club where the team felt right at home.

"What we gonna do with this coke? We can't put it on bubble around here, 'cause Inf will definitely know it's us then," Charisma surmised.

"Man, fuck Inf!" Shamar spat, downing his champagne. "That nigguh don't know shit."

GQ raised his glass. "To Black."

Everybody raised their glass, except Crook.

"Ay yo, fam', you need to get off that bullshit. At least respect that nigguh's memory," Shamar remarked.

"Whateva, yo," Crook mumbled. "Y'all muhfuckas keep actin' like y'all don't know."

"We don't," Shamar retorted.

Crook and Shamar glared across the table at one another.

"That's only 'cause you don't wanna know," Crook growled.

Seeking to change the subject, Charisma broke in. "I got fam' in Delaware. My cousin, Don Pooh, he been wanting me to come down and get in nigguhs' pockets. What y'all think?"

"Shit, I'm wit' it," GQ replied, giving her dap across the table.

"Fuck that. I say we set up shop right here," Shamar objected.

"Word." Crook nodded, giving Shamar dap.

"Ay yo, Sha, why you on shit like that when you know your brother fuck wit' Inf?" GQ questioned.

"I'm telling you like I tell him, Inf a fuckin' pussy! The only reason the nigguh strong is 'cause he got a crazy connect. Whoeva it is, is lacin' that nigguh. But real talk, if nigguhs go at him hard body, nigguh'll fold. Word up!" Shamar explained with malice.

"Speaking of brah, when you heard from him last?" Crook asked.

"He ain't called in a minute, so he probably in the box." Shamar shrugged.

Crook chuckled.

"Yeah, that's brah. The God go hard. You the soft twin."

Shamar smirked and gave him the finger.

"Yeah, my baby do get it in," Charisma added, looking off like she was remembering the time.

"Ay, ma, you ain't gonna start cryin', are you?" GQ joked.

Charisma threw the Moet cork at him. "Grow your eyebrows back, RuPaul lookin' nigguh." She laughed.

They all laughed, despite the fact that they all still looked like RuPaul because their eyebrows hadn't grown back yet.

A thick ass red bone and her friend walked by. Crook eyed her up and down, then reached out and grabbed her wrist as she walked by.

"Ay yo, ma, come 'ere. Lemme holla at you," he remarked.

She snatched her hand away. "Nigguh, you got me fucked up! Don't put yo' goddamn hands on me again, lil' flea ass nigguh?"

Crook was instantly fuming, and the team's laughter was only making it worse.

"Oh shit, she called you a flea, yo!" GQ laughed.

"Goddamn, she chumped you, Crook. I know you ain't gonna let that go!" Charisma goaded him playfully.

"Crook, you gettin' soft," Shamar added. But before the words were fully out of his mouth, Crook had snatched the pistol out of his pants, aimed and shot the girl in the back.

Boc! Boc!

The club went from hysterics to paralyzed shock. The girl's friend couldn't stop screaming amidst the pandemonium and fleeing patrons. "You killed her! You killed her!" she yelled as she tried to escape.

Without hesitation, Crook turned the gun on her and fired.

Boc! Boc! Boc!

The girl's eyes rolled in the back of her head as the right side of her head exploded and splattered across the dance floor. Her body dropped right next to her equally dead friend, whom Crook walked over to and reloaded his clip.

Boc! Boc! Boc! Boc! Boc!

He fired into her, shot after shot, blowing away chunks of her back, neck, and head.

"Man, what the fuck!" Shamar rushed toward Crook, after having fired the final shots. "Well, I guess we goin' out of town now, you stupid muhfucka!"

CHAPTER 5
- Sex and Strangers on Elevators -

"Chanel."

"Mm-hmm?"

"You got some sexy ass feet."

"I know." She giggled.

"Tell me if this tickles."

Chanel squirmed. "You know it does."

They called her Chanel because the Coco part was obvious. She looked like God had dipped her in chocolate, smooth and unblemished. An ebony goddess, that reminded you of Tika Sumpter on first glance, but on second, Chanel had a look all her own. At 5-feet 8-inches tall with long, shapely legs that gave a mean strut to a Coke bottle figure, she was a show stopper that could break the average nigguh.

But don't let her beauty fool you.

She was known to go so hard—the rumor in the streets was that she used to be a man. Her team was that fierce. Some said she had been a child soldier in the Congo that caught the eyes of a gun and drug smuggler who brought her to America. Others said she was the daughter of a drug lord. No one knew. But the one thing they all knew was—not to fuck with Coco Chanel!

Her right hand partner, Kat, was pedicuring Chanel's feet as she lay back on her super king-sized bed. Kat was a Queen Latifah-sized, Amazon dyke that would and had killed for Chanel many times over. She rocked a baldhead better than some nigguhs, but she resembled Jill Scott.

Chanel lay back, watching CNN on her ninety-inch plasma, remote in one hand and a strawberry in the other, wearing a pair of silk white panties that held Kat's eyes.

"Can I have that?" Kat asked, referring to the strawberry.

Chanel took her eyes off the screen and looked at Kat.

"It's the last one."

"And?" Kat smirked.

Chanel smirked back because she knew where Kat was going.

"It's a little tart anyway," she remarked, throwing the double entendre as she handed it to Kat.

Kat took it, then began to kiss up Chanel's calf, stopping to suck the sweet spots that she knew would make Chanel "ohhh."

As she kissed, licked, and sucked up Chanel's thigh, Chanel cocked her legs open and put them on Kat's shoulders.

"Damn, you got my pussy dripping," Chanel whispered with bated breath.

"Well, come out of these panties, so you can drip on my tongue," Kat urged, gripping the elastic of Chanel's panties and pulling them off.

The sweet aroma of Chanel's juices teased Kat's nose and made her dive face first into her garden. She used the gap between her teeth to drive Chanel crazy, putting her clit in the gap and sucking it teasingly.

"Ohh K-Kaaat," Chanel moaned.

At the same time, Kat used the large strawberry like a dick head, penetrating Chanel over and over with it until the strawberry was coated with her juices. Kat devoured the strawberry, then devoured Chanel. She cocked her legs back and ate her from her pussy to her asshole, the whole time fingering her ass with her thick index finger up to the knuckle.

"Oh fuck, I'm about to cum!" Chanel squealed.

Her passionate cries only drove Kat into a state of frenzy, tonguing her pussy down and fingering her asshole. Chanel grabbed the back of her head and wrapped her legs around her neck, then used the position to flip Kat over onto her back, so that Chanel was now vigorously riding her face.

"Right there, right there—I'm about to cum all over your face," Chanel growled, grinding her hips harder. She threw her head back as the orgasm shot through her, and her cream coated Kat's face, giving her a milk-like mustache. Her body still shivering, Chanel straddled Kat and lay back, spent but satisfied. A lazy smile spread across her face.

"That was a helluva pedicure," Chanel cracked.

Kat cracked up, her mouth and chin still slick with Chanel's juices. "You know I got a thing for your feet. You shoulda never got me started."

Chanel picked up the remote and switched to CNBC to check the stock market. The Dow was down and it pissed her off.

"How long has it been since the robbery?" Chanel asked.

"Too long," Kat huffed, suddenly turning serious.

Chanel nodded. "Have you heard from Infinite?"

"Naw."

"Then he should hear from us."

"Done. Clean or messy."

"I think this is a message I should send myself."

∞

Sonja was bone tired. She had been on her feet in her pumps all day, teaching bad ass fifth graders that she loved so much, but who, more often than not, got on her nerves. What bothered her more was the city had cut the school budget, making it damn near impossible to have all the things the kids needed. She even had to go in her pocket sometimes and buy school supplies. But she didn't mind because she loved kids. Since she couldn't have any, she lavished all her love on them. All Sonja had to come home to was her cat and her wild ass sister.

She took the grocery bag out of the passenger seat and carried it toward the door of her building. Shifting the bag against her hip, she unlocked the inner door. The lobby was deserted, the only sound being her high heels tapping against the tile floor. She reached the elevator, pressed the button, and the door slid open as if it had been waiting for her.

As the door began to close, an arm was stuck in the door, causing it to reopen. A well-dressed man with a trimmed beard, baldhead, and glasses got on. He smiled at her.

"What floor, sister?" he asked.

Even though something didn't seem right, the fact that he called her "sister" calmed her somewhat. Plus, he was dressed like a banker, so she returned the smile and replied, "The eighth, thank you."

"No problem." He hit the button for the eighth floor, then stepped back. The door shut and the elevator ascended. The two of them looked up at the floor numbers the way people do in elevators to avoid conversation.

"I hope you had a good day," he remarked.

"It was fine, thank you." Sonja smiled politely.

"How was school?" he asked, no longer looking at the numbers but directly at her.

She frowned subtly and returned his gaze.

"How . . . did you know—"

He smoothly cut her off, saying in an even tone, "I know lots of things, but what I don't know is where Aisha is. Do you? Do you think she's home?" His cold expression belied his calmness.

A chill shot up her spine as the elevator opened on the eighth floor.

"I'm sorry, I don't know if she's home," she replied, trying to get off the elevator.

He grabbed her arm firmly and pulled out a chrome plated nine.

"Mind if I check?"

Sonja thought about screaming, but the look in his eyes dared her to do just that. She knew he'd shoot her dead on the spot.

"If . . . If you must."

"I must."

They walked down the hall with him holding her by the arm. Sonja prayed that someone would enter the hallway, but no one did.

They reached her door and entered. The air felt still and unoccupied.

"Call her," he whispered.

She was scared for her sister, but even more scared for herself. She complied. "Aisha! Aisha, you here?"

No one responded.

"Let's look for ourselves."

Sonja put the bag down on the couch, and they walked through the small two-bedroom apartment. Once he saw that no one was there, he walked back to the living room, sat her on the couch, then sat across from her in the armchair.

"You know her number?"

She nodded.

"Give it to me."

She did. He plugged it into his phone.

"Now, I want you to call her . . . talk regular. Find out where she is and when she's coming home. Can you do that?"

"Please, whatever she did, please don't . . . I don't want anything to happen to her," Sonja begged, nervous tears cascading down her face.

"Do you know what your sister did?"

She shook her head.

"Do you know who I am?"

Again, she shook her head.

I'm Infinite . . . in many ways. My wrath and my mercy. Your sister has earned my wrath—there's nothing you can do about that. But you can earn my mercy. You want to know how?"

Sonja could see whatever her sister had done, there was no saving her. But she hoped she could save herself.

"Yes."

"Call her. Do what I tell you. Now," Infinite instructed her.

She dialed the number with shaky hands. It rang. It rang again. Again and again. Voice mail.

"Voice mail."

"Text her to call."

She did, then lowered the phone. Infinite kept his eyes glued to Sonja. She lowered her head to avoid the coldness of his gaze.

"Look at me."

She did, knowing he was doing it to intimidate her. It was working. She literally began to tremble.

"You got some pretty ass lips," he remarked with a subtle smirk. She didn't know whether to reply or stay silent.

"I give you a compliment and you can't even say thank you?"

"Th—Thank you."

"Like Megan Goode. Now that's a sexy bitch. My wife got lips like that. You know what my wife does with her lips?"

Her phone rang, saving her from having to answer him. She quickly answered. "Aisha, where are you? . . . I–I just want to know . . . No–no, I'm okay, I'm just . . . tired. When are you coming home? . . . Out of town?" she asked, lifting her eyes to Infinite.

He mouthed the word 'where?'

"Where out of town? No, this ain't Twenty Questions. I just . . . need to talk to you. Wilmington,

Delaware? O–okay . . . no, I guess it'll have to wait 'til you come back. When is that? . . . Oh, okay. I love you, too," Sonja replied, then hung up.

"She said she didn't know."

He nodded.

"Did she say anything else?"

"No," she lied.

Aisha had told her she was going to see their cousin, Don Pooh, but she wasn't about to tell Infinite anything she absolutely didn't have to.

Infinite smiled. He could sense she was holding back, but he let it go. He knew all he needed to know.

"You did good. I'm going to kill your sister. You know that, right?" he commented calmly.

Her shoulders shuddered from her silent sobs, and as she wiped her eyes she replied, "Yes . . . I know."

"But you can save yourself. Come here."

She stood on wobbly legs and came to stand in front of him.

"Get on your knees."

Sonja looked in his eyes, and she knew where this was going. She slowly lowered herself to her new position between his legs.

Infinite pulled out his dick, stroked it a couple of times, then said, "Show me what you can do with those pretty ass lips, and do it like your life depends on it." He put the gun to the side of her head. "Because it does."

Sonja gripped his dick by the base, then slid the whole length into her mouth. It instantly began to grow to its full length and hardness, filling her mouth and touching the back of her throat.

"Gag on it," he growled lustfully, moving her hair aside, so he could watch his dick sliding in and out of her lips.

She began gagging, which made him grab a handful of her hair and force-feed her the dick. He sank lower in the chair.

"Yeah, bitch, now relax and lemme fuck that throat."

Sonja deep throated him like her life depended on it, twisting and stretching her neck to match his every thrust. His balls slapped against her chin as he roughly fucked her face, turned on by the slurping sounds her lips were making.

"Wait!" he barked, snatching his dick out of her mouth just when he was about to bust.

Infinite pumped his dick until his cum exploded from his dick and covered Sonja's lips, nose, and cheeks.

"Fuck!" He chuckled. "You a beast! No, don't wipe it—lick it . . . yeah, just like that. Use your hair to get the rest. Good girl. Now . . . you're going to give my message to sis, okay?"

Sonja nodded, trembling and wiping his cum off her cheek and then putting it in her mouth.

"The message is . . . you're dead, got me?" Infinite smirked.

Sonja read his expression and there was a catch. His smirk caused a lone tear to trace her cheek, one that, like a mirror, Infinite saw himself reflected in . . .

CHAPTER 6
- Ultimatum -

Supreme could feel the phone on the side of his face, but the words coming out of it didn't sound real. They couldn't be.

He had been sitting in the driver's seat of Infinite's Benz, waiting for him to come down from Sonja's apartment. Supreme was playing lookout, keeping his eyes open for the police. He had been listening to some throwback Melissa Morgan, when his phone rang. He checked the caller ID. It was his mother. He frowned slightly because she almost never called him; he always called her.

"Hello? Ma?" he answered.

"I was told not to stutter when I read you this," his mother said, her voice sounding weak and strained.

"Who told you to read what?" he questioned intently, leaning forward as if he were about to bounce.

"Dear Son, I have a gun to my head as I read this. It is a big gun and will . . . will—"

"Blow," Chanel chimed in cheerfully as she held the .45 to her head.

"Blow my brains out."

Supreme shut his eyes hard and hit the steering wheel. "How much?" he gritted, thinking she had been kidnapped.

"I don't want my brains blown out, and I'm sure you don't either. At least I hope you don't," his mother read, deadpan.

"That was a joke. Laugh," Chanel ordered.

His mother mustered a nervous titter.

"Ma? Who the hell is there!"

"If we are on the same page, then you have a decision to make. She will blow my brains out if you don't blow out Infinite's."

She . . . Supreme froze, knowing exactly who 'she' was: Coco Chanel. He knew that this was no kidnapping. It was an ultimatum.

"Ma, put her on the phone."

"If you look in the mirror, you will see me."

Supreme glanced in his rearview mirror. Parked three car lengths back was a van. He saw his mother's ashen face, the gleam of a gun to her head and Chanel smiling, waving.

"This is not a game. Choose wisely. I love you, son. Do you love me?" She hung up.

Supreme was stuck. His man or his mother? Not that it was a hard decision, just a fucked up one. He and Infinite had come up together. He loved him like a brother. Now, he would have to kill him.

Several minutes later, Infinite came out of the building and got in the car. "Delaware. The bitch went to Wilmington, Delaware." Infinite chuckled, bringing up the number on his phone. "I even got her number. Yo, why you ain't drivin'? Let's go."

Supreme looked at him, then slowly turned and started the car. He glanced in the rearview mirror and saw Chanel snatch his mother's head back and put the gun under her chin.

"Yo, God, you okay? Fuck is you cryin' for?" Infinite wanted to know.

Supreme shook his head, squeezing his eyes shut tightly against the reality he was facing.

"Forgive me, God," he prayed, but Infinite thought he was talking to him.

"Huh?"

Boom!

Supreme had pulled his gun and pulled the trigger quickly because he wanted to get it over. The gun had been pressed to Infinite's forehead, dead center, blowing his third eye all over the passenger window and roof of the car. Besides a twitch or two, Infinite didn't move. His eyes remained open and dilated, an expression of surprise forever etched on his face. Supreme couldn't even look him in his dead eyes.

As soon as Infinite was dead, the van pulled out and pulled up beside the Benz. The sliding door rolled open and there squatted Kat.

"Get in," she commanded.

Supreme was past the point of caring what happened to him. He had chosen the street life, and he wasn't about to flinch when faced with the consequences. He cut the car's engine off and got out. As he climbed into the van, two dudes quickly jumped out, one carrying a gas can. He doused the car's interior, then poured the rest over the roof. The other tossed a book of matches into Infinite's lap—and voof! The interior went up in a roaring blaze. They jumped in and Chanel drove off. Supreme could see Infinite's burning body in the passenger seat through the van's rear window, then he felt his mother's arm wrapped around him. He hugged her back.

"Now . . . do we understand one another, Supreme?" Chanel questioned, glancing in the rearview mirror.

"We always did."

"Naw, that's not true. You see, when someone steals from you and you work for me, then it's like they stole from me. I can't have that. But yet you and Infinite didn't treat my problem with urgency. That's very disrespectful," Chanel warned.

"Yo, we was on it. We just found out the bitch in Wilmington, Delaware," he replied, holding his sobbing mother.

"Don't use that word. I hate that word. Apologize," Chanel told him.

"I'm sorry."

"Next time, don't hesitate. When a motherfucka violates, punishment is swift. Are we clear?"

"Yeah."

"Then me and you don't have any problems," she responded. A smile spread across her lips and she added, "But since you're no longer employed . . ."

CHAPTER 7
- It Ain't No Game -

Charisma hung up the phone and looked at it strangely.

"Yo ma, what up?" Shamar questioned, reading her expression.

"My sister, yo . . . she sounded bugged."

"Bugged?"

Charisma quickly dialed another number. "Hello, Mrs. Butler? Hey, this is Aisha . . . Yes ma'am, I went last Sunday," she lied, rolling her eyes to the ceiling. "Yes, I was just calling to ask if you would go check on my sister . . . Yes ma'am. Thank you. Have her call me, okay?" She hung up and looked at Shamar.

"That old bitch get on my nerves, but she just nosy enough to go check on Sonja. Just to know what's goin' on."

"She probably just want her rent money," Shamar surmised.

"Shit, I just gave her four stacks last night. Stop here. I need to piss," she told him, pointing to a 7-Eleven convenience store.

They had just exited I-95 and entered Wilmington. Shamar pulled his '06 Cadillac DTS into a parking space and glanced in the backseat at GQ and Crook, sleeping.

"Look at these two dumb muhfuckas." He chuckled.

Charisma opened the door and put her finger to her lips. "Shhhh," she said with a mischievous grin.

Shamar knew exactly what she was doing. He got out, opening the door quietly, then looked at Charisma over the roof of the car.

"On three. One . . . two . . ."

They both slammed the doors as hard as possible, rocking the car with a big *Boom!* GQ and Crook jumped out of their sleep, reaching for their guns, wide-eyed and looking around. Charisma and Shamar cracked up.

"I hate you stupid muhfuckas! Play too fuckin' much!" Crook spazzed, as he jumped out of the car.

GQ got out last. "Muhfuckas need to grow up," he mumbled.

Charisma and Shamar laughed even harder as they went into the store. She headed for the bathroom.

"Umm, excuse me, sir. Are you going to pay for that?"

Shamar heard the words from the cashier and looked to see what was going on. Crook walked out of the store with an XXL magazine and a big bag of potato chips. Shamar shook his head as he walked to the counter and looked at the cashier, giving her a crooked grin.

"Don't sweat that, ma. He's retarded. I'm paying for it. What I owe you?"

She took one look at Shamar's smooth brown skin, charming smile, and gangsta swag and her panties got wet, causing her cheeks to blush crimson. "I—uh—I'm not sure what he took," she replied with a frustrated smile.

He placed a pack of gum and chips on the counter. Then he held out a twenty. "That should cover it."

"Thank you," she said, taking the bill, then adding, "your order is on me."

Shamar knew she was trying to flirt, and he accepted her advance. He didn't really do white girls, but two things made him make an exception. She looked like Taylor Swift, and she put the twenty in her pocket instead of the register, which let him know that she didn't mind getting her hands a little dirty.

"Yo, I 'preciate that. What's your name, shorty?"

"Crystal, Crystal McClain."

"They call me J."

"J?"

"Yeah, J."

Crystal subtly snickered.

"What's so funny?" Shamar asked.

"I bet J's not your real nickname."

"How you figure?" He smirked, impressed by this white girl's bullshit meter.

"It's cool though." She shrugged. "Maybe Crystal's not my real name either." She winked.

Shamar laughed.

"Nigguh, you ain't shit!" Charisma barked, coming out of the bathroom. "I go to the bathroom, and you all up in the next bitch face! Just fuck me and our five kids, huh?" She stopped by the cooler aisle, grabbing a couple of bottles of Vitamin water.

Crystal was wide-eyed, looking from Shamar to the quickly approaching Charisma, but when she saw him laughing, she figured it was a joke.

"Ay yo, ma, just gimme your number so I can get at you when I drop off the short bus riders."

Shamar swiped one of the Vitamin waters from Charisma after she paid for them. Crystal put her number in his Samsung phone, and then Shamar walked with GQ. As he headed for the exit, he turned back and said, "Sha, they call me Sha."

Crystal giggled. "Well, I'm going to call you Slick."

He walked out laughing because he definitely liked the white girl's style.

∞

"Big Cuz, what's good?" Charisma asked as she sat on the passenger side of the Cadillac DTS as it approached the hood.

"What up, baby girl? You here already?" Don Pooh asked with a grin.

"You already know."

"Ai'ight. Well, come all the way down Ninth and you gonna see an abandoned school. I'm back behind it."

"We'll be there in a minute."

Don Pooh hung up and leaned back against the chrome grill of his triple black Chrysler 300, hoisting the forty-ounce Olde English to his lips. He was a chubby Irv Gotti looking dude with massive diamond earrings in both ears.

He was chilling out in the spot with his man, Swifty, a lanky Snoop look-a-like, watching the fiends running back and forth to one of his little mans who was serving them. Two skinny, ashy, dirty fiends they called Mike and Ike shuffled toward them. They called them that because they were always together, like some kind of crack head Batman and Robin.

"Yo, Youngblood, man, we only got thirteen. Look out for us 'til later, man. We got you," Mike begged.

"Man, fuck that! You always short! Get the fuck outta my face!"

"Please, Youngblood, man. This all we got!" Mike stressed, doing a little crack head shuffle that made Don Pooh chuckle.

"Ay yo, Mike, why the fuck you always short, and then in ten more minutes you come back with the other seven and try to get a short with that? You been running that same lame game since I was huggin' the block!" Don Pooh remarked.

"It ain't no game, Pooh. We just tryin' to live," Ike replied.

Don Pooh took a swig of his forty. He was bored and feeling sadistic, so he said, "I'll tell you what . . . Y'all nigguhs want to get high or what?"

"Man, quit bullshittin'. You know we do," Mike whined, grabbing his crotch like he had to piss.

"Ai'ight, fuck it. I'ma give one of y'all a whole ounce, but y'all gotta fight for it," Don Pooh proposed.

"Fight?" Ike echoed, looking at Mike then at Don Pooh.

"And none of that fake shit either . . . if I don't see no blood, the deal's off!"

Mike and Ike looked each other. A car pulled up with Charisma, Crook, GQ, and Shamar as the driver.

The four of them got out and approached Don Pooh. Before he could hug Charisma, Mike hooked off on Ike, staggering him up against the wall. With all his might behind the blow, Mike was definitely trying to draw blood. Mike and Ike's eyes met. They had been hustling together so long, they could communicate without words. They both knew what to do: throw a few blows, get a nose bleeding, and then act like one had knocked the other out. At least, that was the plan.

"Fight! This ain't no goddamn dance!" Don Pooh barked.

The two men were circling each other, hands out, revival style. Ike faked a left then threw a right that caught Mike dead on the nose. In Mike's mind, the blow was harder than it needed to be. Is this nigguh serious? he thought.

Mike thought about the scam they had run a couple of nights ago, when he cuffed on Ike and kept a bigger share. Was he trying to get some get back? But in Mike's mind—at that time—Ike owed him for all those times he had shorted him!

Mike kneed Ike in the nuts hard, doubling him over.

"Owwwww!" all the dudes watching cried out, grabbing their own nuts.

Ike was furious. The pain was fueling his already suspicious mind, thinking Mike was really trying to knock him out, so he could stash some and short his half.

This nigguh's always trying to play me, he thought angrily. When Mike charged, Ike came with a vicious uppercut that dropped Mike on his ass.

"Motherfucka!" Ike bellowed, diving on Mike and sitting on his chest. He commenced to wailing on Mike, pulverizing his face with blow after blow.

"Yeah, Ike! Beat that nigguh ass!" Shifty laughed.

Mike felt himself ready to black out. The only thing keeping him conscious was his urge to get high. He knew if he went out, Ike would keep the whole ounce now that shit was serious. He reached out to grasp something to get this nigguh off his ass. He felt a broken brick against his palm.

Mike wrapped his fingers around the brick and swung with every ounce of energy he had left. The brick broke Ike's jaw on contact, and blood spewed from his mouth so far that the crowd had to jump back.

"Goddamn!" Crook exclaimed, loving the sight of blood.

By the time Mike jumped on Ike, he was in a zone. He beat Ike like Ike had been beating him, but the critical difference was that Mike had a brick and beat him unmercifully, unrelentingly, and non-stop. When he finally ceased beating him, the blood under Ike's head pooled like a miniature lake. There was no question: Ike was dead.

"You . . . you killed him," Don Pooh's young boy said, amazed.

The whole crowd got quiet as Mike struggled to his feet.

He looked down at his dead friend, a man that he had come up with, did time with, and had a certain level of love for. He dropped the brick, wiped blood from his hands onto his pants, and held out his hand. "I won."

The young dude looked at Don Pooh. Don Pooh nodded. The young dude gave Mike the ounce.

"Shit's real, Pooh," Mike remarked, then shuffled off.

"Yo, let's bounce. This nigguh done made the spot hot," Shifty said, heading for the passenger seat of Don Pooh's 300.

Don Pooh looked at Charisma and smirked. "Welcome to Wilmington."

∞

They went to Don Pooh's condo where introductions were made all around. Don Pooh's fiancée, Vanessa, who favored Nia Long but had a body like Deelishis, was on her way out.

"I'm going to the shop, baby. I'll be back," she said, giving him a quick, juicy peck.

On her way out, despite herself, she had to sneak another peek at GQ, only to find that he was peeping her, too. She walked out wearing a smirk.

"Y'all came at the right time. Shit is dry! My Jamaican connect just got hit with a big ass bust! What you workin' wit'?" Don Pooh asked, looking at Shamar the most, but glancing at GQ and Crook.

"We workin' wit' a lil' somethin'." Shamar shrugged.

"What you chargin' for a brick?"

"Twenty-five."

Don Pooh nodded. He snuck a glance at Crook.

"Yo. Me? I ain't tryin' to move my shit in weight. Fuck that! Show me the brick, and I'ma get my grind on," Crook commented.

"Yo, bro, I wouldn't advise that. These nigguhs don't take kindly to strangers," Shifty responded, looking at Crook funny.

"I don't give a fuck! Ain't no man on land that can stop me from eatin', yo," Crook said.

Don Pooh's curiosity couldn't take it any longer. He turned to Charisma and said, "Yo, baby girl, lemme holla at you a sec."

She got up and followed him into the kitchen.

"What's good, Pooh?" she asked.

"You fuck wit' nigguhs like that?"

"Fuck wit' 'em? Cuz, they family! Hell yeah, I fuck wit' 'em," she replied, making sure he understood her emphasis.

"Naw, naw, I ain't mean it like that. I'm just sayin' . . . yo, what kind of shit they on? They some metrosexual thugs or somethin'?"

"Huh?"

"They eyebrows. Why they got them shits arched?"

Charisma burst out laughing. "Yo, Pooh, it's a long story, but believe me. My nigguhs is rock solid. They some of the realest nigguhs you ever gonna meet."

"Yeah, ai'ight," he said, skeptically.

CHAPTER 8
- Say My Name -

Rumors spread fast in prison. As soon as the word spread that Finesse got stabbed up on the yard, convicts already started saying that he was dead. And when a couple of convicts who worked in medical got back to the unit, they confirmed it.

"Yo, the God dead."

The truth was that he had died. Twice. But the prison had airlifted him to an outside hospital where determined doctors had saved his life. He didn't regain consciousness until a few days later, but Finesse was alive . . . and so was his thirst for revenge.

When he first opened his eyes and looked at the all-white surroundings, he thought he was just in the prison infirmary. After all, he didn't know what the infirmary actually looked like. He had been known for sending nigguhs to the infirmary, not going himself. But when he saw that he was handcuffed to the bed and the windows had bars, he knew it was an outside hospital.

He lifted his head and saw Officer Dutton reading an ESPN magazine. He was a white ex-Marine, but he wasn't an asshole.

"Well, if it isn't the cat with nine lives." Dutton chuckled.

"Cut the jokes, Dutton. I need some water," Finesse croaked, his dry-sounding voice scratchy from lack of use.

"Push the little button by the bed."

Finesse pushed his call button. When no one came quickly enough, he pressed it again . . . and again. Several seconds later, a nurse hurried in with a furled brow.

"Is everything okay?"

"Yeah, I'm good. I just need some water."

She looked at him like: I know he didn't . . .

"First off, Mr. Bennett, I'm glad you're awake, but I hope you're not going to become a nuisance," she said firmly, but softened it with a smile.

Finesse eyed her up and down. Her snug white nurse's uniform looked 'right' on her petite frame. Although she had an Asian eye set, she looked more Latino, which made Finesse conclude that she was probably mixed. Either way, she was definitely a dime.

"My bad, yo. I ain't know if this shit was working," he said, holding up the call button.

"Believe me, Mr. Bennett, all you have to do is ring once, and I'll be on my way," she replied.

Finesse smiled flirtatiously. "Word up, I got it like that?"

She giggled.

"All patients do. It's hospital policy. Let me get your water. She walked out just as his lawyer walked in. He was a slim, gray-haired white man, whose boyish features belied his grayness. His expensive suit looked more Wall Street tycoon than a lawyer. He had been assigned to Finesse's case after Finesse filed his appeal.

"Well, DeAngelo, you're looking well for a man that cheated death twice."

"Just call me Steven Segal then."

"Why?"

"'Cause I'm hard to kill," Finesse joked. His lawyer laughed.

"Well, be that as it may, I'm glad you pulled through," the lawyer said.

The nurse walked back in carrying a plastic pitcher and cup. She set them on the table next to the bed.

"There's your water, Mr. Bennett," she remarked.

"Call me Finesse," he replied, squinted at her name tag and added, "Nurse Montoya."

"I'm not calling you Finesse," she protested with a smirk.

"Watch, you gonna call me Finesse," he shot back confidently, watching her walk out and lusting after her short, shapely legs.

"Glad to see you're making yourself right at home," his lawyer quipped.

Finesse used his free hand to pour a cup of water. "Put me anywhere on God's earth, and I'll prove my worth," Finesse jazzed.

"I've been coming by daily, waiting for you to wake up because we need to get these papers signed ASAP." The lawyer handed him several documents.

"What is it?"

"Your release papers."

Finesse stopped cold and looked at his lawyer. "Get the fuck outta here! That quick?"

The lawyer chuckled. "The government knows when it's beaten. They know you have two potential lawsuits: this stabbing and the case itself. So they've agreed not to contest your appeal if you agree not to sue," he explained.

Finesse looked over the documents. "How major?"

"Couple mil' . . . at least."

Finesse whistled. "Now that's major."

"Yeah, but the catch is that you'll stay in prison a few more years, as they fight your appeal tooth and nail."

Finesse thought about it. He knew he had the Feds over a barrel, but they had him over one too. A couple million dollars was a lick, but it wasn't worth his freedom."

"Fuck that, I'll get my own mills. Where do I sign?"

"Smart man. Right here . . . and here . . . and here," his lawyer indicated, flipping the document's pages. "And that'll do it. I have to go before the judge, and part of the agreement is the government foots the hospital bill. But as soon as they discharge you, you'll be a free man."

A free man . . . Finesse couldn't believe his ears. He had spent many nights staring at the ceiling in his cell, wondering if he'd ever hear those words, and now they were a reality. His only regret was that he couldn't get at Everlast, but he could damn sure get at Infinite.

"You hear that, Dutton? I'm a free man! Take these fuckin' handcuffs off!"

"Congrats," Dutton replied, deadpan, not even looking up from the magazine.

"Well, technically, you're still under government supervision, but as soon as I get these filed—"

Finesse didn't even let his lawyer finish.

"Shit, what you still doin' here then?"

His lawyer laughed. "I'm not. I'm on it," he replied, then walked out.

As soon as he left, Finesse pushed the call button.

A few minutes later, Nurse Montoya came and stood in the door. "I know you don't want anything," she remarked.

"Yes I do. I'm looking at it right now." He smiled.

She blushed, shaking her head, and then walked off.

A few days later, Dutton was told to remove the handcuffs and return to Lompoc.

"Well, you're on your own, Bennett. I hope I never see you again," he remarked.

"Believe me, you won't," Finesse replied, vowing if it ever came down to prison or death, he'd hold court in the streets.

Dutton walked out and Finesse looked at his wrists where the handcuffs once were.

"Fuck yeah!" he exclaimed, overwhelmed with the feeling of being free again.

The first thing he did was hit his call button. Then he put both his hands behind his head in a laid-back style.

Nurse Montoya entered the room. "Yes, Mr. Bennett," she sang sarcastically, as if she had been expecting his call.

Over the last couple of days, they had been flirting hard, but being that he was locked up with a life sentence, Finesse had become her fantasy, because she wasn't about to make prison wifey her reality. He never bothered to tell her he was about to get out.

"Notice anything different?"

GAME OF GWOP

She looked at him, then around the room. The Correction Officer was gone. Quickly, she glanced at him and noticed he was no longer handcuffed to the bed. Her eyes got as big as plates.

"Oh my God! What—" She gasped, not understanding what she was seeing. "Did you kill the guard?"

The seriousness with which she said it made him crack up with laughter. "No, I ain't kill the fuckin' guard. Come 'ere, Marissa."

She came over to the bed. "Yes?"

He grabbed her around the waist and palmed her ass, making her jump.

"Stop," she whined, but it sounded more like "don't stop."

"You know how long I've been wanting to do this?" Finesse crooned, slipping his hand under her skirt and feeling her soft ass.

Her eyes fluttered, but she tried to fight the feeling. "DeAngelo, what are you doing? You still haven't told me what's going on," Marissa protested weakly.

"I'm trying to show you what's going on," he shot back smoothly, taking her hand and putting it on his dick. "You know you want this dick."

Marissa squeezed his dick and let out a lip-biting moan. Ever since she had seen his hard dick while he lay in a semi-comatose state, she had fantasized about riding it, right there in the room.

"Somebody might come—come in," she moaned as he slid his fingers inside her wet pussy.

"That makes it even better," he crooned, pulling her close and kissing her neck.

57

The feel of his finger stoking her pussy and his soft lips on her neck drove Marissa over the edge.

"Don't make me scream," she remarked as she hiked up her skirt and climbed on the bed.

Finesse threw the covers aside, and his dick stood straight up. Marissa gripped it as he held her panties to the side and she pushed it up in her, letting out a delicious moan.

"Oh my God, it's so thick!" she gushed. "Go slow."

But Finesse didn't know the meaning of the word. He had been in prison for three years, fucking his hand. Slow was the exact opposite of his full-throttle intent.

"Oh, DeAngelo," Marissa cried out, feeling the full length filling her up.

"Damn this pussy feel good; fuck me back," he demanded, gripping her by the hips, bringing her into every thrust.

"Oh baby, it's too much!"

"Now take this dick! I know you been thinking about me, ain't you?"

She nodded, licking her lips, eyes shut and damn near rolled up in the back of her head.

"Fuck me like that, then."

Marissa began to get used to his size and began to ride him harder. "Like this, daddy? You like it like this?" she groaned.

"Take all this dick!"

"Oh, I am!"

"Say my name!"

"DeAngelo!"

"Naw, mama, you know my name. Say my name," he growled, placing his feet flat on the bed for better leverage and began beating her pussy up.

For a few moments, she couldn't say anything because his thrusts were taking her breath away. Her mouth was open but nothing was coming out.

"Say my name!" he emphasized, putting his finger in her asshole.

The dick was so good she was ready to call him 'god.' "Finesse, oh Finesse, you fuck me sooo good!"

Even before she came, he was half way to his nut. He had done all he could to hold back, but he couldn't hold it anymore and he blew inside of her. Feeling his warm cum coating the walls of her pussy made Marissa explode all over his dick, and then collapse onto his chest.

"Shit!" was all she could say as her body broke out in shivers.

Finesse kissed her on the nose, smirked, and then said, "I told you, you was gonna call me Finesse."

CHAPTER 9
- No Matter Where You Go -

Tyrone would have felt safer in jail. Quickly, he packed his suitcase, stuffing as much as he could into it, and then headed for the door. He knew he had to get the fuck out of Newark. It was too dangerous for him. GQ had played him. He now saw that. The night GQ sat down with him at Four Leaf Deli and Bar was no accident. GQ had been watching him. Tyrone worked at Infinite's strip club, and he knew Tyrone knew how things worked.

"What's up, homie? Long time no see!" GQ had exclaimed, like they were long lost pals, when the closest they had gotten was GQ bullying him back in school.

"GQ, what's good?' Tyrone smiled, glad to be recognized.

"Nigguh, what you drinkin'? Whatever it is, it's on me," GQ proclaimed.

And so it began. GQ supplied the drinks while Tyrone supplied the information, unknowingly.

"Word. I heard that nigguh, um-um, what's his name? Big nigguh used to be up on Avon," GQ prodded.

"Yusuf."

GQ snapped his fingers. "Yusuf, that's it. Nigguhs say he doin' real good. He work at the club too?"

Tyrone downed his drink.

"Yeah, but that nigguh fuck with heroin real heavy. He be slippin'."

GQ nodded, taking it all in. Even though Finesse had turned them on to the lick and they had Charisma on the inside, GQ was the planner in the crew, the details man. It was one thing to know the layout for the plan, but GQ liked to get into people's head, see who posed a problem and who would not. He continued plowing Tyrone with drinks, picking his brain like a lock.

Tyrone downed his last drink. He wobbled as he stood up. "I'm out, yo. I gotta get home."

"Chill, fam', one more," GQ urged.

"Naw, naw, I'm good, really."

GQ shrugged. "Ai'ight, you gotta go, you gotta go. It was good seeing you again."

"You too, G," Tyrone replied, shaking GQ's hand. Before he let go of GQ's hand, he looked him in the eyes and said, "Man, I hope this will stay between me and you."

From the look in his eyes, GQ could tell that Tyrone may have been green, but he wasn't that green. "Naw, fam', chill. I was just getting at you, catching up on lost times. Ain't nothing to it," GQ assured him.

Tyrone nodded and staggered off. That was the last night he had seen or heard of GQ, until the night the police had interrogated him.

"Fuck!" he cried, because if the police knew, who else knew? He hated to think that Infinite knew, so he wasn't about to stick around and find out.

He called a cab and waited in the foyer of the three-bedroom house he lived in on Renner Avenue. He didn't even want to wait on the porch in the open air, because he was that shook.

Beep! Beep!

Tyrone peeped out of the window and saw the cab, then gathered up his suitcase and headed out the door, his neck on swivel, looking for signs of an ambush. He didn't take a breath until he was safely in the cab.

"Penn Station," he told the cabbie.

He arrived at the train/bus station and bought his ticket, a one-way to Richmond, Virginia. He had family there, so he looked forward to wiping the slate clean in VA.

"Hi," a pretty, dark-skinned girl said as he walked away from the ticket window, accompanying her greeting with a smile.

Damn, she bad, he thought as he looked her up and down. Tyrone imagined wrapping those long legs around his head while he sucked her into a frenzy. Her smile lingered as she looked over her shoulder, walking away to buy her ticket. He shook his head. "Next lifetime, mama," he mumbled, because not even a jet-black piece of sweetness could keep him from getting the hell out of dodge.

"The bus is now boarding for Trenton, Philadelphia, and all points South," the P.A. system droned.

Tyrone picked up his suitcase and hurried for the bus. He spotted Miss Chocolate boarding the bus with a baldheaded dude. Naw, that's a chick, he thought, assuming that shorty must be dyking. Still, she was on the same bus. "Shit, maybe this is next lifetime." He snickered.

Almost . . .

She smiled at him again as she got on the bus. When he threaded the narrow aisle, suitcase aloft, he saw her sitting on the left side, two seats from the back.

"I see you goin' my way, huh?" he flirted as he passed her.

"Looks that way," she replied, flirting back.

Just like a nigguh, he took the backseat of the bus. He placed his suitcase in the overhead and sat back. Once the bus took off, his asshole finally relaxed—Tyrone was that tense. He watched the last sights of Newark peel away. He had made a clean get away.

"You mind if I sit with you?"

He broke out of his inner thoughts and looked up at Miss Chocolate. Goddamn! Even in the dark, the bitch shine, he thought, admiring the way the faint light illuminated around her.

"Mind?" he echoed as he slid over to accommodate her. "I would've sat with you, except I see you got your peeps with you."

"You don't have to worry about her. I'm the one you have to worry about." She winked.

"Izzat so?" Tyrone smirked.

She nodded, looking him in the eyes like she was trying to hypnotize. "So where you headed?" she asked.

"Richmond. You?"

"Delaware."

"So, what I gotta do to convince you to come to Richmond?"

They both chuckled.

"Depends on what's in Richmond," she replied, rubbing his knee.

His dick boned off her touch alone. He had to clear his throat to get the dry out. "Just lookin' to start over."

"No matter where you go, there you are," she remarked cryptically.

"Huh?" Tyrone asked, because the comment went right over his head.

She licked her pretty lips and leaned into his air. "Let me rephrase that," she began. Had he been able to see the gleam that suddenly appeared between her teeth, he would have thought she had a platinum grill. But it wasn't platinum, it was steel, a razor expertly clinched between her teeth.

Zzzzzzzzppffffff!

With a vicious flip of her neck, she slit his jugular vein. Blood spewed. She used the collar of his shirt to catch it, so it wouldn't spread. The lights of passing cars lit up Tyrone's face as he gurgled and choked on his own blood.

"No matter where you go, here I am: Coco Chanel, motherfucka. Just thought I'd remind you," she hissed.

Her voice sounded far away, as his life spilled out of him, but the name rang bells: Coco Chanel . . .

Tyrone's head slumped over against the window. In the dark, he looked asleep. His body would be discovered at the Richmond layover.

Chanel got up and returned to her seat, looking forward to her date with Delaware.

CHAPTER 10
- Let the Games Begin -

"Yo, yo, what you need, what you need?"

Crook spat as he ran up on an approaching crack head.

He was on Pine, a spot not too far from Don Pooh's crib, and was known to be a heavy money-making area. Crook was right in the midst of the action, while Shamar sat on the hood of a parked car and kept his eyes out for the police or stickup kids.

They had been in Delaware for three weeks, and the money was lovely. But while Shamar, GQ, and Charisma moved their parts of the lick in weight, Crook was moving his hand to hand. It was more money, but it was also riskier. Not only the risk of the police, but one of the first rules of hustling out of town was that selling weight could be tolerated, whereas hustling the locals' blocks seldom was.

After a week, a couple of goons stepped to Crook as he completed another sale and was counting his money.

"Ay yo, kid, where you from? Who you?" the bigger goon grilled him.

"I'm that nigguh gettin' your money and fuckin' your bitch! Crook, nigguh, who the fuck is you!" Crook growled, pulling his pants up to adjust his sag.

The goon didn't expect Crook to be so blunt. He expected to dominate the situation. But disrespected so openly, he knew he had to save face. Quickly, he reached behind this back and pulled out a pretty chrome Bulldog .357 revolver and aimed it at Crook's face.

"Yeah, muhfucka, talk that shit now!" he growled, emboldened by the feel of the gun in his hand. "Run your pockets!"

Shamar whipped out his nine as he jumped off the car.

"Naw, Sha, chill, chill." Crook laughed, looking the dude in the eyes and adding, "He ain't gonna shoot, pussy ass nigguh!"

"Nigguh, you heard me! Empty your fuckin' pockets!"

Crook took a step closer, so the gun was against his forehead.

"Shoot, faggot! Shoot!"

The gun subtly trembled in his hand. He could see Shamar out the corner of his eye with the nine by his side. He wasn't about to shoot Crook, even if Shamar hadn't been there. He just wanted to rob him, and he figured, once Crook was staring down the barrel of a gun, he would. Now he was stuck.

"Yo, yo, run his pockets," he told his man.

He took one look at the grin Crook gave and the nine in Shamar's hand and quickly replied, "Man, fuck this! Let's bounce."

Crook laughed hard.

"Now what? Huh! Nigga, you's a bitch!" Crook spat, then acted as if he was about to walk away.

He stepped aside so as to be out of the line of fire, then spun, grabbing the wrist of the dude's gun hand with one hand and launching a crushing overhand left with the other.

GAME OF GWOP

Boom!

The pain of the blow made his body tense up, which resulted in his squeezing the trigger. By the time Crook hit him again, he took control of the gun and aimed it in the dude's face.

"Bitch ass nigguh, now run your pockets! Matter of fact, strip! You too!" Crook shouted, pointing the gun at the dude's partner's feet and firing.

Boom!

He jumped back and didn't hesitate to start taking off his clothes. "Come on, man!" the dude protested, mouth bloodied and bruised.

Crook slapped him with his own gun. "You think it's a game? Strip!"

They both stripped down to their boxers. Shamar was laughing, cracking up.

"Muhfucka!" Crook shot at their feet. "I said strip! That means everything!"

They both tossed their boxers and stood there, butt-ass naked.

"Now march!" Crook cracked. He marched them half way up the block, stopping in front of three hustlers standing in front of the corner store.

"Fuck y'all nigguhs lookin' at? Strip!" Crook barked, pointing the gun at them.

One of them grabbed his nuts, spat, then replied, "Nigguh, get the fuck outta my—"

Boom!

The .357 blast to his thigh cut off his slick remark before he could get it out. His leg seemed to him to explode as he dropped to the ground, hollering in excruciating pain.

"Strip!" Crook demanded.

The other two wasted no time getting naked.

"Now, all y'all nigguhs line up!" Crook ordered, and they all did. "This might be your city, but this is my muhfuckin' block! You got a problem with that, come see Crook! Now, when I say go, y'all better run as fast as you can, 'cause I'm shootin' the slowest nigguh in the ass! Ready . . . go!"

Crook squeezed off a round in the air, as four naked dudes streaked down the block as fast as their bare feet could carry them. He fired another round over their heads and all four kicked into high gear.

Shamar had been laughing the whole time. His head and stomach hurt.

"Yo duke," he panted, wiping the tears of laughter from his eyes, "You's a stupid motherfucka."

"Muhfuck them coward ass nigguhs." Crook smirked. "I shoulda made 'em play leap frog up the goddamn street!"

"You know you done started somethin'," Shamar predicted.

Crook shrugged, pulled out a blunt, lit it and then replied, "Let the games begin."

And begin, they did. For the next week, Pine Street was a virtual war zone. Everyday shoot-outs rang out as the four dudes that Crook had run off the block came back with a vengeance and with heavy artillery. Nobody could make any money. Crook was furious.

"Nigguh, you brought this shit on yourself!" GQ told Crook as they rode around in GQ's brand new, burgundy BMW 535 that he had copped with his share of the lick.

"Muhfuck that," Crook grumbled, passing him the blunt.

"Nigguhs been tellin' yo' ass to sell that shit as weight, but you on some Jew shit, wantin' er' break down!"

"I'm not about to let these bitch ass nigguhs run me off the block," Crook shot back.

"So what you gonna do?" GQ asked.

Crook just smiled.

∞

Damn, this white girl pussy creamy as fuck, Shamar thought as he punished Crystal's pussy from the back. He had her legs spread wide, back arched, and pulling her while she bit the pillow to stifle her screams. Shamar slid two fingers in her asshole and her whole body jolted like he had hit the freak switch.

She cried out, looking over her shoulder, eyes glazed and said, "Put it in my ass! Put that big, black dick in my ass!"

Shamar pulled out of her pussy, then ran his dick down the crack of her ass, and stroked it across her tight, pink puckered hole.

"Don't tease me," she groaned, playing feverishly with her own pussy.

Shamar slid his long dick into her asshole, thinking it would be a tight fit, but it slid right in and she took every inch, just like a porno pro.

"Oh, fuck yes! Just like that! Fuck this ass!" She reached back, spreading her own ass cheeks, urging him deeper by throwing it back at him.

"Yeah, you a nasty bitch, ain't you?" Shamar gruffed, biting his bottom lip and putting his back into every stroke.

"I'm a nasty bitch!" she squeaked.

"Tell me whose ass is this!"

"Yours! I'm going to cum! Fuck me harder, baby. Make me cum!"

Shamar made every blow like the blow of a sledgehammer, making Crystal cry out in pleasure and pain. Her pussy exploded, and he was right behind her, pulling out and cumming all over her ass and back.

He had gotten a room with two beds, so they didn't have to lie in the enormous wet spot. They moved over to the dry bed and Crystal threw her leg over his.

"I'm glad you finally got around to calling me. I thought you forgot about me," Crystal remarked, playing with his dick.

"Naw, ma, shit just been crazy, you know? I definitely intended on gettin' at you."

"I can tell you've been busy," she remarked, referring to the fact that he had picked her up in his new cocaine white Lexus F-Sport with dealer tags.

"Why you say that?"

"Hello? Brand new Lex. I may be blonde, but I'm not dumb," she cracked.

He chuckled. "Naw, it ain't that serious."

"I mean, it's cool because being that my job is right off the exit into the city, a lot of out-of-town guys stop there. So I know what's going on," she told him.

"So you used to ballas, huh?"

"Ballers," she echoed with a furled brow.

The way she said it, so proper like, made Shamar laugh. "Not ballers—ballas, hustlas—nigguhs who get money," he replied.

"Don't take this wrong, but I really don't deal with black guys. In fact, truth be told, you're my first," she admitted.

"Well, you know what they say: once you go black, you never go back," he quipped.

She gave his flaccid manhood a squeeze and a pull. "I'm starting to see why they say it."

They both laughed.

"I mean, don't get me wrong, a lot of guys come on to me, but none of them were my type . . . until now." Crystal reached over and kissed him lustfully, her kiss screaming, "I want some dick!" After she broke the kiss she added, "But most of them are like Philly guys and New York guys. I've never seen so many Jersey guys come at the same time.

That got Shamar's attention.

"Jersey guys?"

She nodded.

"Yeah. Like two carloads came into the store today. It made me think about you when I saw the Jersey plates," she flirted.

He sat up on his elbow. "Two car loads?"

She could tell something was wrong. "You okay?" she asked with concern. Shamar's mind was going a hundred miles an hour. How much of a coincidence was it that another crew of Jersey nigguhs had just hit town? Could it be Infinite's squad? And if so, how did they know they were in Delaware?

The last question put his mind to rest. Infinite probably didn't even know they were the ones who robbed the club, and he damn sure didn't know where they were, he thought.

Shamar lay back. "Nothin', I'm good."

"You sure?"

"Yeah, no doubt."

"Well," she replied, biting down on her bottom lip, "I'm not."

With that, she bent down, wrapping her lips around his dick and sucking away the thoughts of the mystery Jersey crew.

CHAPTER 11
- A Gun and a Quick Memory -

Crook parked four blocks away and crept to the block in the dead of night. In his hand, he carried a gas can filled to the brim, and in the other hand was a Mac-11 with an extended clip. He was ready for war.

Climbing fences and skulking through backyards, Crook took extra precautions to make sure he didn't alert anyone to his presence.

Meanwhile, on the block the spot was jumping. The hustlers Crook had stripped naked and run off the block were back and had extra muscle posted everywhere, just in case there was a beef.

"Yo, yo, I got twenty-six, my man. Let me get three dimes," Mike urged the young hustler.

Since he had killed Ike, Mike's stock among crack heads had gone through the roof. They were scared to death of him. Mike even began to believe his own hype, bullying other crack heads into giving up pieces of their score, even threatening one soft dealer with a brick.

"This is what I killed Ike with, nigguh. Don't be next!"

The dealer gave up the goods.

Truth be told, Mike was still the same old coward—he just had the streets believing otherwise.

"Ai'ight, gimme the money," the young hustler agreed.

The exchange was made, and Mike held the baggies up to the light from the lamppost.

"This better be good, too . . . and dig . . . I've got this 50-inch plasma stashed in the alley. What you'll give me for it?"

"Fifty inch? Where? Lemme check it out."

"Come on then." Mike led him into the alley. They approached a large box that Mike had propped up against the wall. As soon as they were deep in the alley, they heard, "Greed'll get 'em every time."

The young hustler turned and saw Crook standing there, gun aimed. He instantly put his hands up. "Yo, you got it, homie."

Mike went straight for his pockets, taking his money and drugs. "Let me get this sucka ass nigguh," Mike cracked.

Crook got in the hustler's face. "First of all, I ain't your homie. Secondly, what I tell yo' bitch ass the last time!" Crook snorted.

"Huh?"

Blah!

Crook slapped him with the Mac, staggering him against the wall. The hustler held his face.

"You remember now?"

"It's your block. You said it's your block!"

Crook chuckled and looked at Mike. "How come a gun in your face make a muhfucka remember ere' thing?" He turned back to the hustler. "Now, if that's what I said, what the fuck you doin' up here?"

"Yo, man, I'm just tryin' to eat!"

"Fuck that. Lay the fuck down! Now!"

He wasted no time getting face down.

"I'm goin' to get the car," Mike remarked, backing away. He could feel what was about to happen next.

Crook gave him a menacing stare. "You better not leave me," he warned, then tossed him the keys.

Mike knew not to try to cross Don Pooh and his people, so leaving Crook was the last thing on his mind. "I ain't," he replied, then jogged off.

"Yo man, I got a safe at the crib!" he offered in a trembling tone. He could feel it coming.

"I do too." Crook laughed, then picked up the gas can. He poured gas all over the young hustler, drenching him from head to toe. As soon as the hustler smelled the gas, he began squirming and flopping like a fish.

"Come on, please, man. Don't do this. I'm all my mama got," he cried.

"Shut the fuck up and get yo' ass up!"

The young hustler struggled to his feet.

"Now walk and keep your goddamn mouth shut!" Crook ordered, walking the dude out of the alley and back toward the block. Quietly, Crook pulled a lighter out of his pocket.

"Just don't kill me," the young hustler begged.

"I ain't gonna kill you, but I need you to show your people . . . the light," Crook remarked, then lit the lighter to the young hustler's shirt.

Voooooofff!

The young hustler ignited into a ball of flames, totally engulfing him so fast that Crook had to jump back.

He let out a scream that sounded inhumane as he stumbled into the street. The whole block turned in his direction. At first, they couldn't figure out what was going on. It took them a couple of seconds to see the ball of fire was a human being.

"Shoot meeeee! Shoot meeeee!" he shrieked, the fire eating his flesh away like the bite of a billion bees all stinging at once. The fire froze them and gave Crook the upper hand.

"I told y'all, this is my block!" he barked, letting the Mac rip. He cut down three dudes before the others returned fire. But they were out in the open and Crook dropped two more. Mike came skidding up in the getaway car and threw open the passenger door. Crook backed toward the car and jumped in.

"God . . . damn!" Mike exclaimed, seeing the body of the young hustler on fire.

"Nigguh, just drive!"

Burning rubber, Mike made their getaway as the young hustler finally dropped to the ground, dead—his body roasting in the cool night air.

∞

"Yes, Steve, this was the scene of a gruesome murder only an hour ago. Witnesses say a man was set on fire and literally burned to death in the street, while a lone gunman shot and killed at least five people in what police are calling a drug war.

"Witnesses say the gunman fled in a dark-colored sedan. Police believe they've located the sedan along with the body of the driver, a Michael Jenkins. Police think Jenkins was the getaway driver and the gunman killed him also. A truly bizarre turn of events."

Chanel stood in front of the TV in the bedroom of her hotel suite. She wore only a fluffy white hotel robe, a drink in her hand, and a smirk on her face.

"That's them!" she remarked.

"How can you be sure?" Kat questioned, sitting the chair against the wall.

"Because that's some Newark shit right there." She snickered. "I see that Charisma and her crew go hard. Too bad we didn't meet under better circumstances."

"You want me to go stake out the block?"

"Naw. Let Supreme earn his keep. Put him on it."

Kat nodded, then eyed Chantel lustfully.

"Now that, that's handled, what you got on under that robe?"

Chanel smirked.

"Not tonight, Kat. I'm expecting company."

"Company?"

A knock was heard at the outer door of the suite.

Matter of fact, they're here."

"Who's here?"

"The strippers," Chanel replied. "Now . . . get the door."

Kat wasn't feeling it, but even she knew not to go against Chanel. She went and answered the door. Three men walked in. One Spanish cat dressed as a cop, a black dude dressed as a bare-chested foreman, and a white dude in a cowboy outfit.

"Are you the birthday girl?" the black dude smirked.

"Do I look like a birthday girl? Come on," Kat huffed and headed for the bedroom. The strippers followed her.

As soon as they entered the bedroom, Chanel's eyes fell upon the Spanish dude dressed as a cop.

"Damn, you fine, but I don't like police, sweetie. Get out," Chanel remarked.

"Huh?" he said.

"Yo, you heard her. Bounce!" Kat gritted.

The Spanish dude wanted to reply, but one look at the .40 caliber that suddenly appeared in Kat's hand, and he did as he was told.

"Okay, now you two . . . strip," Chanel commanded, sitting in the bed and crossing her long, chocolate legs.

"Umm, can we get some music?" the white guy requested.

Chanel chuckled. "I didn't say dance, I said strip. I don't like to be teased."

The two strippers looked at each other, shrugged their shoulders, and then undressed. Once they got down to their G-strings, the black dude asked, "Now what?"

"Mmmm, let's see," Chanel said, standing up and approaching them. She reached inside the white dude's briefs and pulled out his dick. It was thick, long, and heavy. She then stepped to the black dude and pulled his out. It was longer but not as thick.

"Now, you leave," she told the black guy, turning her attention to the white guy. She took his cowboy hat off and put it on her head. "I have a taste for the swirl tonight."

The black dude gathered up his clothes and walked out, grumbling.

"See him out, Kat."

Kat glared at Chanel, who simply smirked back. Kat walked out and semi-slammed the door. Chanel stepped back, took off her robe and let it fall to the floor, revealing her flawless chocolate nakedness.

"You like chocolate?"

"Love it." He smiled, licking his lips.

She led him to the bed, but when he tried to lay her down, she said, "No. You lay down. I want to sit on your face."

"I love a woman that knows what she wants," he remarked as he lay on his back.

Chanel threw her legs across him and sat her already wet pussy right on his lips. He began to run his tongue in and out of her pussy.

"No . . . suck the clit."

He did, using his fingers to push the hood back. He feasted on her pearl like it was an exotic delicacy.

"Mmm yeah, just like that . . . now, run your tongue over it in a cir—ohhh fuck yeah! Damn you've got a golden tongue," she cooed. Chanel began grinding her pussy into his face while she played with her hard, chocolate nipples.

"Sssssss . . . that makes me tingle like I gotta pee. How about it? Can I pee in your face?" Chanel questioned.

"It'll cost you extra," he responded between licks.

She responded with a warm stream of piss that drenched his face like championship winners get drenched in champagne. Even her golden shower tasted sweet.

"I wanna ride that big dick now," she said, scooting back. She grabbed the base of his dick and rubbed it across her pussy lips then slid it inside. His girth was breathtaking, but oh so delicious as she began to rotate her hips, getting increasingly wound up.

"Don't I love a fat dick," she gushed, licking her lips.

He grabbed her by the hips and forced her down on the whole length.

"Oh! That's right, make me take it all!"

"Your pussy is so tight."

"Umm fuck, ooooohhh!" Chanel creamed, her whole body shaking as she came hard.

He kept pumping, but she was done. She rolled off him and lay back on the pillow. He was so close to cumming, his dick was quivering.

"What about me?" he asked.

"What about you?" she countered, eyebrows raised.

Her answer irked him, but he let it go because, after all, this was business.

"Cool. Just give me what you owe me and we'll be done," he remarked, standing and putting on his pants.

"I just did." She giggled with a wink. "Keep the change."

His face turned beet red. "Maybe you didn't hear me. I—"

"Oh, I heard you, but did you hear me?" Chanel shot back, looking delicious against the cream-colored satin sheets.

His face reddened as he frowned. Now he was furious. There was no way he was going to let a woman beat him out of his money.

"Bitch! Where the fuck is my money!" he seethed.

"Don't . . . don't use that word. I don't like it," Chanel warned, the playful expression on her face turning to stone.

"Oh, I'm sorry. How about you dirty black bitch, where's—"

Chanel came from under the pillow with a nickel-plated nine so fast that it froze him in his tracks.

"Say it again . . . please . . . I dare you," she hissed like a cobra with its head spread, ready to strike.

He raised his hands. "Whoa . . . easy."

"Finish what you were saying."

"That I'm going to get my clothes and go."

"Exactly."

And he did just that. But when he reached for the hat, Chanel stopped him.

"Leave the hat."

"No problem," he replied, because the gun in his face made him very agreeable.

"Kat," Chanel called out, and when she came into the room, she added, "show him the door."

Kat was still upset from earlier, and it showed when she sarcastically replied, "Anything else, your highness?"

Chanel hated sarcasm, and Kat knew it, so Chanel decided to make a point. She grabbed the cowboy hat off the bed and flung it to Kat like a Frisbee.

"Yeah, go buy me an outfit to go with my new hat."

CHAPTER 12
- Crack Head Blood Hound -

Once Kat gave Supreme his marching orders, he jumped right on it. He and his lieutenant, Science, rolled through Ninth Street, checking out the scene. The usually booming drug block had slowed to a crawl. A few hard core huggers were out, but for the most part the block was deserted. The police were on orders to come through every ten minutes, and some of the yellow police tape was still up.

Supreme knew the block was hot, so he didn't linger. He drove through once, then circled the block to come through again.

"Ay yo, God, why are we doin' this shit? That's what we brought the soldiers for," Science remarked, his .40 caliber resting in his lap.

"Naw yo, I'ma handle this shit myself," Supreme replied, not letting on that they were the soldiers. Chanel's.

Science didn't know Chanel was in town calling the shots. But as he thought about it, it made sense. "Yeah, yo." Science nodded. "I feel you, B. They killed the God, yo. We gotta serve justice personally for Inf!"

"No doubt," Supreme agreed.

No one knew that he had killed Infinite. The rumor that Shamar and his team had killed Infinite in retaliation for putting the hit on Finesse in the Feds had taken a life of its own, and Supreme did nothing to discourage it because it worked to his advantage.

He came back around the block and spotted a female crack head walking fast in the same direction. He rode up behind her slowly and lowered the passenger window.

"Ay yo, ma, lemme speak with you for a minute," Supreme called out.

She looked at the BMW 850i and it screamed money, so she sashayed over. "What's up, daddy? You like what you see? You tryin' to spend something?" she flirted.

Supreme looked at her. He could tell that she was attractive at one time, but she had smoked that away. "Yeah, yo, get in," he told her, unlocking the back door. She jumped in and he pulled off just as the police patrol was turning onto the block. Supreme played it cool, watching them in the rearview mirror as he rode away.

"So what up? It's just you, or you and your man?" she asked, hungrily.

"Naw, ma, check this out," Supreme said, handing her a fifty over the seat that she quickly took. "I just wanna ask you a few questions."

"You ain't the police, is you?" she asked suspiciously.

He gave her a hard look through the rearview mirror.

"Bitch, do I look like the police? Was you up here last night?"

"What you mean? When K-Nut got set on fire? Hell yeah, I was up here! Why?"

"What you know about the situation?"

"Man, it was crazy! Them Jersey nigguhs is like fuckin' psychos!"

When she said "Jersey," Supreme and Science looked at one another.

"First, a while back they came up here and stripped K and nem' butt-ass naked and made 'em run off the strip. But K and nem' came back and went back and forth, but last night! Man, when K was hollerin' 'Shoot me! Shoot me!' that shit was completely fucked up! Blew my high, too," she explained in rapid fire, crack head fashion.

Supreme was amped on the inside, feeling like he was right on Shamar and his team's asses, but he kept his composure.

"Check this out. You tryin' to make a stack?"

"A stack?"

"A thousand dollars."

"A thousand dollars? Man, I'll suck every dick in town for a thousand dollars. What I gotta do?" she exclaimed.

Supreme handed her a hundred dollar bill and a piece of paper with a number on it. "You see any one of them Jersey nigguhs, you call that number ASAP. We clear?"

"Man, if a muhfucka say the word Jersey, I'ma call you!" she assured him.

Supreme pulled over. "Don't slip, ma. The quicker you find 'em, the quicker you get paid."

When she got out of the car, she took off running like a crack head blood hound, hot on the trail.

CHAPTER 13
- If it ain't Rough, it ain't Right -

"The number you called is no longer in service. If you feel you have reached this number in error, please hang up and dial your call again."

Finesse listened to the recording for the second time, then hung up with a frustrated sigh. It wasn't as if it was unusual for Shamar to change his number since most of his phones were prepaid burnouts, but being way out on the West Coast, Finesse felt disconnected from his twin brother.

He had been out of prison over a month and staying with Marissa, who stayed in an upscale apartment complex that had a pool and a tennis court. He was in white girl heaven, having already fucked two of Marissa's neighbors. He even found an old white man that used to be a hippie, who had a medical marijuana license and blew choice exotic with him.

But Finesse was a hustler, and he was ready to go back on the grind. All he had to his name was a check for $4,100 from his prison account. He hadn't cashed it yet, but he was definitely ready to go back East and put it on the turn.

"Hey baby," Marissa greeted, coming in carrying a tote bag, and adding, "I brought Chinese." Marissa didn't cook, so they ate out every night. That was cool with Finesse, as long as she was paying. She kissed him on the lips and took note of his expression. "What's the matter?"

"My fuckin' brother. Man, I still can't get in touch with him. I thought he would put some money on the number, but now it's off.

"Did you try his Facebook page?"

"Facebook page?" he echoed, face wrinkled up like the very thought stank. "That's some prison shit. Gangstas don't have Facebook pages, yo."

"Half the world has a page, Finesse," Marissa giggled, "and I see thugs up there all the time."

"Digital thugs and nigguhs locked up, but real nigguhs in the free cypher don't go digital," he spat with a cocky demeanor.

"Whatever." She shrugged. "If you did, then you could find your brother."

"True," he admitted.

Finesse watched Marissa as she walked into the kitchen and admired the sway of her hips. He loved her short, shapely legs, and even though she didn't have a Black girl's ass, it definitely wasn't flat either. He liked Marissa, but he was just tired of playing house.

As soon as she disappeared into the kitchen, he took out his dick and laid it in his lap. "Oh shit, 'Rissa! Look!"

She came out of the kitchen stepping quickly, urged on by the urgency in his tone.

"Man down! He looks incapacitated. He may even need mouth to mouth!" he exclaimed.

Once Finesse was within her view, she laughed. "You are so silly."

He picked up his limp dick and let it fall back into his lap. "If you don't hurry, we'll lose the patient."

She sat next to him and began rubbing his dick. "What do you think I should do?"

"Mouth to mouth." He smiled.

Marissa moved her hair out of her face and bent down. "Like this?" She took his dick in her mouth and began sucking the head while she used her hand to pump the shaft.

"Hell yeah!" he replied, closing his eyes and sinking into the sensation of her warm mouth.

Marissa ran her tongue down his shaft, then sucked his balls, something she knew he especially liked. When she stopped, his dick was sticking straight up like a soldier at attention.

"I think I've revived the patient," she said.

"Put that ass in the air," he told her, ready to punish her pussy.

Marissa pulled up her nurse's skirt and pulled her panties off, looking over her shoulder at him, then put her knees on the couch. "Daddy wanna hit it from the back, huh?"

"You already know." He slid his long, hard dick in her tight, wet pussy, spreading her ass cheeks as he did and began to long-dick her, hard and steady.

"Oh yes, daddy! Gimme this dick."

Finesse gripped her by the hips, pulling her back into every stroke.

"Finesse, oh Finesse!" she screamed, loud enough that the neighbors had to know his name. She buried her face in the arm of the couch, biting the fabric while Finesse pounded her pussy until she came. He didn't stop—he kept stroking her until she thought she was going to pass out.

"Oh, baby, I love you so much!" she cooed, tears of orgasmic pleasure streaming down her cheeks.

Finesse felt the rumble in his stomach, so he pushed himself deep inside her until he exploded. "Goddamn, you get a nigguh's knees weak," he remarked, then sat on the couch and pulled his pants up.

Marissa straddled him, then kissed him slowly and passionately. "Funny, you do the same thing to me."

"Oh yeah?"

She nodded, biting her bottom lip. "You know, I meant what I said."

"What's that?" he asked, as if he didn't already know.

She looked at him like: stop playing. "That I love you, and I'm falling in love with you," she replied.

"I love you, too," he lied, simply because he didn't know what else to say.

She snickered. "No you don't, not yet."

"I'm just sayin' . . . you know, it's like—" Finesse stammered, looking for a way to say he was leaving.

She put her finger to his lips to quiet him. "Believe me, baby, I know. I can see it in you. Lompoc isn't quite your speed. I get that. I've always known you'd be going back East."

"Yeah, but that doesn't mean I want us to end," he said, this time a little more sincerely.

Marissa searched his eyes for any sign of deception, and when she found none, she rewarded him with a kiss. "I know . . . I thought about that . . . a lot. I know that you're a hustler, and I know you're getting restless. I'm willing to do for you what I vowed I'd never do."

"What's that?"

She looked him in the eyes, and her expression suddenly darkened. "Go back to the Barrio!"

"Huh?"

"Come on . . . the food's getting cold."

∞

East Los Angeles is primarily a Latino and Asian mix of cultures that symbolically share the same language but not the same perspective. From Nicaraguans, El Salvadorians, Mexicans, Guatemalans to Koreans, Vietnamese, to ethnic Chinese, East LA is California's melting pot.

It is also where Marissa grew up.

They drove to a small apartment complex in the heart of the Guatemalan neighborhood. It had one way in and one way out. The front gate opened onto a small courtyard. Where there was supposed to be grass, only dirt and weeds flourished. Trash, toys, and empty beer cans were everywhere. Marissa surveyed the scene with disgust. "Now you see why I left," she remarked, kicking a can aside as they went up the stairs to the second floor of the complex.

Finesse shrugged. "It looks like Newark."

She gave him a strange look but didn't say anything. They walked along the breezeway several apartments down, until they came to the second to the last. It was open, but the screen door was locked.

Marissa banged on it. "Ma-Ma! Open the door!"

Several moments later, a short, squat woman with strong Indian features came out the back of the apartment. She walked in almost a pained shuffle as she made her way to the door. "Paciencia," the old woman croaked back. She opened the door and stepped back to allow them to enter.

Marissa gave her mother a quick peck on the cheek and a tentative hug. "How are you, Ma-Ma?" she asked.

The old woman didn't answer. She only shrugged, then looked at Finesse. "Quien estel?"

"Ma-Ma, this is a friend of mine, DeAngelo. DeAngelo, this is my madre."

"Como va?" he greeted, using the little Spanish he knew, accompanied by a smile.

The old woman didn't answer, instead turning back to Marissa and unleashing a stream of Spanish.

"Ma-Ma, I haven't seen you in over a year. Don't start already," Marissa whined, regretting that she even came by. "Where is Jorge?"

"En la calle," she spat with disgust, flinging her hand toward the street. "Siempre en la calle."

"Who isn't in the streets around here?" Marissa quipped bitterly. She kissed her mother on the cheek because just being back in the hell hole in which she grew up was beginning to drain her. "I gotta go, Ma-Ma. You take care."

Once again, she didn't answer. She simply turned and shuffled off toward the back.

Marissa and Finesse walked out. "Your mama don't talk much, huh?" he asked.

Marissa shrugged. "She used to, but . . . I don't know . . . She has let life weigh her down."

Finesse thought about it, then replied, "Now I see why you left."

She gave him a grateful smile and a playful bump as they went down the stairs. They walked around the corner to a long, flat building that served as the neighborhood recreation center. The whole front face of the building was covered by a mural of Guatemalan faces, and the block was flooded with gang bangers dressed in and flagging their colors. As the two of them walked toward the entrance of the Rec building, all eyes turned in their direction.

"Yo 'Rissa, these muhfuckas kinda deep. You sure we good?" Finesse asked, staying alert.

"Don't worry, you're with me." She winked.

"Ay homie, you lost?" a dude asked as they entered the building.

"Ignore him," Marissa told Finesse.

They walked through the outer room furnished with domino tables, and out onto the basketball court. It had been converted into a boxing gym, complete with two boxing rings, a weight area, several heavy bags, and six-speed bags. The room smelled like sweat and ambition, as many Guatemalan youth trained to fight their way out of their dismal existence.

Marissa's beauty and Finesse's blackness drew attention like a magnet. She spotted whom she was looking for and walked over to him. He was goading a boxer sparring in the ring with rapid-fire Spanish.

"Spider!" Marissa called out.

He looked and his gruff expression flowered into a smile. "Sobrina!" he sang as she approached. Spider wrapped her in a warm hug. "How's my favorite niece? Back for another lesson?" He chuckled.

Marissa snickered. I'm still sore from the last one. Where's Jorge?"

"Eh, he's around," Spider replied, purposefully being vague as he gazed at Finesse.

"Spider, this is Finesse. Finesse, this is Uncle Spider."

Finesse noticed how she introduced him with his nickname, whereas she used his real name with her mother. He took it to mean that this introduction was on some hood shit, and it peaked his interest.

He and Spider shook hands. "Nice to meet you," Finesse said.

"Same here," Spider replied, slyly sizing him up. He turned to Marissa. "Jorge expecting you?"

Marissa put her hands on her hips. "Since when do I need an appointment to see my own brother?"

Spider laughed. "No, Sobrina, I didn't mean it like that. It's just . . . never mind, I'll call him." Spider pulled out his phone and called Jorge. "Marissa's here . . . okay, but she's got company . . . moreno," Spider explained.

Finesse knew when he said "moreno" he was referring to him.

"Tambien," Spider concluded, then hung up. "Follow me." He walked them through the gym to a back door that led to a dimly lit hallway. The hallway led to a set of stairs that descended into the bowels of the building. The only light was the red bulb that led to a cavernous room. Even though it was bright and sunny outside, down there you didn't know if it was day or night. The room was packed and it smelled of blood and money, both of which were present in the room—blood on the floor and money in many hands. It was obvious to Finesse that the men were gambling, but it wasn't clear what they were gambling on. Finesse looked at the blood on the floor. It looked fresh. He thought about cock fights.

He was wrong.

"Jorge!" Marissa cried out and jumped into her brother's arms.

"I missed you, Sonrisa," Jorge replied, using his nickname for her.

It was obvious they were brother and sister. The main difference was the darker Indian complexion that Jorge had.

She led him by the hand over to Finesse. "Jorge, this is Finesse, a very good friend of mine," she said.

Jorge and Finesse shook hands, looking each other in the eyes. "Is that right? A very good friend?" Jorge smirked. "How'd you meet?"

"In the hospital," Finesse replied.

"You a doctor?" Jorge joked.

Finesse chuckled. "No, I'm a chef."

Jorge got the joke immediately and laughed. "I guess that's why mi hermana wanted us to meet, eh?" Jorge surmised.

"It is. I think you two can make some things happen," Marissa chimed in.

"Yeah?" Jorge remarked with a nod. He started to say something else, but someone stepped in the middle of the crowd and began talking loudly in Spanish.

"Excuse me one second, my fighter's about to go on."

Money began to change hands all around them. Marissa and Finesse elbowed their way to the front of the crowd. Finesse could understand very little of what was being said, but when a hefty girl in gold shorts and a black sports bra stepped into the circle, he knew he was introducing the fighter.

It was clear she was the favorite, as men started shouting and more money changed hands. She looked like a bruiser, with a build that indicated that she could beat a man. In this type of fight, Layla Ali didn't stand a chance.

The next person to step into the ring was a girl who barely looked twenty, even though she was twenty-four. She was muscular, but not to the extreme. At 5-feet 9-inches tall, she was built more like a brawny track star than a boxer, and her face reminded Finesse of Michelle Rodriguez.

"She gonna fight her?" Finesse laughed. "Ma, you got some money? Big Girl gonna mash Shorty."

"No." Marissa smirked, looking the girl in the eyes. "Never bet against her."

When the girl saw Marissa, she smiled subtly and winked.

The bell rang and the girls moved to the center of the ring. Big Girl came on like a rushing bull and caught Shorty with an overhand right that staggered her.

"Owww!" the crowd cried collectively.

"Damn, that would've dropped the average dude!" Finesse exclaimed.

"Just watch," Marissa said with a smile that said she knew something he didn't.

And she was right, because after the first blow, Shorty moved in for the kill. It was like she wanted to see how hard Big Girl hit, and then she went to work.

The next blow that Big Girl threw, Shorty ducked and caught her with a two piece to the gut that took the wind out of Big Girl. Shorty danced to the side and landed a pretty two piece, then an upper cut, then another two piece and an overhand right and—

Big Girl dropped to the asphalt floor, bloodied and bruised. But Shorty wasn't finished. She sat on Big Girl, pinning her arms beneath her and drilled her repeatedly, dropping blows like a swarm of angry bees.

"Matala!"

"Kill her!"

"Matala!"

Shorty pulverized Big Girl, who could take no more. "No mas!" she cried out in a weakened and hoarse tone.

Shorty stopped the next blow in midair, stood up, and walked out of the ring. The crowd went crazy. Losers cursed and ranted while winners raved and waved money.

Jorge came over, counting a fat stack of bills, licking his thumb. "So what you think? I made her a beast, huh?" Jorge smiled proudly.

"She already was. You just unleashed it. Excuse me," Marissa said as she went after Shorty.

"So . . . you like my sister?"

"No doubt," Finesse replied.

"Yeah? You love her?"

"Of course," Finesse lied, but looked Jorge straight in the eyes when he did. He couldn't tell if Jorge believed him when he responded.

"Well, she loves you. She's never brought one of her boyfriend's home, you know? That means a lot, because my sister is, how you say, Americanized. She don't like to remember the slime she climbed out of. Me? The slimier, the better!" Jorge laughed and Finesse joined him.

"If it ain't rough, it ain't right," Finesse remarked.

Jorge nodded. "Exactly! So . . . you're a . . . businessman?"

"Indeed."

"You ever do time?"

"I just got out. I did three in Terre Haute, Atlanta, and Lompoc."

"I'ma check you out, and if you're good, we're good. But if you ain't good, tell me now because I'd hate to find out on my own," Jorge warned.

"Believe me, I'm official tissue. The brick don't raise no rats," Finesse shot back, letting his pedigree be known.

"That's good to hear, because I love my sister. But I love money too. I'd chop a muhfucka up and eat his heart over my money, so just imagine what I'd do to a nigger over my sister," Jorge hissed.

Finesse could tell by the way he said the word "nigger," that he was being derogatory but not malicious. He simply wanted to make his point as blunt as possible.

"I hear you, yo," Finesse replied, meeting Jorge's stone gaze with a steel gaze of his own.

Jorge smiled evilly. "Naw, I don't think you do, so let me be more direct. If you try and play my sister, I'll kill you. Now, as a man, I'm sure you feel untouchable. Maybe you are . . . maybe you'll kill me. But one thing is for sure, we will find out."

"Yo, I respect that. Just make sure you respect me and we won't have no problems."

Jorge laughed. "I like you, Finesse. You walked into the lion's den and didn't flinch. That takes heart. You box?"

Finesse looked at Jorge. It sounded like a simple question, but he knew it wasn't. It had a menacing edge to it. "I know a little sumthin'."

"Yeah? You nice or what?"

Marissa and Shorty walked up. "Nice at what?" Marissa wanted to know, but Jorge and Finesse were on their macho shit and ignored her.

"Like I said, I know a little sumthin'," Finesse repeated.

"You think you can handle my ring? It's about as rough as it gets," Jorge remarked, purposefully using the word rough to remind Finesse of his own earlier statement.

"Like I said, if it ain't rough, it ain't right," he replied, showing Jorge he stood behind it.

Marissa caught on. "Finesse, what are you doing? I know you're not talking about fighting."

She turned to Jorge. "Jorge!" Marissa emphasized.

Jorge chuckled. "Cállate, Sonrisa, he's a big boy. Chino!" Jorge called out, without taking his eyes off Finesse.

A muscular, yet wiry young Guatemalan stepped into the ring. He was bare-chested, revealing all his tattoos that literally covered him from head to toe.

"Que va!" Chino spat arrogantly.

"I got a thousand on my man here says he kicks your ass, homes," Jorge yelled, still looking Finesse in the eyes.

"Then you just lost it, homes," Chino joked, and a few others laughed.

Jorge smiled, then counted off ten 100 dollar bills.

"You lose my money, and I'll consider you a bad investment."

Finesse knew what was going on. He was being tested, thrown into the forging fire to test his mettle. Finesse took off his shirt and handed it to Marissa.

"You don't have to do this," she protested weakly, hating that she had brought him to this.

Finesse stepped into the circle, bouncing around to get his blood flowing and loosening himself up. Chino stretched and contorted his neck from side to side. Money began to quickly change hands. The bell rang.

Ding!

"Matalo!"

"Mata el moreno!"

"Kill the nigguh!"

Finesse was clearly not the crowd's favorite, and that was proven as soon as Chino moved in. Finesse threw a jab that missed, and Chino countered with a powerful kidney shot.

"Yeah!" the crowd cried in broken unity.

Finesse grimaced in pain but ignored it and caught Chino with a pretty two-piece, drawing first blood.

Chino spat blood.

"That all you got, homes?"

"Muhfucka, I ain't the one spittin' blood," Finesse shot back.

But Chino would soon change that. He charged in, taking two powerful hooks from Finesse in order to get in a body-rocking gut shot that bent Finesse over. Then he followed it with a stinging uppercut that knocked Finesse backward into the crowd. The crowd caught him and flung him back as quickly as if he had bounced off the ropes. He flew back into a Chino jab that punched him drunk. He had to grab onto Chino to keep from going down.

"Oh my God!" Marissa gasped, covering her mouth.

"Get off me!" Chino gruffed, shoving Finesse back, then switching to southpaw to finish him.

Finesse bounced around the ring, getting his head together, so that, by the time Chino moved in, Finesse had his second wind. The two of them went toe to toe, exchanging thunderous blows.

Crack!

The breaking of Finesse's jaw rang throughout the room, but he kept swinging and connecting, and when Chino dropped his left, Finesse hit him with a hook that dropped him to the ground.

"No!" someone yelled.

"Chino, get up!" a random voice shouted.

Finesse got on top of Chino and went to work. Chino's defense was almost nonexistent. As much as his ego didn't want to, he knew he had to.

"No, m—" Chino started to say, but Finesse grabbed him by the throat and choked the words back. Chino had broken his jaw. He was totally enraged. Fuck "no mas!" Death was on his mind. He choked Chino with one hand and pounded him with the other, over and over and over and over and—Jorge caught his bloodied hand by the wrist. Finesse looked at him.

"No mas," Jorge said.

Finesse held his gaze for a moment, then he looked down at Chino. He was out cold and his face looked like raw meat. He couldn't take any more blows and live. Jorge stopped the fight just in time, unfortunately for Finesse.

"You win, homes. Congratulations," Jorge said, handing in a bundle of money.

Finesse damn sure didn't feel like a winner. His jaw was broken, and his left eye was swollen shut, but he had earned the connect of a lifetime.

Finesse stood to his feet, dropping his arm over Marissa for support.

"Yeah, Finesse, I think we can do business, but let's go before things get out of hand," Jorge remarked.

The crowd was deathly silent, watching Finesse, Jorge, Marissa, and Shorty walk out of the basement with all eyes on them, while several men carried Chino out of the circle.

CHAPTER 14
- Playing with Prey -

"Slurp! Slurp! Mmmmm—Slurp!"

Were the sounds that filled the car as GQ drove around Market Street in his new, all-black Land Rover.

Don Pooh's fiancée, Vanessa, had her face in his lap and his dick down her throat. Her head game was so good, it damn near had GQ cockeyed.

"Goddamn, ma, fuck!" he grunted, his toes curled up in his Timbs.

This was the second time she had given him brains in the whip. Ever since she first laid eyes on him, she was feeling him. On GQ's behalf, he was simply feeling being felt. He was used to females being all over him, so when Vanessa finally made her move, he was almost expecting it.

∞

"Yo, ain't that GQ?" one of Supreme's goons barked, as they passed him going the other way. "Yo, bust a U! Bust a U!"

"I am, nigguh. Hol' the fuck up!" the driver growled, waiting for a break in traffic to do just that.

The passenger goon used his speed dial on his cell. "Yo, 'Preme, we on it, God! We see GQ!"

Supreme jumped up and grabbed his car keys. "Where you at?"

101

"Where I'm at? I don't know where the fuck I'm at, but we followin' the nigguh."

"A street sign! Read a fuckin' street sign!"

The passenger goon looked around, then turned to the driver. "You see a street sign?"

"Market Street . . . We on Market Street," the goon repeated.

Supreme hurried for his car, tucking his pistol in his pants.

"Where at on Mar—never mind."

"What you want us to do? Blast the nigguh or what?"

Supreme thought about it. As bad as he wanted to show Chanel that he was making some progress, he knew that if he killed GQ on the spot the rest of the team would scatter.

"Naw, naw, follow 'im. See where he leads you. If you can, snatch his ass up," Supreme ordered, jumping in his car.

"What if we can't do neither one?"

"Then murder the bastard!" Supreme growled.

∞

"Yo, ma, do it wit' no hands," GQ commanded, taking her by the back of the neck and guiding her motions.

"Okay, daddy."

GQ was in heaven, but he didn't know he was slipping, too. Usually, he kept a check in the rearview mirror, but the face in his lap had him distracted.

Vanessa was giving a porn performance on his dick. Her pussy was dripping wet. She wanted to fuck him so badly.

"Oh shit, yo! Yo, swallow this shit!" he grunted, feeling the rumble build in his gut.

He was coming to an intersection and the light was green. That was the last thing he saw before his eyes rolled up in the back of his head. He fought to keep focus, but when he looked up, the light had just turned red, and he entered the intersection.

"Oh shit!" he exclaimed, because he was cumming and because traffic was coming. He knew if he hit the brakes, he'd have an accident, so he floored it and narrowly missed being side-swiped by an oncoming bus.

"Fuck!" the driver spat as he watched GQ run the red light and disappear on the other side of the busy intersection.

"You run it! Run it! Nigguh gettin' away!" the passenger goon urged.

"You crazy as fuck! I ain't running this shit! Look!" the driver said, referring to his rearview.

The passenger goon looked over his shoulder and saw, four or five cars back, the dormant lights of a patrol car, waiting on the green.

"Damn yo, he ran the red light, 'Preme! He musta seen us, plus po-po right behind us!"

"You stupid motherfucka!" Supreme blasted. "How the fuck you let the nigguh get away?"

"He–he ran the light!" the goon repeated.

Supreme shook his head, hung up, and turned back toward the motel.

Vanessa sat up, not knowing they had just run a red light. She swallowed all of GQ's cum, but she used her pinkie to wipe the corner of her mouth. "You gotta drop me off back at the salon," she told him as she pulled the visor down to use the vanity mirror.

"Come on, ma. You know I'm tryin' to fuck. What's up?"

"I know, baby, but I can't," she whined as she applied her lipstick. "Don be on some real possessive shit. He might be sitting in front of the salon right now."

"Goddamn, the nigguh be on it like that?"

She shook her head and rolled her eyes. "You don't know the half."

Two blocks later, they were back at the salon. "Pull around back," she instructed him. Vanessa got out her phone and hit a number.

"Pam, it's V. Open the back door," she said and then hung up.

GQ chuckled. "You've done this before, huh?"

She giggled to play it off as the car came to a stop. "Whateva. I'll call you," she replied, opening the door and leaning toward him for a kiss.

GQ leaned away.

"It's yours," she sassed.

"So is my piss, but I don't drink it."

"You so stupid."

"For real, for real, get at me, yo."

"You know I will, wit' that sweet dick," she replied with a sexy smile.

GQ watched her get out, admiring the way that plump, apple bottom ass looked in her jeans.

"I see why Don fucked up." He chuckled as he pulled off.

Vanessa walked in through the back door and straight out the front door, where her Benz was parked. As soon as she was about to get in, her phone rang.

It was Don Pooh. "Yo, where you?"

"I told you I had to go to the salon."

"Fuck takin' you so long?"

"I'm leavin' now," she sang cheerfully to keep the strain out of her voice.

"Well, hurry up and bring me a fish dinner."

"Okay, daddy."

"I love you."

"I love you, too," she replied with another man's cum on her breath.

∞

"He got away?"

Those were the three words that Supreme didn't want to say or hear, but he thought it sounded better than nothing. But the way Chanel spat it back at him, now he wasn't so sure.

He was in the outer room of Chanel's suite sitting on the couch facing her as she sat across from him. But Kat was pacing behind him, and it had him nervous.

"Ma, I'm tellin' you, we got this—"

"But he got away," she repeated.

"I'm sayin', he ran the red light and—"

"So you're sayin' he spotted you?" she questioned.

"Naw, yo, he might've thought he was being followed," Supreme said.

Chanel smirked. She loved to make people squirm. "But he was being followed."

Realizing that he had backed himself into a corner, he took a deep breath and reset. "Believe me, ma, I got these muhfuckas. I got my team on call 24/7, and I got these bitches on—"

"Don't . . . use that word."

"My bad, these chicks off the block."

"What chicks?" she probed.

"They be on the block all the time," he replied.

"You mean, like . . . crack heads?"

He realized how feeble it sounded, but at the moment it was all he had, so he tried to make it sound good. "Shit, ma, you know them crack bit—I mean—fiends be on it." He laughed.

Chanel didn't. She rubbed her head like she had a headache, and he was the cause.

"Crack heads." She chuckled, shaking her head. "Supreme, I told you . . . the longer these nigguhs breathe, the worse the organization looks. You understand that, right?"

"My word, Chanel. These nigguhs won't live."

"Oh, I already know that. If I wanted to, I could dead them like"—she snapped her fingers—"that."

"I know."

"But then, what would I need you for?"

Supreme sensed that Kat had stopped pacing and felt her standing behind him. He held his composure, but inside he was shook. "I'ma take care of it."

"Supreme, you're making me regret my decision. Infinite was a good money maker, but he lacked that—umph, you know—the killer instinct. I thought you had it," Chanel remarked.

"I do."

"Prove it," she replied, looking him dead in the eyes. "Burn the city down if you have to, but handle your business. Are we clear?" she questioned.

GAME OF GWOP

"No doubt."

"Good, now get out," she spat, waving him off dismissively.

He got up without another word and left.

As soon as he was gone, Kat turned to Chanel. "Yo, Co, why the fuck are we playing with these lames? Let's handle it and go home," Kat growled.

Chanel shrugged. "We could . . . but to play chess, one must have pawns, no?"

"It's starting to get on my fuckin' nerves."

"It's not that bad. Besides, it feels good to be on the hunt again. It keeps you on your toes. It's been a while since we've had a target this swift. I'm having fun." Chanel giggled.

She had the power to crush the crew, but like a lioness, she was playing with her prey, toying with them . . . but only for a short moment.

CHAPTER 15
- Double Cross -

"Aw, who dis?"

"What you mean, who dis? You called me," Supreme stated.

"Oh yeah. This Bev, the chick you met on the Ave. The one who look like Halle Berry."

Despite his aggravation, Supreme had to chuckle to himself because this was the smoker chick that he had paid to be the lookout, and she looked more like Halle Scary than Halle Berry.

"Yeah, ma, what up?"

"They here! Them Jersey nigguhs here!" she exclaimed in a forced whisper.

"Where?"

"You know where Shabazz barbershop at?"

"Naw, but I'm on my way!" Supreme replied, hitting Science's knee and waving him on.

Supreme, Science, and two of his goons had been playing cards. They quickly jumped up and grabbed weapons as they headed out of the motel room door.

"Where you comin' from?" she asked.

Supreme was hesitant to tell her what motel he was in. "Just gimme the address. I'll GPS it."

"It's on Market Street."

"I'm on my way."

"Big Daddy!" Bev shouted, trying to catch him before he hung up.

"Don't worry, ma, I got you."

"Bet. I'll be right here, too!"

GPS took them straight to the barbershop. As soon as they pulled onto Market Street, the BMW with Jersey plates was just pulling off. Inside, Supreme could see three heads.

"There they go!" Science said, loading the AR-15.

"Pull up beside 'em, God, and it's over!" one of the goons in the back said, letting his window down. He placed the muzzle of the SK-47 out of the window.

"Whateva you do, don't miss!" Supreme warned.

He didn't have to tell them twice.

As soon as he pulled up next to the BMW, he suddenly cut them off. The occupants never had a chance. Science stuck the AR-15 out of the window and aimed at the driver and shotgun passenger. Supreme's goon did better, stepping out of the car and letting loose on the dude in the backseat at almost point blank range, exploding his head and face all over the rear interior of the car.

"Go! Go!" the goon bellowed as he jumped back in.

Supreme screeched off.

"Yeah yo! We got them nigguhs!" Science exclaimed.

"But it was the wrong muhfuckas! That wasn't GQ!" Supreme cursed.

∞

"Ay yo, you shoulda seen it! Muhfuckas put in work up at the barbershop! Somebody murdered the shit outta them Trenton nigguhs that be wit' Lucky and them." Shifty chuckled as he walked in the door of Charisma's apartment.

It was a nice-sized condominium. The only problem was, there was no furniture. She had spent all her money on a brand new Silver Mercedes S-Class and a pink diamond watch she just had to have. But of the team, she was the only one smart enough to even rent a place, while Shamar, GQ, and Crook still stayed in hotels, when they weren't sleeping on her living room floor. The three of them each had a fifty thousand dollar car, but they were basically homeless.

Don Pooh sat on a milk crate in the corner, and when Shifty entered talking about the shooting, he replied, "Goddamn, you Jersey nigguhs got shit hot as fuck!"

Crook closed the door behind Shifty. "Them nigguhs probably thought it was us," he cracked, not knowing how right he was.

"Naw, 'er body know them Trenton nigguhs, yo. They know they ain't you," Shifty replied.

Shamar hit the blunt, but his mind went back to what Crystal had told him. Charisma peeped the look on his face.

"What?"

He started to say something, but decided against it. "Nothin'"

"Yeah, and that's just what I got left. Nothin'," GQ remarked.

"You ain't the only one," Charisma added. "I done had five muhfuckas holla, but I ain't got shit to sell 'em."

"We need to re-up." Crook nodded.

"Yo, I got an ill connect in Philly. He kinda expensive, but shit, we can eat," Don Pooh told them.

"What's his number?" Shamar asked.

"Twenty-eight a key."

"Twenty-eight?" Crook echoed. "Fuck that, we can do better in Jersey."

GQ nodded in agreement.

"Yeah, but Philly right next door, plus we spendin' over two hundred stacks. I'm sure we can get him down," Charisma replied, looking at Don Pooh.

"Nigguh tight, but we might get him to do twenty-six," Don Pooh surmised.

Shamar thought for a moment. His not hearing from Finesse, and Charisma still not hearing from her sister Sonja had him feeling bad vibes coming from Newark, so the Philly connect played right into the situation. "Yo, I say fuck it. Let's fuck wit' the Philly nigguh, and if his shit straight then we good," Shamar suggested.

They looked around at each other. Then Crook replied and cracked, "Yeah, yeah, I'm wit' it. I need to get back on my block."

Ever since he had burnt up that dude K-Nut, the other dudes decided they didn't want a war. So he knew that as soon as the heat died down, he'd have the block on lock.

"Yo Pooh, call your man. Let him know we lookin' for that Brotherly Love!" GQ remarked with a chuckle.

Don Pooh nodded and laughed, hoping he hadn't tripped himself up by putting them on with his Philly connect. He knew, based on Crook's actions alone, that a double cross was very probable.

CHAPTER 16
- Out of the Loop -

For the past three and a half days, Finesse's asshole had been so tight that he couldn't shit a mustard seed. He was tense all while riding the Greyhound bus from Los Angeles to Newark with a kilo of uncut heroin in his book bag. At every stop or changeover, he half expected the police to ask the dreaded question: "Sir, may I check your bag?"

He hadn't eaten except for snacks, because he didn't want to get off the bus.

Jorge had come through like a champ, estimating the kilo of heroin, if cut right, could bring Finesse over a million dollars. It was his "wedding gift," Jorge had said, referring to his relationship with Marissa. Finesse couldn't lie. He was definitely feeling Marissa, especially after she had helped him become a millionaire overnight. They had talked about the future the night that he left.

"So Monday, I'll be able to contact some hospitals in New Jersey and New York and see if they have any openings," she told him with her head on his chest. She lifted up to look him in the eyes. "Please stop me if I'm making a mistake."

He brushed her hair out of her face, caressed her cheek, and kissed her forehead.

"No, ma, everything with us is one hundred percent."

She smiled. "Okay . . . because, believe me, I'm not feeling the East. I hate the cold." She giggled.

He pulled her close and wrapped her in his embrace. "Don't worry, I'ma hold you so tight that you won't even feel it."

"I love you, baby."

"I love you, too," he replied, meaning it a little bit more.

Finesse was looking forward to bringing Marissa East, but first he had to make it there himself.

"Next stop, Newark, New Jersey!" the bus driver announced through the P.A. system, bringing Finesse back to the present. He breathed a sigh of relief.

As he looked out the window at his hometown, smiling from ear to ear, he marveled at the changes. It had been almost four years since he had seen Newark. Gentrification seemed to be on the cusp. It was partly fixed and mostly broken.

"I'm 'bout to turn this shit the fuck up," he whispered into his reflection in the window.

The bus stopped. He grabbed his book bag and headed for the front door, moving fast so as not to get caught up in the crunch of people getting off the bus. He stepped down and took a deep lungful of Newark air. It smelled less than pure, but it smelled like home. Despite being gone for so long, he remembered one of Newark's golden rules of smuggling: never get a cab right in front of Penn Station because the police can be waiting for you.

He began to walk along the busy sidewalk in front of the station when he heard, "Excuse me, sir." His blood froze in his veins as he turned toward the direction of the voice.

It was the police—actually, two of them, plain clothes and headed right for him. Finesse knew what it was. There was no mistaking the look in their eyes. He hadn't been in Newark but a few minutes, and he was already facing another prison bid.

He wasn't about to let it go down like that. "Why? What's up?" Finesse asked, buying time until they got close enough.

As soon as they were, one of the officer's said, "I'd like to see your—" That's all he got out before Finesse caught him with a vicious left, then hit his partner with a right cross.

He struck with sufficient force to stun them both long enough to snatch the first cop's gun from his holster and take off running.

By the time the second cop regained his composure sufficiently to pull his gun, Finesse was already sliding into the driver's seat of a cab. The cabbie had just put his fare's luggage in the trunk and left the driver's door open, when Finesse ran up on him, gun aimed straight in his face, barking, "Get back! Move!"

The cabbie damn near broke his neck to comply with Finesse's order.

"Freeze!" the second cop yelled, taking aim as Finesse threw the car into drive and barreled forward.

Finesse ducked down as he mashed the accelerator, heading straight for the cop. The cop let off two shots that pierced the windshield and then the head rest, right where Finesse's head would have been if he hadn't been ducking. The cop dove out of the way of the cab just in a nick of time.

The other cop had gotten the unmarked car, and once the second cop jumped in they were in hot pursuit. Finesse had them by half a block, but their car radio evened the score.

"All units! All units! We've got a suspect in a stolen cab. He is armed and dangerous, I repeat, armed and dangerous! He's heading west on Raymond Boulevard and just made a left onto Broad Street!"

Finesse had been gone so long, he didn't know about the police substation on Broad and Market Streets, and he was headed straight for it. Several police cars buzzed out like angry bees from a hive to join the chase.

"Fuck!" Finesse bellowed, seeing the odds stack against him. He slung a hard right on a small one way side street and hit the gas until he felt the floor, but he had to slam on the brakes because a cop car blocked him in. He quickly got out, dumping shots, ducking and running.

The cop got low but came up firing, as Finesse disappeared down an alley between two buildings.

"He's in the alley!" a cop yelled.

His own breathing, footsteps, and heartbeat were the only audible sounds. Everything else was background noise. "I ain't going back, I ain't going back," he kept repeating in his mind. He was glad he had the gun because true to his word, if he got cornered, he was holding court in the streets.

He leaped and grabbed a hanging fire escape ladder and scurried up, thankful for all those prison pull ups.

"Don't move!" a cop yelled who spotted Finesse a second before he dove through a window as the sound of shattering glass filled the air.

The cop, who was quickly joined by five more tried to pull himself up, but too many donuts weighed him down.

"Shit!" he cursed, then tried the back door only to find it locked.

"Go around front! Hurry up!" he yelled.

The delay gave Finesse the needed respite as he walked the darkened hallway of the building. He thought he would never catch his breath, but when he heard the muffled sounds of footsteps on the floor below, he caught it quickly, taking the steps to the roof two at a time.

Finesse burst out onto the roof, knowing exactly why he was there. He flung his book bag to the roof of the building across the alley. He knew the cops had concentrated on the one building, so if they were all in that one, then he could easily elude them in the other—if he could make the leap. He and his brother had grown up jumping roof to roof, but the distance in this situation was a little greater than he was accustomed to. He backed up and took off running, and as soon as his foot hit the edge and he felt himself in flight, the police burst out of the door.

"He jumped!"

"Fire!"

The bullets from several guns blasted off at the same time, piercing the air and narrowly missing Finesse as he hit the roof on the other side. He grabbed his book bag then stayed low, bullets whizzing over his head as he duck-walked to the fire escape.

"Suspect just jumped to the building directly opposite of us. He's using the fire escape on the north face of the building. All units' coverage!"

Finesse kicked in a window on the top landing of the building and entered a darkened office. He quickly moved through and out of the door, heading for the elevator, which he saw down the hall. He hit the button and the elevator door opened. As soon as he was in the elevator, he stood on the metal handrail, bracing himself against the diagonal wall and opened the trap door in the roof of the elevator. After throwing the book bag through, he climbed up after it and lay on top of the elevator, shutting the trap door behind him. Several seconds later, the elevator started to descend to the first floor. The police had summoned it.

Once it reached the lobby, as Finesse felt the weight shift, he knew several police had gotten on, and then the elevator began to ascend.

"Well, I guess Bennett definitely doesn't want to go back, huh?"

Finesse heard the words and peeped down through the crack of the trap door. He could see that it was one of the plain clothes officers from Penn Station.

But how the fuck they know my name? he thought. Something wasn't right. He knew there was no way the police could have identified him, or had a way to know his name.

Unless someone told them.

The police scoured the building for two hours before concluding that he had somehow gotten away.

Finesse waited another hour until he heard no more muffled voices coming from any floor. Then he took the elevator to the first floor, left the building, and hopped on the first bus that came. He sat in the back of the bus and pulled out his phone. "Goddamn!" he cursed when he discovered that he had broken his phone. "This ain't my fuckin' day," he added.

Without his phone, he was without any contacts, including Marissa, which he would realize later. He vowed to himself to start remembering numbers and not just relying on the wonders of modern technology. He decided to head to the one address he knew wouldn't change.

Charisma's.

∞

By the time Finesse reached her block, it was dark. He trudged up the block, tired, hungry, and paranoid. He half expected every car to be an undercover cop and every cop car to be looking for him. As he approached the building, a money-green Cadillac CTS with chrome rims blinding, passed him on his side of the street. He didn't pay much attention until he saw the vehicle brake and then come to a complete stop. When Finesse saw that, he too stopped and put his hand on the gun in his waistband. He only had two bullets left in the clip, so he knew he had to make every shot count.

The car backed up, and the passenger window came down, but it was so dark he couldn't see inside.

"Yo Shamar, what you doin', God?" the voice inside called out.

Finesse bent over and squinted, his hand firmly around the butt of the gun.

"Yo, who dat?" Finesse called back.

"Who?" the voice barked back. Then Bam got out of the driver's seat and looked over the roof of the car. "Nigguh, this Bam! Fuck is you, blind?"

As soon as Finesse saw Bam, a big smile spread across his face. "My nigguh!" Finesse exclaimed and approached Bam.

Bam met him halfway and gave him a gangsta hug.

"And I ain't Shamar, nigguh. This Finesse."

Bam frowned. "Fuck outta here, Sha. Stop playin'."

"Dead ass, nigguh. Finesse!" Finesse stepped back and pulled up his shirt, revealing the tattoo "Finesse" across his stomach.

Bam's eyes bucked wide and he hugged Finesse again. "Oh shit, Finesse! What the fuck! When you get home?"

"Today!"

"Muhfuckas said you had a 'L', my nig?" Bam questioned.

"I got my shit overturned, yo. Ain't no funny shit. I'm still official!" Finesse boasted, just in case Bam thought he got out for cooperating.

"Naw, fam', I already know you solid. I'm just tellin' you what the word is. What up? You heard about Sha?"

Finesse froze up and looked Bam in the eyes.

Bam read his expression. "Naw, it ain't nothin' like that, but shit is real out here! Muhfuckas say he murdered Infinite!"

"Murdered?"

"Get in. I'll pour you a drink," Bam said, heading back around the car.

"Hol' up, I'm 'bout to go up and holla at Charisma," Finesse explained.

Bam stopped at the open door and looked at him. "Damn, you really is out of the loop, huh? Charisma gone and her sister dead!"

Finesse couldn't believe his ears. But since he had nowhere else to go, he decided to go with Bam. He started to get in the passenger seat, but there was a female sitting there, so he jumped in the backseat, ready to learn what was going on with his brother.

CHAPTER 17
- Riding Dirty -

Crook grabbed his gun and started to get out of the car, but Shamar grabbed his arm.

"No, yo, chill," Shamar told him.

"Nigguh, you crazy as fuck! These nigguhs takin' our money, and all I'm 'posed to do is watch?" Crook barked.

Shamar shook his head. "Yeah, yo . . . yeah." He had to fight the same urge as Crook, but he knew that to move was foolish because he couldn't just kill cops.

The day had started off normal. They were preparing to make the trip to Philly. Knowing that a car full of black dudes would draw too much heat, they decided to have Charisma and Vanessa drive the money car.

"Whenever I make the trip, I always let 'Nessa take the paper," Don Pooh had said.

But Shamar wasn't about to send two females all alone, so they decided to trail them in GQ's Land Rover. GQ drove while Don Pooh rode shotgun, with Shamar and Crook in the back. They were heading for the highway, when a patrol car threw on its flashing cherries and pulled the two girls over in their rented Prius.

"Fuck!" GQ exclaimed.

"Probably just a routine stop," Don Pooh surmised.

Charisma thought the same thing. She was in the passenger seat while Vanessa drove. She made sure the car was extra clean—she didn't even have a cigar on her, let alone weed. The only thing dirty that they were carrying was the three hundred and fifty grand in the duffle bag in the backseat.

"You good?" Charisma asked Vanessa as the policemen got out and approached the car.

"Yeah," Vanessa responded, but her tone of voice sounded nervous.

Red flags started jumping all around in Charisma's head, but before she could say anything, the cop approached the driver's side. He was a tall, black dude with a name tag that read 'Jefferies,' and his partner Rodriguez was a Puerto Rican who approached the passenger side from the rear of the Prius.

"License and registration, please ma'am," Jefferies requested firmly but politely.

"Umm, was I speeding, officer?" Vanessa asked.

Jefferies smiled and replied, "Just license and registration, if you don't mind."

Vanessa sighed hard, then went in her purse and handed him the license.

Jefferies took the license, then bent over and looked at Charisma. "And you, ma'am. Do you have an ID on you?"

"I'm not driving," Charisma replied, keeping her tone neutral.

"I can see that, but I'd still like to know who you are."

Charisma handed him her ID because she wanted to get it over with. Besides, it was fake, so she knew it would come back clean.

Jefferies walked back to the squad car.

"You okay, right?" Charisma asked Vanessa.

"I should be. I think I have a couple of parking tickets though.

∞

"Yo, what they pull 'em for?" Shamar questioned.

"Dog, this Delaware. Police be on it. Especially how hot shit been lately," Don Pooh explained.

"Yo, this some bullshit!" Crook gruffed.

"Shamar just watched, feeling bad vibes about the whole situation.

"Yo! He putting handcuffs on your girl, Pooh!" GQ exclaimed.

∞

Charisma couldn't believe her ears when Jefferies said, "Miss McCrae, step out of the car please."

"Why?"

"You have an outstanding warrant for your arrest."

Charisma wanted to punch her in the face on the spot. "Bitch, I thought you were straight!" she hissed.

"I am!" Vanessa cried as they handcuffed her. "It's a mistake."

Jefferies led a sobbing Vanessa to the backseat of the squad car.

Rodriguez opened Charisma's door. "Ma'am, I'm going to have to ask you to step out of the car, please."

"For what!" Charisma snapped.

Rodriguez's hand hovered above his gun. "Ma'am, I'm not going to ask you again."

Charisma looked at him through angry eyes, then she got out.

"Please turn around and place your hands on the roof of the car," he told her, and she reluctantly complied.

After he frisked her, he cuffed her up.

"Yo, what are you arresting me for?" Charisma questioned with mad attitude.

"You're not under arrest, but this is for your own safety." Rodriguez walked her to the squad car and put her in the backseat next to Vanessa. When Charisma glared at her, Vanessa couldn't even meet her gaze.

"I-I swear, it's a mistake," Vanessa mumbled.

"Nope, no mistake. Vanessa McCrae, you were supposed to be in court on a simple possession charge. You didn't appear, hence the warrant."

"Yeah, well, I ain't got a warrant. Why are you holding me?" Charisma probed.

"Because, Miss . . ." Jefferies looked at her ID "Young from Roselle, I'm wondering what you're doing in Delaware."

"Visiting."

"Or trafficking?" He smirked, looking at her through the rearview mirror. "Because I've seen it a million times. Pretty, young girls like you, bringing drugs into my fair city. And with this recent slew of killings, two and two ain't twenty-two, you follow me?"

Charisma didn't reply.

"I thought you did," he continued. "So if I search the car, will I find any drugs?"

"No!" Vanessa blurted out. "We don't have any drugs."

"And you ain't got no warrant," Charisma added.

"But I have probable cause," he shot back. "Now . .
. before I search the car, anything you want to tell me?"

∞

"It's over." GQ shook his head, feeling sick to his stomach.

As soon as he saw Jefferies get out and head for the Prius, he knew what was about to happen.

"Fuck that!" Crook growled and grabbed his gun. He started to get out, but Shamar grabbed his arm

"No, yo, chill," Shamar told him.

"Nigguh, you crazy as fuck! These nigguhs takin' our money, and all I'm 'posed to do is watch?" Crook barked.

Shamar shook his head.

"Yeah, yo . . . yeah."

They watched as Jefferies carried the bag back to the squad car and got in.

∞

Jefferies got in the car and closed the door. "Wow," was all he said, then handed the bag to Rodriguez.

Rodriguez unzipped it and peeped inside, then whistled. "Double wow. You girls must be Queenpins, huh?"

Charisma could see where this was going, so she cut straight to the chase.

"Okay, look, we do promotions, no biggie. But it's gonna be a big headache for us to explain all that. So look, we'll give y'all fifty stacks to let us go."

Jefferies and Rodriguez looked at each other and burst out laughing.

"How are you going to give us half, when we have all of it?" Jefferies cracked.

"That's legit money."

"You have receipts?"

"Yeah," she lied.

"Bullshit." Jefferies chuckled. "But just in case you can, this'll be down at the precinct for you to reclaim.

"Then we're gonna need a receipt," Charisma replied.

Jefferies looked at Rodriguez. "Partner, do we have any receipts?"

"Fresh out." Rodriguez smiled.

"Sorry," Jefferies said, looking at Charisma through the rearview mirror.

"So you're gonna just take our money?" she remarked.

"Yeah." Jefferies shrugged. "Pretty much. But at least I'm leaving you with drugs. I'm sure they're in there somewhere."

Jeffries got out and opened Vanessa's door. He helped her out of the vehicle and uncuffed her. Then he walked around the car and opened Charisma's door. She didn't move, but she did, however, glare at him.

"Either get out, or you can come with us," he told her.

Charisma's face broke into an evil-looking smirk as she got out. She turned so he could uncuff her. "You sure you want to do this?" she asked coldly.

"I can't think of a reason why I wouldn't. Can you?" he shot back.

"Naw, me neither," she replied, already planning his death.

He took the cuffs off, and she turned to face him.

"And if I see you in my city again, I have a few unsolved murders just dying for a pretty face to wear," Jefferies threatened, then walked away.

Without another word, he got in the car and pulled off. As soon as he did and Vanessa turned to Charisma to speak, Charisma punched her dead in the mouth and commenced wailing on her. By the time GQ skidded up, less than a minute later, Vanessa was already dazed and bloodied.

Shamar pulled her off Vanessa as she continued to curse and kick.

"Get off me, Sha! I'ma kill that bitch!"

"What the fuck happened?" Don Pooh asked.

"This dumb bitch had a warrant!" Charisma spazzed.

"I didn't know," Vanessa cried.

"Yo, we gotta get off the street," GQ warned.

"Pooh, you ride with Vanessa. I got 'Riz."

∞

As soon as they got back to Charisma's condo, and she saw Don Pooh and Vanessa walk in, Charisma said, "Bitch, be here when I get back." She took off for the back.

"Yo, 'Nessa, wait in the car," Don Pooh said.

He didn't have to tell her twice. She disappeared as fast as her feet would carry her. When Charisma came back into the room, she had the Glock cocked.

"Pooh, I'm tellin' you, keep that bitch the fuck away from me," Charisma fumed.

"Ma, listen, I just lost a hundred stacks my goddamn self, but it wasn't 'Nessa's fault. She ain't got no charges. Wilmington police dirty like that. They spotted y'all on the way to Philly and figured you was movin' somethin'," Don Pooh surmised.

"All I wanna know is the cop's name," Crook grumbled, pacing the floor.

"Jefferies, yo, fuckin' Jefferies, and his bitch-ass partner was named Rodriguez!" Charisma spat, pacing the floor in the opposite direction. She and Crook were two high energy book ends.

"Yo, we can't kill no cop," Don Pooh exclaimed, looking from face to face as if they had lost their collective mind.

"Naw, nigguh, you can't kill no cops. I kill who the fuck I wanna kill, and that includes that dumb bitch of yours!" Crook said.

"Nigguh, what you say?" Don Pooh spat right back and lurched toward Crook.

Crook came at him, but GQ and Shamar got between them. Don Pooh may have outweighed Crook by over a hundred pounds, but the .45 in Crook's waistband weighed a ton.

"Nigguh what!" Crook replied.

"Yo chill. Y'all muhfuckas chill, goddamn it!" Shamar blasted both of them. "Pooh, as far as you, if you ain't trying to make moves, then I suggest you bounce because we ain't about to take this shit on the humble."

Don Pooh thought about it, then replied, "Yo dog, I'm wit' whateva, but we need to move right."

"We always do," Charisma chimed in.

"Bottom line is, I'm fuckin' broke!" GQ spat. "I got less than a grand to my name."

Everybody looked at everybody else, because they were all in the same boat. They all had bought fancy cars, jewelry, and splurged like real ballas, when in actuality, they weren't.

"So what we gonna do?" Charisma questioned.

"I say we start layin' these Wilmington nigguhs down. Pooh, who your biggest competition?"

"Naw, we goin' back to the brick. This is a sweet spot, so ain't no need in blowin' it. Besides, if we gonna catch them cops slippin', it's best that they think we ghost," Shamar surmised.

Charisma nodded. "No doubt. I'm feeling that."

"Shit, plus we sittin' on damn near two hundred grand in our whips. We go see Bam and trade a whip or two and we right back on," Shamar added.

"What about that thing, yo?" GQ reminded them, and they all knew he was talking about the bodies Crook caught in the club.

Chances were that some snitch nigguh had already dropped a dime. Shamar looked at Crook. "Then you stayin' here."

"I don't give a fuck, it's whateva," Crook replied.

Charisma looked at Crook. "And stay your little ass out of trouble!"

He smiled an evil grin with his mouthful of gold teeth because they all knew telling Crook to stay out of trouble was like telling him not to breathe.

CHAPTER 18
- A Mercy Killing -

It was good to be home.

That's what the smile on Finesse's face seemed to say as he lay back on the firm hotel bed while a dark, chocolate stallion and a honey-brown Beyoncé look alike sucked his dick. He had scooped them up at a club in Paterson that Bam had taken him to and couldn't decide which to take, so he took them both . . . hence the results.

Beyoncé popped his dick out of her mouth and cooed, "I wanna ride this big motherfucka."

"Shit, you already know." Finesse smirked.

She tongue kissed Chocolate, and then straddled Finesse, gripping his dick and sliding it in with a gush and a groan. Finesse took one look at Chocolate's pretty, pink pussy and decided to taste it.

"Come here, ma. I got a ride for you, too."

She smiled seductively, then slithered up the side of the bed and sat on his face, reverse cowgirl style, facing Beyoncé. The chorus of "oohs" and "aahs" Finesse had them singing sounded like an orgasmic orchestra. The Chocolate sitting all over his face was beginning to melt as her pussy got wetter and wetter.

"Ooohhh yes, yes, right there!" she moaned, leaning over to lick Beyoncés pert nipple.

"Damn, this dick feel so goood," Beyoncé cooed, as Finesse bounced her harder and harder.

"I–I'm–I'm about to—" Chocolate stammered.

"—cummin!" Beyoncé squealed, as both girls came back to back, damn near like synchronized swimmers.

Finesse got up and bent Chocolate over, grabbing a fistful of her hair and beating her pretty, pink pussy red. He cries were muffled by the pillow, into which, her face was buried, but Finesse pulled her up by the ponytail.

"Naw bitch, sing for daddy. Say my name," he grunted.

"Oh God! Fuck me. God!" Her pleas and super soft pussy made Finesse squeeze and bust before he wanted to, but he damn near came a bucketfull. Both girls were exhausted and satisfied as he collapsed between them.

"Damn, you gotta come home from prison more often." Beyoncé giggled, stroking his chest and his ego.

"Believe me, ma, the God's stamina is crazy. Gimme ten minutes and I'll show you," he boasted.

His phone rang. "Yo, hand me that," he told Chocolate.

She got up and got his pants, then handed them to him. His new phone was just a flip phone, because he hadn't had time to get a permanent one.

"Yes," he answered.

"Yo, my nig, we all set. Where you?" Bam inquired.

"Word? Shit, say no mo'. I'm on my way," he replied, and then hung up.

Finesse turned to the chicks. "Yo, y'all put your numbers in my phone. I'ma have to take a rain check on round two.

"Oh, believe me. I will hold you to that." Chocolate winked.

Finesse winked back, but quickly got dressed and hit the door.

∞

"You—ohh—you hear my pussy, daddy?" she moaned on the phone line.

"Hell yeah, I hear it. Slide your fingers in that pussy." Everlast lusted, his cell phone in one hand and his dick in the other.

He was trying to talk low so his voice wouldn't carry through the vent into the next cell. Having a cell phone in prison was dangerous enough because the police could do a major shakedown at any time, so you definitely didn't want another convict hearing you. If he was a rat, he would definitely tell. But the chick on the other end had him so fucked up, he didn't really care.

"It's too tight," she said lustfully.

"Push it in."

Her guttural moans let him know she was forcing it in. He gripped his dick tightly, pumping it faster and harder while the chick on the other end panted and squealed. He erupted with a toe-curling grunt, catching his seed in a shower. Once the bodily spasm had subsided and his toes uncurled, he whispered, "Police comin'. I'll call you back!"

He was lying, but the females never seemed to catch on. For Everlast, it was just like on the streets: "After the nut, what do I need you for?" Everlast got up and checked, just in case the police were coming, but all was quiet. It was the middle of the night, and everyone was asleep or on their own phone. He heard his phone buzz under the pillow. He knew it was a text, so he pulled it out and the text read: Can I call you?

It was from Carmen, his baby mother, wifey, and chick holding him down during his bid. He smiled and texted: Yes.

Several seconds later, the phone vibrated with her call and he picked up instantly.

"What's up, pretty—" Everlast started to say, but his words were cut off by a blood curdling scream coming through the phone. It seemed to fill his cell, and he quickly pressed end. "What the fuck?" he gruffed, dialing her number. This time, there was no answer. He frowned, knowing something was not right, but before he could call again, a picture text came through from Carmen. He pressed to receive, and after the picture was processed, it came through.

Everlast dropped the phone.

The picture was of Carmen, butt naked and spread eagle with her whole stomach blown out. She had been shot, point blank with a shotgun. The whole bed was red from her blood. Stuffed down her throat was a twelve-inch dildo, the one she had used many nights to play in her pussy while he masturbated to her moans. Her glossy, wide-eyed stare told him she was definitely dead.

"Oh my . . . God!" he gasped, sitting down on the bunk with a thud.

The phone vibrated again. It was another picture text. With a trembling finger, he pushed to receive it. When he saw the picture, his heart almost collapsed. It was a picture of his mother—what was left of her. Her body was on the bathroom floor, her whole face and half of her head were gone. She too had been shot with a shotgun at close range. The only way he knew for sure it was his mother was the housecoat she wore. It was the same one she wore in the picture on his wall that showed her holding his son.

He rocked on the bed, eyes shut tight, crying so deep down that no sounds or tears came out. The pain he felt was unbearable.

Then the phone vibrated again.

He knew what the picture would be—felt it in his bones. His heart told him to delete it, don't look. But he ignored his heart and pressed to receive.

"Oh God noooooo!" he bellowed loud enough for the whole dorm to hear.

His son was in the bathtub. It was full of water and so were his little, two-year-old lungs. He had been drowned. The expression on his face seemed to ask, why? His large, adorable eyes stared lifelessly into the camera.

In waves of helplessness, rage, and futility, Everlast wanted to kill himself and whoever did this and the whole world. He had never felt so powerless. His head throbbed unceasingly.

The phone vibrated with a call. He knew that whoever did it would be on the other end. He quickly pressed send and barked, "You killed my family! You killed my family! I swear I'ma kill you, I swear!"

"Justice must be served. Ain't that what you told me, nigguh? You bitch ass nigguh, you next!" Finesse seethed into the phone.

"Finesse?"

Finesse laughed.

"I swear on my dead seed, you cock suckin' faggot. I'ma murder you! I swear on everything!" he yelled into the phone, then flung it with all his might at the wall, exploding it in a shower of pieces. Then he went to pieces, falling to his knees and crying uncontrollably for his slain family.

∞

Finesse hung up the phone and looked down at the dead baby floating in the tub. Truth be told, he hadn't wanted to kill the child, but after he had gunned down his mother and grandmother, he felt like he didn't have much choice.

He knew that Everlast didn't have much of a family. His mother and his girl were all he had. So with them gone, he envisioned the child growing up in foster homes, then group homes, and then juvenile centers. Then he'd probably be killed or kill someone and end up in prison like his father. A life of pain was not life at all, so to Finesse, it was a mercy killing.

"Yo, let's go," Bam said, sticking his head in the bathroom door.

Finesse took one last look at the dead child and walked out, being careful not to step in the splattered blood.

"You think he got the message?" Bam chuckled as they walked out.

Finesse laughed.

CHAPTER 19
- Rage Broke Like Clouds -

As soon as Charisma got back to Newark, she hit up White Castle for a couple of surf and turf burgers, then headed home. She tried to reach out to her sister Sonja and Mrs. Butler while she was in Delaware, but got no answers. What really worried her was the fact her sister's phone had been cut off.

When she reached her building, everything seemed fine. She grabbed her White Castle burgers and, not being able to wait, devoured one of the burgers and a handful of fries. By the time she got off the elevator on her floor, all she had left were fries. Charisma licked her fingers, then fingered through the key ring for the apartment key. She stuck it in the lock, but it wouldn't turn. She frowned and tried again. Same result. She checked to make sure it was the right key, and then started to try it again. But the door opened and a slim, Spanish woman with a scowl on her face asked with attitude, "What the hell are you doing?"

Charisma was taken aback, not only by the woman's attitude, but also by the fact that she had answered her door. She looked at the number of the door to confirm that she was at her apartment, then replied, "My key wouldn't work."

"It ain't 'posed to work. This is my apartment!"

"Your apartment?"

"Do I stutter?"

Any other time, Charisma would have already smacked her, but she was too focused upon trying to figure out the situation.

"Wait . . . doesn't Sonja live here?"

"I don't know no Sonja, and she damn sure don't live here," the woman shot back, then slammed the door in Charisma's face.

Charisma's stomach sank because she knew something wasn't right. Her sister wouldn't just move and change her number, unless . . .

She hurried down the hall to Mrs. Butler's door and knocked on it heavily. A few moments later, she heard slippers sliding up to the door.

"Who is it?" she called out, as if she wasn't already peeping out the peephole.

"Chari—Aisha."

She heard several locks being opened in succession, and then the door swung open with a creak.

"How are you, baby?" Mrs. Butler asked with matronly concern.

Skipping all the small talk, Charisma said, "Mrs. Butler, I just came from my sister's apartment—"

Tears formed in Mrs. Butler's eyes as she replied, "Bless your soul. So then you know?"

Charisma's whole body tensed up, as if preparing herself for a physical blow. "Know what?"

Mrs. Butler held out her hand and tried to take Charisma's. "You better come inside, chile."

Charisma stepped out of her reach. "No," she stated firmly, "tell me now. Here."

"Baby, it's so terrible that I think—"

"Fuckin' tell me!" Charisma blazed, but deep down she already knew.

"She's . . . she's dead, Aisha. Your sister's dead, baby."

Charisma looked at Mrs. Butler, her expression blank. Then she staggered back shaking her head. "No . . . no," she whispered as her stomach became queasy.

Mrs. Butler stepped toward her to hug her tightly, but Charisma lurched to the side and threw up, hard and long. She didn't stop until her stomach was emptied, and then she fell against the opposite wall and slid to the floor, sitting with her knees up and her head in her hands.

"When . . . how did it happen?" she whispered, unable to muster the energy to be heard.

"The day you called," Mrs. Butler began, "I-I went to the door and knocked, but no one answered. The door was open so I went in."

Mrs. Butler's mind traveled back to that moment as she explained it to Charisma. She had walked in, calling out, "Sonja? Sonja, baby, are you here?"

When she walked into the living room, she saw the most gruesome sight ever seen. Sonja was sitting on the couch, mouth and eyes open, along with the back of her head. Infinite had put the gun in her mouth and blew her brains all over the wall, drapes, and window. "Oh my Lord Jesus!" She shivered, covering her mouth and backing out of the room.

Standing in the hallway, completing the recitation of events to Charisma, she shivered again.

"I didn't know what to do," she said.

Charisma could almost picture it as Mrs. Butler spoke, and all she kept thinking was, The bullet should've been for me.

"I didn't know at the time that someone had been shot right outside. Some man, and . . . after they shot him, they set him on fire," Mrs. Butler said, shaking her head and wiping tears from her eyes. "I saw it on the news."

Charisma hardly heard the part about the burning man. She was concentrating on her sister, and her mind was too dazed to make the connection.

"Why didn't you tell me?" Charisma asked, looking up at Mrs. Butler with red-rimmed eyes.

"I didn't know how, baby. I–I just left it in the Lord's hands."

Charisma nodded. She knew what Mrs. Butler really meant, because it was written all over her face. She didn't want to get involved. That was the real reason she didn't call Charisma back and tell her. She had found the body and figured she knew too much. Therefore, she certainly didn't want to put out how much she really knew. For all she knew, maybe Charisma herself had something to do with it.

She didn't blame Mrs. Butler. This was on her to handle, and she intended on doing just that. She rose to her feet and gave her a short, comforting hug.

"Thank you."

"Thank the Lord," Mrs. Butler replied softy, trying to comfort Charisma in her time of need.

Fuck the Lord! Charisma's mind spat, but she held her tongue and walked away.

Mrs. Butler watched her walk down the hall toward the elevator, and then she went back into her apartment.

Charisma pressed the elevator button and waited. The elevator came. She paused. She turned and went to the door of her former apartment and knocked.

"Bitch, didn't I—" was all the Spanish woman got out before Charisma punched her dead in the mouth.

The blow staggered her back, allowing Charisma to step inside. She pulled out her pistol and began to pistol whip the woman, over and over and over until the rage broke like clouds in the sky and unleashed a torrent of tears.

The woman, half conscious, moaned in agony. Charisma struggled to her feet, tears streaming down her face. She staggered down the apartment hallway drunken with grief and fury, unable to get her bearings. Looking at the door, she saw how everything had changed, as if she and her sister had never lived there. She looked at where the couch used to sit, which was now replaced by a small table with a computer on it. Charisma imagined the couch there and saw her sister sprawled on it, mouth agape, brains dripping off the window behind her, and it made Charisma's body wrack with sobs.

She headed for her bedroom. Inside, she found a baby's crib with an infant lying in it. The baby, sensing her vibes, began to cry and kick. Charisma stopped and looked down at the child turning red in the face. She bent down and picked up the baby, putting him on her shoulder and bouncing him gently and rubbing his back.

"Shhh, it's gonna be all right. Don't cry, it's gonna be all right," she whispered softly. But the more she said the words, the more it felt like she was talking to herself and it brought her comfort as well. The baby quieted down and then slowly drifted off to sleep. She laid him down, and then went to the closet. She reached into the back of the closet in the corner and banged the butt of the gun against it hard, until the opposite edge popped loose. Then she pried it up with her fingers. Underneath the floor board was her stash, which contained two 9-millimeter pistols and $7,500. Charisma grabbed the baby's diaper bag, threw the guns and money into it, then headed for the door. The woman was still lying there, moaning and writhing in pain. When she saw Charisma coming with the gun in her hand, she began begging, "No . . . please don't kill me."

Charisma stopped and stood over her, looking at her as if she was an ant that she had inadvertently stepped on.

"I'm not gonna kill you . . . that mouth is," Charisma replied, then turned and walked out of the door, closing it behind her.

∞

"I'm sorry, Miss, but we cremated her body over a month ago," the woman at the city morgue told her after looking at her computer.

Charisma looked at her and shook her head. "But she had insurance—it wasn't enough?"

"Regular insurance wouldn't have covered it, and evidently, she didn't have a life insurance policy. What did you say your name was again?"

"Aisha Mitchell."

The woman looked at the screen, then turned the computer so Charisma could see the screen as well.

"Is this your number?"

Aisha vaguely remembered it being her number at some point. The life she led forced her to change numbers almost as frequently as she did her underwear. It kept her one step ahead of the game, but this time it had put her one step ahead of her sister, too.

"Yeah . . . it was."

"Well, she had you down as the contact in case of an emergency so . . ." the woman said, leaving the conclusion up to Charisma to reach.

"Yeah . . . thanks," Charisma replied, turning toward the door to leave.

"Don't you want the ashes?"

Without turning back, Charisma mumbled, "For what?" She walked out.

When she got outside, the first person she called was Shamar, but she got no answer. She then texted him: Call me.

∞

Shamar's phone buzzed like a tree in the forest, because he had left it in the car. Besides, he was too preoccupied to pay attention. As soon as he got back to Newark, he headed to the chick's apartment where he was laying his head at. When he walked through the door, the first thing he heard was, "Motherfucka, where you been! You been gone since goddamn ever, and you think you can just waltz your happy ass in here like it's all good?" she spazzed.

Shamar smirked, admiring her shapely figure clad in pink boy shorts and a white tank top, looking like a thicker version of Kerry Washington. She was sexy when she was mad and she knew it, too.

"And what the fuck is you laughin' at? Shit ain't funny!"

He walked up to her and wrapped his arms around her. "I missed you, too." He smiled, poised to kiss her neck.

She pushed him away. "Nigguh, get your goddamn hands off me! You ain't shit, Shamar!"

He pushed up on her, grabbing her ass and using his weight to pin her against the wall. "Oh, so you want it rough, huh?"

"Get off me, Sha!" She struggled, but he could feel the sexual energy in her fight.

He slid his finger under her boy shorts and found her pussy so wet that it had already coated her inner thighs. He put two fingers in her and began to finger fuck her while sucking roughly on her neck.

"Damn this pussy wet," he grunted.

"So? It ain't for you," she huffed, but her fight was already becoming decidedly less intense.

Shamar put his other hand under her tank top and began playing with her hard nipples, as she moaned with pleasure.

"Sha stooooooppp," she whined, her defense getting weak.

Suddenly, he flung her over the arm of the couch, slapping her ass.

"Owwww!" she cried out.

Shamar dropped his pants, dick sticking straight out and rammed it up in her, not even bothering to take off her boy shorts. He slapped her ass again as he pounded her relentlessly.

"This was what you wanted, ain't it? You wanted Daddy to beat this pussy, didn't you?"

"Yeeessss, oh yes, daddy, ohh right . . . there!" she moaned, pussy so wet and creamy that she had cum as soon as he penetrated her.

"Tell me you missed me!"

"I did, I did, I missed you soooo much!" she cried, gripping the back of the couch for support.

The fight part of the fucking had Shamar's adrenaline on one thousand, so it didn't take long for him to cum all in her pussy. As soon as she felt his hot cum coat her walls, it made her cum all over his dick a second time.

She turned and wrapped her arms around his neck. "You know I love you, right?" She smiled.

Oh, now you love me?" He chuckled. "A minute ago, I wasn't shit."

She sucked her teeth and then giggled. "You ain't." She pecked him on the lips. "But I love you anyway."

He slapped her on the ass. "I know that's right. Go fix me a sandwich, then get dressed. We goin' out."

"Okay, baby," she sang, then sashayed off to the kitchen.

Shamar took a shower, and by the time he came out, his sandwich was ready. While she jumped in the shower, he jumped on the phone.

"Yo Bam, what up?"

"Sha, what up, my nig? How you?" Bam returned as he drove.

"You already know, fam'. I need to holla at you."

"Okay, okay, no prob. But check, when the last time you holla at brah?" Bam asked, smiling to himself.

Shamar frowned. "Finesse? It's been a minute. I lost my phone, so I need to write that nigguh and give 'im my new one. Why? You talked to him?"

"Yeah, yeah, I got word from him," Bam replied, holding in his laughter, then he added, "but yo, meet me at my spot on Avon in like twenty minutes."

"Ai'ight," Shamar replied, and then hung up.

Bam hung up, laughing. "I'ma blow that nigguh's mind," he said as he pulled up in front of his spot on Avon Avenue.

He spotted Finesse's '05 Buick LeSabre that he had just copped. It was a hooptie, but the way Finesse was moving his heroin, it was just a matter of time before he was back on balling status.

Bam walked around back where one of his young boys was guarding, with a Mac-11 tucked in the bushes beside him.

"What's up, Bam-a-lam?" he greeted.

Bam gave him dap.

"Shit look hectic."

"No doubt, we killin' 'em out here!" Bam went up to the second floor to find Finesse on the phone and counting money.

Finesse looked up. "Why you ain't bring back nothin' to eat?"

"'Cause I drive a Cadillac, not a delivery truck, nigguh." Bam sat down, grabbing the remote and flipping to ESPN.

"That's that bullshit, Bam."

"It is what it is."

Finesse hung up the phone. "Yo, that was my man from B-More. He said shit's a go! We can get rich down that muhfucka!"

Bam waved him off. "That outta town shit is always a fuckin' headache. Half the nigguhs in prison down there from up here!"

"True, true," Finesse conceded, "but they probably went to jail up here, too."

"Whateva. Check, I got this nigguh comin' over here I've been havin' a problem wit'."

"Who? What you tryin' to slump 'im?" Finesse asked, always down with getting his hands dirty.

"Naw, naw, it ain't like that. I just wanna slap the shit outta him, yo," Bam replied, holding back his smile.

"Say no more."

Ten minutes later, Shamar knocked on the door.

"There go that nigguh now," Bam grunted as he got up and opened the door.

Shamar walked in.

"Here we go, Finesse. Smack the shit out this nigguh!" Bam laughed.

Neither brother could believe their eyes, but Shamar was especially stuck because he thought Finesse was still in prison.

"Yo!" Finesse exclaimed.

"What the fuck!" Shamar gasped.

They rushed each other and embraced one another with intense brotherly love.

"Nigguh, what the fuck you doin' here!"

"I beat my case!"

They embraced again.

"Goddamn, it's good to see you!" Shamar beamed.

"Nigguh, I can't tell. Why the fuck you ain't write me and send me your new number?" Finesse complained, snapping a quick but playful jab at Shamar, which he easily blocked.

Shamar threw a jab back that Finesse just as easily weaved. They were so alike they could anticipate the other's move.

"Ay yo, come downstairs. I need to holler at you," Finesse remarked.

"Naw, y'all nigguhs chill. I gotta go handle something anyway," Bam said, grabbing his keys from the table and heading out of the door.

As soon as Bam left, Finesse turned to his brother and said, "Yo, Inf found out the club robbery was y'all."

"How?" Shamar questioned.

"I don't know but he knew. Nigguh put a hit on me on the yard. Nigguh named Everlast from Jersey City tried to murder me," Finesse explained, pulling up his shirt and showing Shamar the multiple stab wounds.

Shamar was seeing red. "Fuck that bitch ass nigguh! He dead!" he vowed.

"You right," Finesse smirked.

"Huh?"

"You right, he is dead. Somebody killed that nigguh already. Hit 'im up and set him on fire," Finesse replied.

"Goddamn! Word? Who?"

"Don't know. Nigguhs think you did it because he killed Aisha's sister," Finesse answered, thinking that Shamar really did do it, but was playing coy.

Shamar's eyes widened. "Killed Aisha's sister? When?"

Finesse could tell by his expression that he was serious. "You ain't know?"

"We been in Delaware since the lick. Fuck! Where's my phone?" he said, patting his pockets till he remembered. "Fuckin phone's in the car," he said aloud. "I gotta call Charisma. I know she's fucked up."

"Use mine."

"Naw, I got it on speed dial."

Finesse nodded. "Goddam, God, if y'all ain't hit that nigguh, who did?"

Shamar shook his head, then a thought hit him. He remembered what Crystal had said about the Jersey dudes and what Swifty said about the barbershop hit.

"The nigguhs in Delaware!" he blurted, turning for the door.

"What nigguhs?" Finesse questioned, coming behind him.

"Motherfuckin' Infinite's people . . . and Crook still down there, in the blind."

Shamar's mind was going a mile a minute. Now he understood. That barbershop hit was intended for them, and Crook was still down there, not knowing that sharks were in the water.

When Shamar got to the car, his girl said, "Are we still going shopping?"

"Hold up," he replied, reaching through the window and grabbing his phone. That's when he noticed that Charisma had called. He hit speed dial and tried to call Crook, but he got no answer. He texted him, then called Don Pooh.

"Yo," Don Pooh answered.

"Pooh, what up? This Sha. Is Crook wit' you?"

"Naw, yo. Why? What's good?"

"Yo, tell him to hit me ASAP, but let him know Supreme and Science down there and be on point," Shamar emphasized.

"Yo, is it a problem?"

"Hell yeah! Put my man on point, ai'ight, and make sure he call me."

"No doubt."

Shamar hung up, then quickly went through his contacts and found Crystal's number. He waited for her to answer, while his girl kicked it with Finesse.

"Hello?"

"What's good, beautiful?" Shamar greeted.

"Wow, I'm surprised you remembered my number," Crystal replied.

Shamar chuckled. "Come on, ma, don't be like that. I just lead a hectic life."

"I can see that."

"Listen, remember you told me about those Jersey guys that came in the store?"

"Yeah."

"Listen, if they come in again, make—"

"They came in this morning. They're stayin' at the Ramada across the street," she told him.

Bingo! his mind exclaimed.

"Do me a favor. I need you to . . . like—kinda come at one of 'em."

"Come at?" Crystal echoed.

"You like—come on to him—not on some fuckin' shit, but I need to get his number."

There was a pause, and it grew so long that he thought the call had dropped.

"Crystal?"

"I'm here . . . what's going on, Shamar?"

"Nothin' . . . Put it like this: nothing you need to worry about. I just need you to flash that Hollywood smile and get a number," he explained.

"Just a number?"

"Just a number."

"Okay, when am I going to see you again?" she asked, already missing that long, black dick.

"As soon as I'm back in town."

"It better be soon."

Shamar chuckled and hung up.

Finesse came over to him. "Crook good?" he asked.

"I ain't speak to him, but I left word."

Finesse lowered his voice. "I ain't know you was fuckin' Salena."

Shamar snapped his fingers like something had just hit him. "That's her name! I been trying to think of that shit all day!"

Finesse laughed hard. "Lil' brah, you been livin' with this bitch. How the fuck you forget her name?"

Shamar shrugged and replied, "I just call the bitch boo." Charisma's state of mind and Crook's safety were more important than a chick whose name meant very little to him at that moment. Would they both be okay?

CHAPTER 20
- Your poker face is cracking -

GQ cursed the fact that he hadn't used his fake ID, but ironically, he was more worried about having a charge he didn't know about on his fake ID than on his real one. He knew he didn't have any charges under his real name because he never used it.

He was wrong.

GQ had been driving his Land Rover up Springfield Avenue when the police had passed him going the other way. They quickly swooped a U-turn and threw on the cherries, pulling him over.

"License and registration."

"Is there a problem, officer?"

"Yeah, you. Now shut the fuck up."

GQ was burning on the inside, but he knew to hold his tongue.

Several minutes later, he was cuffed and on his way to the precinct.

He sat in the interrogation room, the same one that Tyrone had sat in and helped put the finger on him.

The door opened and in walked Detective Simmons. GQ just shook his head. They knew each other well enough because Simmons had been a Narcotics Detective before he switched to

Robbery/Homicide, and had arrested GQ numerous times.

Simmons looked at GQ, his hands behind his back while GQ sat cuffed in the chair.

"Didn't I tell you I'd get you one day, Quincy?" Simmons gloated.

"Man, this some bullshit. I ain't got no drug charge," GQ fumed.

"Oh, you didn't hear? I got promoted. I'm now Head Detective of Robbery/Homicide. Aren't you gonna congratulate me?" Simmons quipped.

"Big Head Detective," GQ mumbled.

"Exactly. Wanna see it?" Simmons shot back.

GQ glared at him, wishing he didn't have the cuffs on.

"Anyway, I just wanted to return your property," Simmons remarked, then came from behind his back with a large plastic bag, and in it was the Mac-11 that he had dropped at the robbery.

"I think maybe you dropped this," Simmons said, tossing it on the table.

"I don't know what you're talking about," GQ lied, but Simmons had seen all that he needed to see.

As soon as he had shown GQ the gun, his shoulders sagged. It wasn't much, but Simmons was a great reader of body language.

He sat down. "Come on, G. We've been doing this too long. You know I know your tells by now. Your poker face is crackin'," Simmons commented.

"Fuck you. I want a lawyer," GQ spat, seeing that shit was deeper than he thought.

"You lawyerin' up already, G? How are we supposed to make a deal?"

GQ looked him dead in the eyes. "You already know how I get down. Have we ever made a deal in the past?"

"No, but I've never had you for three homicides and a smoking gun before either. The stakes are too high for you to tough-talk shit. We're talking about the rest of your life here. Don't lawyer up until you hear me out," Simmons proposed.

He could tell by GQ's expression that he was thinking; he just didn't know what about. But since GQ didn't say anything, he continued. "You fucked up, G. You fucked up bad. But maybe, just maybe we can help each other . . . Now, I'm sure you know Malik Thompson is dead."

"Who?"

"Thompson. You know him as Infinite."

"Yeah, what about it?" GQ replied calmly, but inside he was shocked. Infinite dead? His mind wandered, but he kept his poker face and let Simmons do the talking.

"Who hit him?"

"I wouldn't tell you if I knew."

Simmons smiled. "Oh, you know. Matter of fact, word on the streets is your man Shamar Bennett did it in retaliation for killing Sonja Mitchell."

"Sonja Mitchell!" GQ scowled. Even he couldn't keep his poker face when he heard Sonja's name. He knew she was Charisma's sister, and if Infinite was involved in her death, it was because of them.

Simmons peeped his reaction. "Ooooh, you didn't know that? Yeah, Thompson blew her brains out, then got his blown out in his car in front of her building. Set him on fire, too. I'd say whoever did it had a message to send, wouldn't you?"

"I done said all I'ma say. Now, get me to the County before I miss lunch. They usually have fish sandwiches on Wednesday," GQ spat contemptuously.

Simmons chuckled, but GQ could tell he was getting frustrated.

"Lemme put it like this, Quincy: If you don't tell me who did it, then I'll make sure Shamar wears it. But don't worry, you two can be cellies because you have a couple of bodies of your own. Now, if you don't like that crystal ball, then let's work together. Tell me about Coco Chanel."

When Simmons said that name, GQ just looked at him and smirked. He knew the stories well—he just didn't believe them. He thought Infinite used the name as a smoke screen because there was no way he'd believe a chick could do all that they said Coco Chanel had done. But he saw an angle, so he played along.

"Coco Chanel? You wanna know about Coco Chanel?"

Simmons nodded, watching his expression like a hawk.

"Is that the deal? I tell you how to get Chanel and you let me walk?" GQ probed.

"It won't be that simple, believe me. But if you help me, I'll help you."

"I can't do it from a cell."

"I know . . . I thought of that. I also thought, if I leave you on the streets, you can just disappear. But if you did, I'd find you . . . one day . . . and then I'd make sure you never see the streets again," Simmons warned.

GAME OF GWOP

Even though GQ felt that he could get away, he wasn't about to try it. He could see the greed in Simmons' eyes, like catching Coco Chanel would make him Mayor. It would be his biggest catch, and GQ planned on milking him for everything.

"What makes you so sure I can catch her?" GQ questioned.

"Because your crew is the only one even remotely close to Infinite's. Besides, we go way back." Simmons winked.

"Okay, so how about you uncuff me and we can talk?" GQ replied, but on the inside he was dying laughing, because he thought Coco Chanel didn't exist.

∞

"You hit . . . the wrong people?" Chanel asked Supreme as he stood in front of her.

They were in her suite, and he stood in the middle of the floor. Chanel sat cross-legged on the couch while an Asian woman painted her nails.

Supreme rocked from foot to foot, exuding nervous energy.

"Yo, Chanel, that's my word. I thought—"

"You thought?" Chanel cut him off. "Kat, haven't we heard that song before?"

"It's like a broken record," Kat said, eyeing Supreme hard.

"I despise incompetence, Supreme, and I despise excuses and justifications," Chanel remarked.

"Look, yo, you told me to burn down the city, so that's what I'm doin'. Any Jersey nigguh in the city is dead, until I get the right one," Supreme replied, trying to put some umph in his stance.

Chanel smiled at his bravado.

"That's the best thing you've said all day . . . but there's no need. I'm taking over from here. You will be my . . . back up. Can you handle that?"

"All day," he replied cockily.

"We'll see. Is there anything else?"

"Naw."

"Good. Then lay low and wait for my call," Chanel told him.

Kat walked him to the door and closed it behind him.

"Kat, find the biggest club in the city, rent it. Then get me every stripper around and book them. We're throwing a party . . . absolutely free. Drinks on the house. I want it all over the radio. See if Drake is available to host. If not, get Nikki Minaj. If we can't find them, then we'll help them find us." Chanel smiled, looking like a black widow spinning a silky, seductive web.

∞

Shamar told Charisma to meet him back at Salena's house. She told him about her sister, but he didn't tell her about his brother. He wanted to surprise her, and from the sound of her voice, he could tell she needed one.

She pulled in front of Salena's building, went inside and knocked. Several seconds later, Shamar opened the door. The first thing he did was give her a big hug. It felt good, but she kept her composure.

"Yeah, ma, I know you messed up right now, but whatever you need, you know I got you. You like a sister to me," Shamar said.

"Thank you, Sha. My mind is just crazy right now," Charisma replied, running her hand through her hair as she stepped inside. Shamar closed the door behind her.

"You know I'm here."

"I know."

"I'm here too."

She heard the voice and her knees instantly got weak. She quickly turned her head and saw Finesse standing there. Tears welled in her eyes. She covered her mouth and looked at Shamar, whose smile touched his eyes.

"He wanted to surprise you."

Her heart beat so fast, she was afraid to take a breath. She wanted to run to him, but she was scared that her legs would give out. It was what she needed most when she most needed it, and the overwhelming emotions of the moment almost made her break down.

Finesse crossed the room, wrapping her in his embrace and picking her up off her feet.

Charisma instantly wrapped her legs around him and sobbed into his neck, tears of simultaneous joy and sadness.

"Oh my God, oh my God! I can't believe this," she cried.

"Believe it, baby girl, you know them people couldn't hold me down," Finesse replied, feeling just as good holding her as she did being held.

He put her down, and she gazed at him in awe.

"How . . . when?" she stammered, a flood of questions rushing through her mind.

"Shhh," Finesses answered, putting his finger to her lips. "We'll talk about all that later. Just know, I'm here now and I ain't going nowhere," he promised.

Charisma nodded and smiled through her tears. "Okay. I love you."

"I love you too." He kissed her passionately.

When it ended, she wrapped her arms around his neck and held on for dear life.

"I'm so glad you're home."

"That makes two of us."

They laughed and then he sat her on the couch.

"Did you hear what happened?" he asked.

"Naw, I just know she got shot."

"It was Infinite. He found out about the robbery. He even tried to get me hit up on the yard," Finesse expressed.

The tears on Charisma's face then melted in her mounting anger. "Then why we sittin' here?" she asked, tone full of venom.

"'Cause he already dead. Nobody know who hit him, but they think y'all did it because of sis. God bless the dead."

"Then where Supreme? He dead too?" she probed.

"Naw," Shamar cut in, "he in Delaware lookin' for us."

"How he—" she started to ask, but then the answer hit her like a slap in the face.

Sonja.

Now she understood why she got the vibe from her sister's phone call. Infinite had been sitting right there.

"Damn!" Charisma shook her head, her anger mixing with guilt. "He killed Sonja lookin' for me."

Finesse put his arm around her, but she calmly shrugged it off.

"Naw, baby . . . I'm good. They lookin' for me. They 'bout to find me, too," she vowed.

"No doubt," Finesse seconded her emotion. "Besides, we need to get outta Newark, 'cause if nigguhs think y'all drilled Inf, then it won't be long before the police do, too."

"True indeed." Shamar nodded.

Shamar's phone rang. He checked the caller ID. It was GQ.

"Yo."

"Where you at?" GQ inquired.

"At my rest in Hooterville."

"I'm on my way."

"Say no more."

∞

GQ hung up and adjusted the small, metallic box strapped to the inside of his pants, flicking it on with his thumb.

"This is Quincy, check one-two, recording number one. I'm on my way to meet up with Shamar and the rest of the crew. If anybody can get close to Coco Chanel, it's him," GQ said aloud, barely holding in his laughter. He tried to spin the situation in his own mind, but the bottom line was, he was working for the police.

CHAPTER 21
- Linked Up -

"Y'all nigguhs ready?"

Crook questioned as he rode shotgun in the hooptie that Shifty was driving.

The dude in the backseat named Tech replied, "No doubt." Then he cocked his pistol in emphasis.

They were in Trenton on a robbery mission. The blackness of the Buick hooptie blended right into the blackness of the night as they followed an unsuspecting female to their victim.

"I'm tellin' you, that nigguh gettin' it!" Tech had stressed to Shifty and Crook, in order to get them to go along with his robbery plan. They didn't need much convincing because they were both broke. There was a virtual drought of cocaine in Wilmington, so the three of them linked up.

Whereas Crook didn't like Don Pooh, he loved Shifty. They were just alike. Grimy.

"Yo, we gotta move quick once the bitch get out," Tech emphasized.

"I got you." Crook nodded, pulling the blue bandana over his face.

The woman they were following turned onto her street and pulled over in front of a brick, two-family unit home. As soon as she did, Shifty quickly parked three car lengths down. By the time she got the grocery bag out of the passenger seat and got out of the car, three masked gunmen were on her, guns in her face.

"You know what it is. Play fair and so will we," Shifty hissed through the mask.

"O–okay," she said, sounding nervous but keeping her composure.

Crook could tell she had probably done this before. She reacted calmly but carefully. They walked her up the stairs to the porch, head on swivel, looking for any activity up and down the darkened block.

"He here alone?" Crook questioned.

"I don't know," she replied.

"Okay, open the door and be easy, you got me?" Crook ordered.

"You not gonna shoot me?"

"As long as you don't need to be shot. Open the door."

She used her key to unlock the door. Tech gripped her around the throat, keeping her body in front of his as a shield. Crook and Shifty entered right behind them.

Inside, two dudes were sitting on the couch playing Madden. If Crook thought they had caught them slipping, he was sadly mistaken, and if Tech thought using her as a shield would keep them from shooting, he was even more mistaken. As soon as they saw the masked men, both men grabbed pistols that were lying next to them and opened fire, aiming straight at the chick and hitting her three times in the chest, until she dropped to the floor, leaving Tech dangerously exposed. If it hadn't been for Shifty, Tech would've been a dead man, but Shifty happened to shoot the second dude before he got off a shot, while the first dude dove over the couch, busting shots the whole time.

Boc! Boc! Boc!

The shots rang back and forth. Crook caught the movement out the corner of his eye. Another dude was coming down the stairs, sawed-off in hand.

Bloka! Bloka!

Crook squeezed twice, hitting the dude in the throat and forehead. He keeled forward and tumbled down the stairs. His neck broke on the way down, but he was dead before it cracked. Crook took the stairs, two at a time, head up and eyes peeled for anyone else.

"Ggggrrrrrr!" He heard as he hit the second floor, looking straight into the sinister eyes of a red-nosed pit bull. The pit came straight at him and leaped.

Bloka!

"Errrrrrreeeee," the beast hollered as the bullet tore out his midsection. He hit the ground at Crook's feet, still whimpering and kicking his legs.

Bloka!

Crook blew off his nose and part of his face, taking him out of his misery. He quickly went room to room, opening closed doors and looking under beds, gun aimed and ready. He didn't find anybody, but he did find a dresser full of jewelry.

"Bingo!" He chuckled.

There were several rings with various colored diamonds, a diamond-encrusted Rolex and three platinum, forty-inch links with pendants containing diamonds. He quickly stuffed his pockets, having no intention of splitting his find with anyone.

When he got back downstairs, Shifty and Tech had the first dude, bloody-nosed and dazed on the couch. As soon as Crook came in the room, he shot the dude in the knee. He howled in pain.

"Who the fuck punched this nigguh in the face?" Crook growled. "That shit ain't worth a fuck! Keep shooting him until he give it up."

With that, he shot him in the other knee.

"Fuck! Okay, okay! Flip the couch, it's under the couch!" the dude bellowed, giving up his stash.

Shifty snatched him off the couch and dumped him on the floor while Crook and Tech turned the couch over. They found six bricks of cocaine, prepackaged in one-ounce baggies affixed to the underside of the couch.

"Ha! I told y'all this nigguh had it!" Tech greedily declared.

Crook wasn't satisfied. "Where's the money?"

"Rip the lining!" the dude yelled quickly, knowing Crook wouldn't ask twice.

Crook ripped the lining and found several stacks of money. Shifty began scooping up the money and drugs. Tech snatched off his mask and got in the dude's face.

"Yeah muhfucka, it's Tech! You thought it was a game, nigguh! You mighta fucked my broad, but now I'm fuckin' you!" He cackled.

Shifty and Crook stopped dead in their tracks and looked at each other. They couldn't believe their ears. Tech had exposed himself, just because he wanted revenge over a bitch? They had already planned on killing the dude, but that wasn't the point. If Tech could be so easily swayed emotionally, who else would he tell and what? They seemed to have the same thought at the same time. They both raised their guns and aimed at him.

"Yo Shifty, don't—" Tech tried to plead, but his words were cut short by a rain of bullets. Tech slumped, body still convulsing.

Crook looked at the dude and shrugged. "At least you get to see him in hell," he remarked, then blew the dude's brains all over Tech's dead face.

"Come on, nigguh. We out!" Shifty urged.

The two of them headed for the door, stepping over the girl on the way out. Neither of them knew she was still alive and had caught Tech's last words on her phone's voice recorder.

Once outside, they pulled off and made their getaway, but as they did, they saw the police heading toward the street, a heavy presence.

"Neighbor musta called," Crook surmised, not knowing that it had been the girl.

"Fuck it, somebody gotta clean up the mess," Shifty joked.

They both laughed.

"Yo, I love this nigguh! You sure you ain't from Newark?" Crook chuckled.

"Naw, I'm just showin' you how real Delaware nigguhs get down."

Thirty minutes later, Shifty dropped Crook off at Charisma's condo and left, feeling as if they had overlooked something or someone.

∞

Once Crook was inside, he dumped his take on the floor. All in all, it had been a good day, especially since he kept all the jewelry. Crook eyed the quality of the diamonds and the gleam on the platinum.

"Shit, I'ma get more of this jewelry," he said, putting the three chains around his neck and practicing his chain-swinging walk.

His phone rang. It was Shamar and he remembered that he was supposed to call him.

"Yo! I was just about to hit you," Crook lied.

"Lyin' muhfucka, you just forgot," Shamar shot back, knowing Crook well. "But yo, did Pooh tell you what I said?"

"About 'Preme and Science? Yeah, but what the fuck you talkin' about?" Crook questioned, admiring himself with the chains around his neck in the full-length mirror.

"The nigguhs know about the fuckin' jooks! Be on point!" Shamar stressed.

"Word?" Crook replied calmly, caught up in his own reflection. "Fuck 'em."

"Yeah, ai'ight fuck 'em. Just keep your eyes open."

"Oh yeah, yo. I don't trust that nigguh Pooh. The nigguh ain't right. You want me to do somethin' to him?" Crook suggested.

"Naw, nigguh, what the fuck you talkin' 'bout? That's 'Riz cousin."

"Man, fuck that shit. She just related to that nigguh. She love me," Crook replied, heading for the refrigerator.

"Just chill till we get down there."

"Yeah, ai'ight. I ain't gonna do nothin' to him," Crook said, hanging up and adding, "yet."

He took off two of the chains, but kept one on. "I'm rockin' this one," he said proudly. The thought of another lick just like tonight's made his smile widen and his heart tingle.

CHAPTER 22
- Ain't Nothing Changed -

Charisma followed Finesse through the door of his abode, a rooming house, a two-room walkup in the Ironbound section of Newark. The passing trains rattled the window panes constantly, and it was overrun with rats and roaches, but it was all he could get with no ID.

"This place is a shack." Charisma chuckled as she looked around, then stepped on a roach.

"Yeah, but it's better than a cell."

"I know that's right."

He took his gun out of his pants and laid it on the table, then took hers and laid it next to his. Then he pulled her to him.

"No, Finesse, I didn't come here for that."

"Yes you did. You just wanna hear me beg like Keith Sweat," he replied, kissing her on the neck, then singing, "Girrll, I been thinkin' 'bout you all day loonnggg!"

Charisma laughed like only Finesse could make her. Still, she pulled away. "No. What I tell you before you got locked up?"

"I can't recall right now," he mumbled, because he had pulled her close again and was kissing her neck again.

It felt good. Her eyes fluttered. Her defenses lowered. "Finesse," she whined, "this is wrong."

"Does it feel wrong?"

She couldn't answer because it didn't. He was touching her like she liked to be touched, kissing her like she liked to be kissed. The only parts of her body saying "no" were her lips, and Finesse's tongue between them had ended that as well.

He laid her on the bed, never breaking the kiss, while he ran his hands under her shirt and then unhooked her front-snapping bra. Charisma liked his lips, loving the way his tongue felt on her nipples.

"Mmmm, you're makin' me wet."

"I can't wait to taste it," Finesse answered, running his tongue down her stomach, then darting it in and out of her belly button. She giggled and squeezed her legs together, because the tingly feeling shot straight to her pussy.

"Stooopp," she playfully whined.

"Say please," he teased, doing it again and making her squirm.

"Now you wanna hear me beg?" Charisma moaned as she reached back and grabbed the head rail.

"Yep," he replied, unbuttoning her jeans.

"Please," she whispered so sensually that it made Finesse's hard dick jump in his pants.

She lifted her hips as Finesse pulled her jeans and panties over her shapely ass and stopped mid-thigh. Her fragrance filled his nostrils, making him want to dive right in. He ran his tongue along the full length of her swollen pussy lips and up to her clit, taking it in his mouth and sucking it until she started singing: "Oh Finesse, Finesse, don't stop. Baby, don't stop."

He had no intention to. He spread her pussy lips with two fingers, inserting them, then taking them out only to insert them again, stimulating her pussy while he feasted on her clit.

"That dick," she gasped, "stop teasing me and give me that dick."

Finesse was in such a rush, he didn't even take her jeans all the way off. He pulled them down to her ankles, as well as his, and slid his hard, throbbing dick into her wet pussy.

"Oh fuck!" she squeaked, arching her back to meet his thrusts.

"This pussy still feel like butter," he grunted, putting his back into it.

"Damn, I missed you," Charisma sang, wrapping her entangled legs behind his back.

"I thought about fuckin' you every night."

"Yeah?" she moaned, fucking him back harder, because she was turned on by the thought of him jacking off to her as his fantasy.

Finesse sucked and bit on her nipples, sliding his finger in and out of her asshole, driving her wild.

"Oh shit, here it comes," she growled. "Fuck me harder, baby . . . fuck this pussy!" He got in pushup position and drilled her hard and fast until they both came, back to back, then lay in each other's arms, their bodies spasming.

"Finesse." She giggled.

"Hmmm?" he replied lazily, nuzzling her neck.

"What are my pants doing around my ankles?"

"I was too lazy to take 'em off."

They both laughed.

"We're tangled up like a pretzel," Charisma remarked.

"A nasty, sexy pretzel," he added, giving her a kiss.

"I have to pee. Where's the bathroom?"

"At the end of the hall. It's a community toilet."

"Never mind, I'll hold it."

Finesse found his way out of the twisted position they were in and pulled up his pants, sitting on the side of the bed. Charisma pulled hers up without getting up, then pulled him back down beside her.

"I missed you like crazy, you know that, right?" she told him, forehead to forehead.

"Then why you ain't write me?"

"Nigguh, you know why," she shot back.

Finesse sucked his teeth and rolled over on his back. "Ma, I know you ain't still buggin' off that shit, yo."

"How can I not be, Finesse? You got a bitch pregnant," she reminded him, propping up on her elbow.

"It might not be mine," he protested.

"But you don't deny fuckin' the bitch." She humphed, rolling her eyes.

He tried to rub her back, but she elbowed him off. She could feel the old anger trying to rear its ugly head. "You know what? I ain't gonna let you take me there," Charisma said, taking a deep breath and getting up to sit on the side of the bed.

Finesse got up and sat beside her. "Riz, listen. I'ma do better this time, ai'ight? I just get—you know—distracted some time."

GAME OF GWOP

Charisma looked at him. "This time? Ain't no this time, Finesse. Ain't nothin' changed. As much as I love you, I'm not puttin' up with your shit no more."

"Then what was all this about?" he asked, referring to the bed and what they had just done.

"I just wanted you to see what you missin'," she said. "You just my jump off now."

Finesse threw his head back, laughing. "Word? So you gonna treat me like the big dick, cockeyed nigguh, huh?"

"Basically." She giggled.

"Well, I guess beggars can't be choosy," he replied, putting his hand under her ass and squeezing it.

She put her head on his shoulder and took a deep breath. They sat wordlessly for a few moments, as a train rumbled by. She watched a large roach crawl into the barrel of her gun.

"I'm tired of living like this, baby."

Finesse nodded. "Yeah, ma, I feel you. But we gonna be good, I'm tellin' you. I got a ill connect out Cali, and B-More wide open. We just gotta—"

She shook her head while keeping her head on his shoulder. "That's what I meant. I'm tired of living connect to connect, town to town, lick to lick. Having a hundred grand one day and the next, can't even pay the rent . . . nowhere to call home. Sonja put me down as her contact in case of an emergency and the number I gave her was a burnout. I couldn't even give her a fuckin' number," she cried into his shoulder.

Finesse didn't truly understand all she had said. He just thought it was the guilt from her sister's death. As he hugged and rocked her, letting her get it all out, a rat

171

scurried along the wall and disappeared into his hole. That sight alone pressed him to keep his stay there as short as possible.

CHAPTER 23
- Get this Gwop -

"Fam', what's good?"

GQ greeted Shamar, giving him a pound and a gangsta hug as GQ walked into the apartment.

"I'm good," Shamar replied, closing the door.

When he turned back to GQ, GQ had his finger pressed to his lips. "Yeah, yeah, that's what's up," he said, making small talk while motioning like he was writing something. "So what's going down tonight?"

Shamar frowned, totally thrown. "Wha—"

GQ scowled and put his finger to his lips again, then made the scribble motion.

Shamar caught it and gave him a pen.

"Yo, fam', we need to make a power move, yo. My pockets is touchin'. Who got the coke?" GQ asked, while he wrote.

Shamar had a bad feeling. He totally didn't get how GQ was acting. "Yo . . . I don't know," he replied, hesitantly.

GQ slid him the note. It read: I'm wearing a wire.

"What!" Shamar spazzed, but GQ got animated too, making frantic charade-like gestures for him to calm down.

"I'm tellin' you, fam'. I need a nice package. We gotta get this GWOP, kid!" GQ exclaimed, then passed Shamar another note: Yo. Play along! I'll explain in a minute.

Shamar eyed GQ hard, but he trusted him. He was family. So he reluctantly replied, "Yeah, I do too."

GQ smiled and gave him a thumbs-up. Shamar snatched the pen and wrote a note of his own: What the fuck goin' on?

GQ read it while saying, "We need to get up with Supreme. We need to get in touch with the Big Lady.

Say Coco Chanel, GQ wrote.

Shamar read it and frowned.

Frantically, GQ pointed at the paper.

Finally, Shamar, sounding like a bad actor, said, "Who? Coco Chanel?"

GQ smiled hard and gave him another thumbs-up. Shit was comical, but Shamar was in no mood to laugh. "Shit, who else? I need to get at Supreme. Tell that nigguh we need to make a move, ai'ight?"

Shamar glared at him.

"Ai'ight?" GQ repeated, motioning Shamar to answer—again frantically.

"Yeah, yo, I get you," Shamar deadpanned.

"Cool. I'm out," GQ replied. He went to the door, opened and closed it and said, "Recording one. I just met with Shamar. If anybody can get me close to Chanel, it's him. I'll record more later."

As soon as GQ cut the recorder off, Shamar was in his face. "Nigguh, what the fuck is you doin'? Why you wearing a wire and why the fuck you say my name!" Shamar was so mad, he was ready to hook off on GQ.

"First off, back the fuck off me, 'cause your breath smell like you been eatin' shitty Bon Bons," GQ joked, trying to lighten the mood, but Shamar wasn't going for it.

"Yo, G, that's my word—"

"Man, just listen, ai'ight. Remember Detective Simmons from Narcotics?"

"Yeah, what about him?"

"I got pulled. Long and short, he head of Homicide now, and he got the Mac from the robbery. Shit is bodied up. But he offered me a way out. He want me to work for him to bring him Coco Chanel!" GQ explained, then burst out laughing.

"What's so funny?" Shamar wanted to know.

"Man, you know ain't no Coco Chanel! The bitch don't exist!"

"Regardless, why the fuck is you wearin' a goddamn wire?"

GQ shook his head. "Man, don't you see? It's free fuckin' money! I'ma make the muhfucka think I'm snitchin' until he give me a lump of buy money. Once he do, I'm gone!"

Shamar saw his point, but couldn't stomach his method. "Yo, G. I know you solid, but I don't know. What if the bitch is real?"

GQ waved him off. "Fuck outta here . . . ain't no bitch gone do all that shit nigguhs be talkin'. Breakin' out of a Haitian prison and coming to America with the warden's head in a bag, or taking over the Haitian cartel by murdering his whole team. Really?"

Shamar chuckled. "You know motherfuckas exaggerate, but the bitch could still be real."

"Inf made the bitch up to make muhfuckas think he wasn't the boss, which was smart, because the police believe that shit and I'ma cash in!" GQ concluded.

"It's still some bullshit, yo."

"Fam', the police been playin' us for years . . . it's time we play them," GQ replied, then added with his megawatt smile, "Besides, what can go wrong?"

∞

Science was getting burnt out on Delaware. Nothing was going right, and he was missing a lot of money back in the bricks. Supreme had banned them from hustling in Delaware because he didn't want them to bring attention to themselves.

"But yet and still, this muhfucka gonna throw a mega party," he grumbled to himself as he entered the 7-Eleven across from the motel.

He thought the idea was Supreme's, not knowing that Supreme wasn't calling the shots. Science had never seen Coco Chanel, so since Supreme never used the name like Infinite used it, Science had forgotten all about her. All he knew was that he was ready to go back to the brick.

"Good morning."

He only half heard the words as he brought his orange juice and three honey buns to the counter.

"Good morning," Crystal repeated, a little louder and a little crispier.

She felt nervous, knowing why she was speaking to Science, but at the same time, it was exciting to be involved. Crystal had never been involved in anything remotely close to drama, but she was no dummy either. She knew she was being the femme fatale of something street and sinister.

"Huh? Yeah, yeah, good morning," Science replied without paying her much attention.

"I–um–notice you usually buy honey buns when you come in. What's the matter, you're not getting enough sweets?" she flirted.

Science looked up from pulling a twenty out of his roll and smirked. He didn't do white girls, but she wasn't half bad.

"What kind of sweets you talkin' about?"

She smiled and took the bill. "Your friends always try to come on to me when they come in here, but you never have. Why is that?"

He shrugged. "I ain't tryin' to end up like Emmett Till."

"Who?"

"Nothing." He chuckled.

She handed him his change. "Aren't you going to ask me my name?"

"What is it?"

"Crystal. What's yours?"

"They call me Science."

She cocked her head to the side, trying to give off a vibe of innocence.

"Because I'm a mastermind," he smoothly replied with an arrogant grin.

"What a coincidence. I am too."

Science chuckled.

"So, if I give you my number, will you give me yours?" Crystal requested.

Science assessed her frame then answered, "Sure, why not?"

Gotcha! Her mind giggled with glee.

∞

"I got it, baby," Crystal told Shamar.

"Good girl. Give it to me."

"It's 555-3316," Crystal replied.

Shamar smiled as he wrote the number down.

This white girl is pretty sharp, he thought.

"Okay, keep him on the hook. Text 'im, be casual, but leave the door open. Got me?"

"I thought you said, just the number," she reminded him.

"Yeah, but I can see you're enjoying yourself." He laughed, reading her correctly.

Chrstal chuckled too.

"I plead the fifth—on everything."

Shamar smiled, taking the last comment to mean that she knew how to keep her mouth closed.

"No doubt. I'll see you when I hit town."

"You better."

They hung up. He turned his attention back to the table. GQ, Finesse, Charisma, and Shamar were having dinner in a back booth of Finesse's favorite Italian restaurant. It was cozy, low-key, and expensive, but GQ was so happy to see Finesse that he offered to pay for everyone.

Shamar tucked his phone just as GQ was saying, "You lost it!"

Finesse couldn't do anything but shake his head. "Yo, I'm sayin', I can easily get at him through my chick out in Lompoc," Finesse replied.

"But goddamn, fam', you walk right outta prison and into the connect of a lifetime, and you lost your fuckin' phone? What are you, a buzzard?" GQ cracked.

Finesse stuffed his mouth with pasta as he reached for the bread basket.

"Fuck outta here . . . I'ma get 'im once I finish the brick."

"Yeah, but what if he think you hopped the fence on him?" Charisma probed, grabbing the garlic shaker.

Finesse shrugged and changed the subject once he saw that Shamar was off the phone.

"What up wit' 'Preme?"

"I got my snow bunny on him. She just gave me the number," Shamar answered.

"So what's the plan?" Charisma wanted to know because the pasta had done nothing for her hunger for revenge.

"We got his number, and we can use the Silk Road app to GPS his every move. Then we hit 'im when the time is right," Shamar explained.

"Yo," Finesse said, chewing a mouthful of food, "you like a fuckin' gangsta nerd or something. Because what Wall Street nigguh know about the secret Internet?"

"Don't sleep, God. That shit pay off. Right now, if the police was trackin' your phone through GPS, they'd know exactly where you are. Me? I got this GPS spoofer, so they would think I'm driving through Harlem right now," Shamar said.

"You never know, the police could be closer than you think," Charisma remarked, leaning over to GQ and speaking into his chest as if he was wearing a wire.

"Ay yo, 'Riz, don't play wit' me, ai'ight? I told you this is a fuckin fool-proof plan to get GWOP. I'm still official tissue," GQ snapped, feeling his gangsta being tested.

GQ had already told Charisma and Finesse about his police scam, and although they didn't want anything to do with it, they knew GQ would never switch for real.

"Yo, later for that, we got to concentrate on Wilmington," Finesse reminded them. Then he turned to Shamar and said, "I'm tellin' you, God, just 'cause we get Science don't mean shit. We gotta make sure we hit 'em all, or we could have a problem. Inf left Supreme a hell of a team."

"No doubt, that's why I got shorty on 'em."

"Naw, God, I got a better idea." Finesse grinned mischievously.

"What?"

"A rocket launcher."

"A rocket launcher?"

"Yo, hear me out," Finesse stressed, hit his drink, and then said, "You said she said they stayin' in the motel across the street, right?"

"Yeah."

"So instead of trackin' son, we hit 'em where they rest. But instead of a long shout out, we him 'em once with some Afghanistan type shit," Finesse surmised.

"Okay, genius, where we gonna get a fuckin' rocket launcher?" Charisma asked, taking a bread stick off Finesse's plate.

"Bam. He just copped one, but he scared to shoot it," Finesse replied.

"Shit, I would be too. Feds'll be all over that shit," GQ remarked.

Finesse shrugged.

"So we burn the town down. We'll be in Baltimore once shit get hot."

Around the table, they all looked at each other.

"Yeah, but who gonna shoot it?" Shamar asked.

"Finesse." Charisma snickered.

"I don't know how to shoot no goddamn rocket launcher."

"It's your idea."

"Fuck knowin' how. I ain't shootin' it. What if that shit blow up in your face?" GQ protested.

"I can see my cousin. He did a tour in Iraq back in the day. I know he'll do it," Charisma suggested.

"Yeah, but will he?" Shamar inquired.

"If the money right, hell yeah!" Charisma confirmed.

"Then let's go holler at cuz," Finesse concluded, wiping his mouth and getting up.

Everyone else followed suit.

"Ay yo, I said I'd pay for the meal. Can't one of y'all pay the tip?" GQ asked.

"Man, I'm broke."

"I left my money at home."

"No."

"Cheap muhfuckas," GQ grumbled, tossing a ten dollar bill on the table.

Shamar, Charisma, and Finesse walked out, and as soon as no one was looking, GQ dipped out of the door behind them, tossing the unpaid bill aside to flutter down the street in the wind.

CHAPTER 24
- A Woman Scorned -

Kat slurped, licked, and hummed as she feasted on Chanel's pink, juicy pussy. She had her legs around her ears as she zoned out on Chanel's fragrance. But it was when she tried to insert her finger in her that she got a rude awakening.

Chanel's pussy was bone dry.

Kat glanced up at Chanel, only to find Chanel gazing down at her with a bored expression.

"What's the matter, baby? You okay? You got something on your mind? Don't worry, we gonna get those nigguhs for sho'," Kat rattled off, thinking her words could comfort Chanel.

Chanel waved her off, contemptuously.

"Please. They're the furthest thing from my mind."

"Then what's the problem?"

"You."

"Me?"

"Actually I said you." Chanel smirked. "But, you got the point."

Chanel passed her leg over Kat's head and got up, her smooth, naked, chocolate skin being kissed by the sunlight coming through the window, right before she put on the white hotel robe.

Kat stood up. "What did I do, Chanel?" Kat questioned in Creole, using their mother tongue, hoping to evoke Chanel's sympathy.

"Nothing," Chanel replied in English, rejecting Kat's linguistic plea.

In that one word, Kat understood that she meant everything and nothing. It was one of Chanel's mind fucks that Kat so resented.

"You know how I feel about you, Chanel. Please, can we work this out?"

Chanel broke her cold expression and gave her older friend a warm smile. She stepped toward Kat, reached up and caressed her cheek, then spoke softly in Creole. "Katerina, seasons change, mon chéri. We will always be friends, but I've simply grown tired of you as a lover. There's nothing to work out—this is just . . . it."

By the time she finished, tears were streaming down Kat's face. "Don't . . . do this to me. I love you. I would die for you."

"Would you?" Chanel asked, then turned and grabbed Kat's gun off the dresser. "Then die for me."

Chanel handed her the gun. Kat looked at it in her hands, then looked at Chanel, who watched her with a slight grin.

Kat knew that Chanel had allowed her to paint herself into the corner. If she made good on her words, then she'd simply be dead. But if she didn't kill herself on the spot, her inability to act would make her a liar.

She tossed the gun on the bed with disgust. "You can't just throw people away, Chanel, or are you going to do me like Cassandra?"

As soon as the name was out of Kat's mouth, Chanel grabbed her by the throat with an iron grip. Kat clawed at her hand but it was like a vise. Kat outweighed Chanel easily, but Kat knew what the petite, smaller woman could do. She had been in a Haitian prison with her.

"Don't ever say her name again," Chanel seethed in cold Creole.

All Kat could do was nod. Chanel let her go.

"From now on, it is strictly business between us. You can have the operation in New York and New Jersey. I don't plan on going back. Cheer up." Chanel smiled. "I'm making you a boss."

Kat glared at her coldly.

"Whatever you say . . . Mademoiselle."

"Now go. Make sure everything is in order for our coming out party."

Kat walked out without saying another word, but inside she was boiling. She may have been a dyke, but she was still a woman—scorned.

CHAPTER 25
- Alqaeda Did it -

GQ and Charisma's cousin, Drake, drove the whole trip to Delaware in silence. Finesse had bought a jalopy of a van so they would be in an inconspicuous vehicle transporting the rocket launcher.

"Why the fuck I gotta drive?" He had initially protested.

"Because you said you stayin' in Jersey. You drive Calvin down, handle your b.i. then y'all get back on the road," Shamar reasoned.

"That's that bullshit," GQ complained, but he couldn't argue with the logic, so he did it.

When they finally got to Wilmington, Calvin broke the silence. "I gotta piss like a muhfucka," he remarked.

"We almost to the spot. You can piss then," GQ replied.

He glanced over at Calvin as the headlights of oncoming cars illuminated his bearded face. If Calvin was nervous, GQ couldn't see it. If anything, he looked eager. GQ knew then that he was looking in the face of a killer—not a wild, street killer but a government-trained one.

"Ay yo, what was it like in Iraq?" GQ asked.

Calvin's face broke out in a slight grin. "Heaven!"

"Heaven?" GQ echoed with a chuckle.

185

"Bombs exploding over your head, everywhere you look a motherfucka gettin' his head blown off, his guts ripped out, but at the end of the day, you survive. You ain't lived until you've almost died," Calvin explained.

GQ didn't ask him anything else.

∞

Shamar, Finesse, and Charisma rode behind the van in Charisma's Benz. Shamar was in the backseat on the phone.

"I just need to know if the whole crew at the motel, ma. Call son and tell him you and your friends wanna come over and party, feel me? Text me and let me know what's good."

"Shamar, what are you up to?" Crystal asked.

"Nothin', just handle that," he replied, then hung up.

∞

"What up?" Finesse asked Shamar.

"She'll do it."

"We might have to murder that bitch after this," Finesse warned.

Shamar shrugged. "It is what it is."

∞

Science hung up the phone and walked over to the small motel table where Supreme and one of the goons were playing cards.

"Yo, that white bitch say she got a bunch of freaky friends, and they tryin' to come through. What up?"

Supreme shrugged and played his ace of hearts. "I don't give a fuck as long as nigguhs stay on point," he replied.

Chanel had given him strict orders to stay low at the hotel, not only because of the botched barbershop hit; she wanted them ready for the party.

"Indeed, God, indeed," Science replied and then texted Crystal: Come thru!

∞

Crystal smiled at the text and forwarded it to Shamar, who chuckled and then replied, "I will."

∞

GQ and Calvin pulled into the 7-11 parking lot, but continued around back, as Charisma pulled up front. She looked inside and saw some freckled-faced white boy working behind the counter.

"Handle your business, ma." Finesse winked.

She got out of the car and went inside.

∞

Calvin opened the rear doors of the van. The way GQ had parked, the rear wall of the 7-11 was right there. The door had barely enough room to open all the way, but that is how Calvin had told him to park.

Calvin pulled back the blanket from the rocket launcher and the rocket shell.

"Yo, we only got one," GQ warned.

"That's all we need."

He tossed the binoculars to GQ and motioned with his head for GQ to follow him. Calvin swung his body up to the top of the van, and then onto the roof.

"Hand me the baby," Calvin requested.

GQ complied. He handed him the rocket launcher and shell, then put the binoculars around his neck and climbed up onto the van. By the time he positioned himself beside Calvin, he was already loading the shell.

"Yo, what if that shit jam?"

"Then we two dead nigguhs."

GQ's face took on a shocked expression that Calvin found hilarious.

"I'm just kidding. It won't jam."

"Yeah, I was about to say you'd be a dead nigguh. I was gettin' back in the van." GQ laughed even though he was dead serious.

Calvin lay down on his stomach with the rocket launcher beside him. He gazed out at the motel across the wide boulevard.

"This is a good height, but I wish we could get closer for maximum impact," Calvin remarked.

"How close?"

"From the middle of the street, I could bring the whole goddamn motel down," Calvin said, "but we should still be good from here."

GQ checked his watch. Peering over the edge of the roof, he could see the top of Charisma's Benz.

"We got the green light?" Calvin inquired.

"Whenever you ready."

"Then check the target. Let's get it over with."

GQ looked through the binoculars at the motel. He could see three vehicles with Jersey license plates, a couple of goons outside smoking blunts, and movement inside the three rooms the team had.

"It's the last three rooms on the end," GQ told Calvin.

"I got a visual on the enemy," Calvin replied, peeping through the electronic viewfinder of the rocket launcher.

The enemy? GQ thought. I hope this nigguh don't have no fuckin' flashback. GQ gripped the butt of the gun in his pants, fully prepared to leave Calvin's body dead on the roof if he started acting crazy.

Calvin got up on one knee, the rocket launcher balanced on his shoulder. "Say hello to my lil' friend!" he said, then pressed the trigger.

Fffffsshhheeeeeeeee!

The rocket exploded the pipe-like barrel of the launcher and screamed like an angry banshee destined for its target.

∞

"So you said to make a right at the next light?" Charisma asked the guy behind the counter.

Her job was to make sure the cashier didn't somehow catch on that the roof of the store was being used. Shamar worried that Freckle-Face didn't see the rocket launch, put two and two together, and then run outside and see the van pull off and get the license plate number. There was only a slight chance that this would have happened, but Shamar was taking no chances.

"No, the second light, then make a—"

Boom!

The impact across the street sent a slight tremor to the store. It was that powerful. The cashier looked around and saw the motel across the street on fire.

"Holy shit!" the cashier exclaimed, straining his neck to see what was going on.

"Did you see that!" Charisma asked with mock amazement. She wanted to make sure they didn't have a knowledgeable witness on their hands.

"Wow! I don't know. I just heard the explosion! What happened?" he asked her.

Charisma smiled inside because she could hear him giving the same vague description to the police.

"I don't know. I hope it ain't no terrorism shit," she replied, planting the suggestion in his mind. "I'm gone!"

Charisma headed straight out the door. As she jumped into her car she could see the taillights of the van disappearing in the distance.

"What he say?" Finesse asked.

"He'll probably tell the police Al Qaeda did it." She giggled as she started the car.

"Mission accomplished," Shamar remarked, then sat back relaxed as she pulled off.

CHAPTER 26
- Intruder -

The first impression that Federal Agent James Myers had of the crime scene was that it looked like a miniature ground zero. The motel had all but collapsed. The whole right side of the building was nothing but a pile of rubble. The rescue workers weren't finding bodies—they were finding body parts: arms, legs, bloody torsos and head fragments. The local police had set up barricades and the yellow tape characteristic of crime scenes, but they were only gate keepers. It was totally a Federal show.

Myers hopped out of his vehicle and strolled toward the wreckage, casually flashing his badge as he ducked under the yellow tape. He had a walk like Denzel, and many women said he even resembled a young Denzel. In his mind, he thought he looked like his father, an ex-Eagle linebacker that he idolized.

He approached an Asian woman, Agent Yaun and shook her hand. "What you got for me, Ming?"

She sighed hard. "It's not good. There were no survivors. Twenty-seven dead, including four infants and a toddler," she replied.

Myers shook his head. "Bomb?"

"We're not sure, but we think it was some kind of missile or projectile."

"Missile?" he echoed with astonishment.

"Maybe a rocket launcher," Yaun suggested, "too early to tell."

"This place is a mess."

Both Yaun and Myers looked in the same direction, but Myers did a double-take because she was so gorgeous, even in the drab, blue suit favored by Federal Agents.

"Agent Lisa Murray," she said, flashing her shield.

She shook Yaun's hand then Myers'.

"Agent Murray, I don't think I've had the pleasure before." Myers smiled.

"I'm in the Philadelphia office. I just transferred from the Wisconsin field office."

"Go Packers, huh?"

"No, go away Packers." She giggled. "I hope I'm not intruding, but my Agent-in-Charge thought I'd be of some assistance.

"Oh?" he said.

She nodded. "We've had some problems with gangs and drug dealers getting their hands on heavy weaponry."

"Well, that's what it looks like we have here. Agent Yaun was just bringing me up to speed. Yaun," Myers said, nodding at Yaun to continue.

Yaun looked at Murray skeptically, but since Myers was the ranking agent, she continued. "Yes . . . so, we've learned that there was a large group of black males from Jersey here at the motel, and they had been here for several weeks. We think they were the target."

Murray nodded. "Out-of-towners usually mean drugs. Maybe they're connected to the spate of violence you've been seeing recently," she surmised.

"Possibly," Myers conceded.

Murray handed him her card. "Well, thanks for the heads up. If you need me to link our offices, just give me a call."

"I'll do that. Hey, what if you need me?" Myers asked, subtly flirting.

Murray looked over her shoulder as she walked away, smiled, and said, "I've already got your number." She disappeared into the crowd.

Several minutes later, Myers wanted to know if Murray had heard of any gangs with access to rocket launchers, so he called the number.

"Domino's. May I take your order?"

He looked at the phone and frowned. "Sorry, I guess I dialed wrong," he said, then hung up. He dialed again, this time checking each number against the card as he dialed, then he pushed send. They answered.

"Domino's."

That's when he knew that he had been had.

∞

Chanel drove away from the motel, loosening her tie. She hated wearing blue, but the disguise called for it. She couldn't wait to get out of it. She picked up her burner cell and hit the only number in the contacts.

"Was it them?" Kat questioned, after picking up on the second ring.

"Definitely."

"All dead?"

"Every last one of them."

"Good. Now we send in the heavy hitters."

Chanel thought for a moment, then replied, "No, not yet. I'm starting to like these nigguhs. Anybody that can set a man on fire and rocket a whole building is worth getting to know," Chanel surmised with a devilish grin.

CHAPTER 27
- Too Hot in the Spot -

"My muhfuckin' nigguh!"

Crook roared as soon as Finesse came into Charisma's condo.

He and Shifty had been sitting on the couch with two chicks, watching the big screen that he had bought. He didn't know Finesse was home, so seeing him walk through the door threw him for a loop. Finesse was just as happy to see him. Of the whole crowd, besides Shamar, he was closest to Crook.

"What's up, fam'? How you?" Finesse greeted with emphasis.

"Uh-uh, oh hell no! This ain't no hotel. Crook, get these bitches out of my crib!" Charisma spazzed.

"Bitches!" one of the girls echoed, jumping up, shaking her neck.

"And what!" Charisma barked, heading in her direction.

Shamar held Charisma.

Crook turned to the girl, saying, "Chill, ma, 'Riz ain't got 'em all. Yo, Shift, this my nigguh Finesse, but get these bitches out of here, then come back."

Shifty began walking the girls out, but got too close to Charisma, who slapped the shit out of the

Indian-looking girl, the one who had jumped up before. She went wild; Shifty had to carry her out.

"That bitch hit me! Get off me, nigguh! Bitch, it ain't over! I'ma see you again!" she screamed.

Charisma started to follow them out, but Shamar stopped her. She started laughing.

"Yo, 'Riz, you fuckin nuts!" Crook said, turning back to Finesse. "When you get home?"

"It's been a little minute. I wanted to surprise you, my nigguh."

"You ain't see the look on his face?" Shamar laughed. "That nigguh was surprised as fuck, damn near had an 'aha' moment!

Everybody laughed.

"Get the fuck outta here," Crook replied, swinging on Shamar hard but playfully.

"That's my word. Your upper lip quivered! Nigguh, I thought you was gonna take off runnin' to the nigguh in slow motion!" Shamar added.

Everybody laughed so hard that they were in tears.

"Fuck that. Yo, my muhfuckin' nigguh home! Yo, it's about to be a big ass party! Nicki Minaj 'posed to be there. I'ma fuck that bitch, too. Nigguh, you just in time!" Crook exclaimed.

"Naw, yo, I'm on my way to B-More. Shit too hot in this spot," Finesse protested.

"B-More? What's good?" Crook wanted to know.

"Nigguh, we just nuked this muhfuckin' place!" Finesse said.

"Huh?" Crook was totally out of the loop.

Shamar flipped the remote until he came across the news channel and a shot of the smoldering motel.

"That," Shamar pointed out.

Crook looked at the screen, mouth agape. The big screen plasma had the scene looking so crisp, it seemed as if he could just walk into the scene.

"Man! What the fuck y'all hit that shit wit'? A tank!"

"Close, yo, a fuckin' rocket launcher," Finesse boasted.

Crook looked at Finesse, wide-eyed.

"Word up! Get the fuck outta here! I wanna shoot that shit!"

"Too late. It's on its way back to Jersey," Charisma told him, sitting down on the fake leather L-shaped sectional. "Crook, where you get this tacky ass couch?"

He ignored her and turned to Shamar. "What, y'all got them nigguhs? That's that bullshit, yo! And y'all had a goddamn rocket launcher! Where the fuck is GQ?"

"Goin' back to the brick. Man, fuck Delaware—B-More is fuckin' bubblin'! What up?" You wit' it?" Finesse questioned.

"Not right now, fam. I got pups now, my nigguh. Them lil' nigguhs I got on the block is soldiers," Crook bragged proudly.

"I can dig that, but yo, as soon as you can, come through."

"Indeed."

"Yo, ma, you ready?" Finesse asked Charisma.

"Now? Nigguh, I'm tired," she protested.

"I'm drivin', just bring your lazy ass on, yo. I got a trunk full of heroin. I ain't stayin' in this hot ass city."

Charisma sucked her teeth, but she knew he was right. She got up, throwing him the keys.

"Damn skippy you drivin'."

Charisma and Finesse walked out.

Shamar looked at Crook's chain. "Ay yo, when you get that?"

Crook laughed and told him the story.

Once Crook finished with the details, Shamar concluded, "It's just you, me, and your lil' soldiers now since er' body else heading out."

"That's all we need to take over the entire city," Crook said.

"And what about Don Pooh?" Shamar asked.

"What about that nigguh? Like I said, we can take over this entire city."

∞

GQ puffed on his cigarette and paced the parking lot back and forth. Detective Simmons leaned against the car, listening to GQ talk a hole in his head. GQ was playing the role to a tee.

"Simmons, I'm tellin' you, man, you start throwin' Coco Chanel's name around, nigguhs shut down shop. I'm tellin you, this ain't a game. I'ma need witness protection after this or somethin'," GQ explained in rapid-fire fashion.

"What have you found out?"

"That damn near er' piece of coke movin' in the city belong to her. She even got them Spanish nigguhs working for her, and you know they grow the shit!" he emphasized.

Inside, GQ was dying laughing, especially seeing the intense look in Simmons' eyes. To him, this was the ticket to the Chief of Police desk. If he could bring down the infamous Coco Chanel, he knew even the

Mayor's office wasn't out of reach. He just didn't know he was being played in the game of GWOP.

"How many layers of insulation?" Simmons probed.

"Huh?"

"How many people between Chanel and the street?"

GQ hit his cigarette one last time and thunked it away. "See, that's the thing, the bitch like to get her hands dirty, so if she likes you, you know, think you a stand-up muhfucka, she'd come out the shadows and put you on the team," GQ explained, simply regurgitating one of the many street myths about Coco Chanel.

Simmons nodded, intrigued. GQ knew he had him, so he kept going. "Simmons, I'm tellin' you, I can get at this bitch, but I'm gonna need buy money."

"Buy money?" Simmons echoed with an amused expression. "You think I'm gonna trust you with buy money?"

Simmons broke out laughing, just like GQ knew he would, so he hit him with the real scam. "How else am I 'posed to get close to her?"

"I don't know, but buy money is out of the question."

GQ pinched his lip, paced, and pretended to think. "Okay, how 'bout this. I'll buy the shit with my own money, but you gotta reimburse me," GQ suggested.

Simmons looked at him, but GQ could tell he was thinking.

"How much are we talkin'?"

"Coupla thousand at the most." GQ shrugged. "But if I get a hook in this bitch, she won't show her face unless I make it worth her while."

Simmons nodded.

"You get me results, Quincy, and I'll see what I can do. Don't buy shit until I tell you, and when you do, I want you wired. You got me?"

Inside, GQ was jumping for joy. Simmons had swallowed the scam, hook, line and sinker. But on the outside, he kept his swagger.

"No problem, yo. You're the boss," GQ replied as he opened his car door.

"And Quincy?"

"Yeah."

"I've got my eye on you."

Yeah, cracka, GQ thought, too bad you can't see me.

CHAPTER 28
- Opportunity -

The party was one of the largest parties that Wilmington had ever seen. It was held at the biggest club in the city, Moodswing, and it was supposed to be free until it reached capacity and a few dudes in line started acting like doormen and began charging people to get in.

"Yo, I thought it was free?" some dude said.

"We reached capacity, yo. Extra heads gotta pay. You goin' in or what? Nicki Minaj about to go on!"

The fake bouncers made over a thousand dollars before the real bouncers put them out. It was the game of gwop.

Inside, the party was packed and pumping. Nicki Minaj came through, took pics, and even performed a song. Everybody who was anybody in the city was there, diamonds blinging and chrome shining. Half-naked strippers walked around, working the place like it was a strip club. Coco Chanel had planned the party to a tee. Originally, the plan had been to lure Shamar and his team into the open, so Supreme and his goons could murder them on the spot. It would have worked because Shamar and Crook were up in the club like they owned the place.

Crook's young soldiers were deep, drunk, and disruptive—just like he liked them. The only flaw in her plan was that Supreme and his goons were dead. Still, Chanel wasn't going to waste the opportunity that the party presented.

She tried to make her entrance as low key as possible, keeping her hair in a simple ponytail, wearing jeans, Timberland stiletto boots and no jewelry. But hiding her beauty was like trying to hide a diamond among lumps of glass. She consistently turned heads, making nigguhs ask, "Who that?" with lustful exuberance, while females asked the same thing, but with their tone filled with insecure attitude. But Chanel kept it moving, because tonight was about business. Reading the room, she saw 'hos flanking one chubby, Irv Gotti-looking dude and his Snoop lookalike partner was playing the cut in a corner booth, but a lot of dudes were coming through to pay homage and chicks were flirting hard. They already had a table full of females and champagne, but that didn't stop more from coming through. That told Chanel that Don Pooh was the man in the city, and she was right.

Word on the street had it that Don Pooh was behind the Jersey nigguhs infiltrating the city. They even said he was behind burning up young K-Nut, the barbershop shooting, and the motel explosion. He did nothing to waylay the rumors because he understood that perception was power, so he played it for all it was worth.

Now Chanel set her sights on him.

"Blend in," Chanel told Kat, and without hesitation, Kat melted into the crowd, but kept her eyes on Chanel.

Chanel caught Don Pooh's eye before she reached his table, and like a magnetic reaction, he couldn't tear his eyes away. He had never seen ebony skin that seemed to glow in the dark. Despite being fully dressed, her sultry walk made her seem as if she were naked, and picturing her that way made Don Pooh as hard as a rock. By the time she reached the table, she had him right where she wanted him.

"What's up, ma? I know you gonna have a drink with a nigguh," Don Pooh flirted, holding up the bottle of Moet.

Chanel smiled, then looked around the crowded table.

"I don't have anywhere to sit."

Without hesitation, Don Pooh took his arm from around the little light-skinned broad beside him and said, "Ay yo, Mimi, I'll holler at you later, ai'ight?"

"What!" Mimi snapped.

"Bounce, bitch, goddamn it!" Don Pooh gruffed, clearly aggravated.

Mimi sucked her teeth and rolled her eyes, but she still got up. She grabbed her drink, and as she turned, she acted as if she had tripped and spilled it all over Chanel's blouse.

She gasped. "Oh my God! I'm so sorry." But her eyes said, "Yeah bitch, what?"

If it hadn't been so dark in the club, the girl may have seen the fire in Chanel's eyes, but Chanel's body language hid it well.

"Don't worry, accidents happen," Chanel replied, grabbing a napkin off the table and dabbing at her blouse.

The girl smiled, satisfied as she walked away. Chanel and Kat made eye contact and Chanel made a subtle motion with her head in the girl's direction. Kat nodded and followed her. Chanel slid in the booth next to Don Pooh.

"Naw ma, you ain't gotta worry about that, 'cause I'ma buy you a new one in the mornin'," Don Pooh said.

Chanel laughed. "Along with breakfast, huh?"

"Baby girl, you are breakfast, lunch, and dinner. What's your name?" Don Pooh asked, looking her up and down.

"Angel," Chanel replied, extending her hand.

Don Pooh kissed it instead of shaking it. "They call me Don," he replied arrogantly, filling a champagne glass and sliding it in front of her. "But you're not from around here."

"Oh? How can you tell?"

"Because you would'a already knew my name if you were."

She giggled.

"Aren't you the cocky one?"

He shrugged and sipped his champagne. "It is what it is. This is my party. I'm showing love to the city," he lied, waving his glass, gesturing to encompass the club.

Chanel smiled to herself, imagining how many chicks he had already run that line on, but since she was the one who actually paid for the party, she was the only one who knew better.

"Wow, this is definitely in the right place, huh?" she remarked, cuddling up closer to him.

Don Pooh smiled because he was feeling himself. Chanel was the baddest chick in the club and he had pulled her . . . or so he thought.

∞

"I'm sayin', I'm tryin' to leave wit' you too, but I can't leave my girl," the red-headed, brown-skinned chick replied to Shamar, who was all in her ear, hand on her ass, trying to convince her to leave with him. Shamar wanted to fuck her badly. She may have been super ghetto, but she was Luke-Dancer-thick, with an ass so fat and waist so thin that she looked like a porn star ready to perform.

"That ain't no problem, 'cause my man is with me. He can rock wit' your girl."

"Where he at? I hope he ain't ugly, 'cause she ain't even about to play herself," she responded.

"I don't be judging nigguhs like that, ma, but he official," Shamar remarked.

"We'll see."

"Come on."

"Ay, Candy! Candy, come on!" the girl called out to her friend.

When Shamar saw Candy, he wanted to fuck her too. She wasn't as thick as her friend, but she could still give K. Michelle a run for her money.

"What's up, Nita?" Candy asked.

"We about to get something to eat. You comin'?"

"We who?" Candy wanted to know.

"Hol' up, I'm lookin' for my man now," Shamar said, thinking, Where the fuck is Crook?

∞

Crook was staggering through the crowd with a bottle of Moet in each hand, drunk out of his mind. He was dancing on the asses of females, regardless of whether they were with a man, because word was quickly spreading about the wild little Jersey nigguh and his team of young Wilmington goons. He made his way to Don Pooh's table, and when he saw Coco Chanel, he was stuck. Mesmerized in his drunken state of mind, she looked like the most beautiful woman in the world. He approached the table, looking dead at Chanel

"Fam', what up?" Shifty greeted, but Crook didn't even hear him—he was locked in.

"Yo, ma, come on. Let's dance," Crook said, setting both bottles on the table and jacking up his pants, staggering.

Chanel eyed him with a curious, amused expression. "Excuse me, I'm with somebody."

"Man, fuck that!" Crook spat back, in his mind thinking, Fuck him. I'm tryin' to dance wit' you.

Don Pooh felt like Crook was disrespecting him, but truth be told he was a little shook of Crook, so he played it off.

"Yo fam', you drunk. Chill," he said. "I'm hollerin' at shorty."

"Oh, he's your little friend?" Chanel questioned.

Crook spazzed. "Little!"

Without hesitation, he reached in his pants and pulled out his dick, then slapped it on the table. It hit the wood like a slab of meat, right next to Chanel's forearm. Everybody at the table reacted except Chanel. The three other girls marveled.

"Damn, that lil' nigguh holdin' like that?"

"I'll dance with you!"

"What's your name?"

Shifty and Don Pooh looked away, disgusted.

"Goddamn, nigguh, fuck kinda shit you into?" Shifty barked.

"This nigguh put his dick on the table! I don't want to sit here no more!" Don Pooh growled.

Chanel and Crook's eyes met. She was definitely feeling his swagger. She simply glanced at his dick, smirked, and said, "I'll keep that in mind."

Satisfied, Crook smiled and put his dick back in his pants. "You do that. Now, 'bout that dance?"

Before she could respond, they heard, "Yo Crook!"

It was Shamar. He walked up to Crook and said, "Let me holla at you, yo." He put his arm around Crook's neck and walked him away from the table.

"Yo, you see them two bitches over there?" he asked, pointing at Candy and Nita.

'What about 'em?"

"Fam', I told shorty in the 'fuck me' skirt all about you! She on your dick like a muhfucka!" Shamar commented, shooting Crook the bullshit.

"Man, fuck her. You see that," Crook countered, pointing at Chanel.

When Shamar looked, it was as if Chanel was expecting it, because she looked dead at him.

"Damn!" Shamar remarked, eyebrows raised, impressed.

"I'm 'bout to bag that," Crook remarked proudly.

"Come on, fam'. I need you, yo. Fuck wit' me on this, ai'ight?" Shamar pleaded, ready to fuck Nita.

"Ai'ight, yo, but you owe me."

He and Crook walked out of the club with Candy and Nita in tow. On the way out, a big, bald, dyke-looking chick was carrying a drunken chick out of the club and bumped into Shamar.

"She drunk," the big dyke explained.

"Whateva," Shamar replied and kept moving.

The girl wasn't drunk, she was out cold. Kat had followed her around the club, waiting for her opportunity. The girl went into the bathroom and Kat followed. As soon as she entered, two other chicks were leaving out. Only Kat and the girl remained. The girl was in the stall and Kat kicked open the stall door. To the girl's credit, she didn't kick and scream. She jumped up, letting her skirt fall back in place and hooked off on Kat, punching her dead in the face.

Kat took it and smiled.

The girl swung harder, but this punch was caught by Kat's massive hand, and then flung back at the girl. Kat spun her around and yanked her off her feet in a suffocating arm lock around her neck.

"Get ahhhggh!" the girl said, trying to resist, but once the handkerchief soaked in chloroform went over her mouth and nose, it was only a matter of seconds before her body went limp.

Kat picked her up, placing the girl's arm over her neck and carried her out, as if she was drunk. The girl never saw Wilmington again.

CHAPTER 29
- No Witnesses -

As soon as they got back to Nita's apartment, she and Shamar were all over each other. He closed the door of her bedroom by swinging her body against it and pinning her right there.

She reached in Shamar's pants and gave his dick a lustful squeeze. "Damn, your dick thick," she groaned breathlessly.

"Get on your knees," Shamar growled, dropping his pants and letting his gun hit the floor.

Nita suddenly dropped to her knees.

Shamar gripped a handful of her hair and angled her face up, while he rubbed his dick across her lips and cheeks.

"Mmmmm," she moaned as she finally wrapped her lips around his shaft.

"Yo, ma, eat that dick," he said, palming the back of her head and fucking her face.

Nita's head game was average, but that wasn't what Shamar was on for. All he could think about was watching that ass jiggle while he hit her from the back.

"Come 'ere, ma," he ordered, pulling her to her feet.

She quickly shed her clothes, and Shamar bent her over the bed. He eyed her ass lustfully. It was perfect.

He slapped it once and it jiggled and wobbled just like he knew it would.

Nita looked over her shoulder, biting her bottom lip. "Oh, I love gettin' my ass spanked, daddy."

Shamar spread her pussy lips and filled her full of hard dick. She moaned and thrashed like he was killing her, filling the room with cries.

The sounds of fucking bled through the walls and into the living room where Crook and Candy were sitting on the couch on opposite ends. Every time Nita cried out, Crook got more heated.

"Ay yo, this some bullshit," he mumbled, glancing over at Candy.

She had her legs crossed, swinging one sexy ass foot, impatiently.

"I'm ready to go," she huffed.

Crook slid over a little closer. "I'm sayin', ma, it's like that? I'm tryin' to holla at you," he said, trying the smooth approach, which was totally not him.

"Like I said, I don't get down like that."

"Why not? Your friend do."

"I ain't my friend," she shot back, rolling her eyes.

"I know, you prettier." He smiled, but she didn't respond. "So it's like that?"

"I'm ready to go."

"Oh daddy, fuck this pussy! Ah fuck, yeah!"

Crook got more heated. "Goddamn, it wasn't like that when you was eatin' up my food and drinkin' my drinks," Crook snarled, referring to the meal and drinks that he paid for at the restaurant where they ate before coming to Nita's apartment.

Candy looked at him with disgust. "Nigguh, please, I know you ain't about to go there."

"It's—it's yours! Oh damn, I'm 'bout to come again!"

Crook slid over next to Candy.

She jumped up. "Fuck it, I'll take a cab."

"Naw, yo, you ain't goin' nowhere," Crook retorted, grabbing her wrist.

She snatched away. "Nigguh, who the fuck you grabbin'!"

"Come 'ere, bitch!" Crook huffed.

"Ohhhh, I feel it in my stomach."

Crook grabbed Candy by the back of the neck and flung her on the couch.

"Get off me!" Candy yelled, trying to sound tough, but inside she was petrified.

"Bitch, you about to do somethin'!' Crook demanded, snatching at her tiny skirt, which hiked up enough to reveal the camel toe print in her black panties.

"Fuck me, baby, fuck meeeee!"

"Stop!" Candy yelled, but Crook was in a zone.

The more she fought, the harder his dick got. He ripped her panties off, then snatched her down onto the floor between the couch and the coffee table. She dug her nails on both hands into his face.

"Aaaafffgh!" he cried out and back-handed blood out of her mouth.

He pried open her legs and forced the engorged head of his dick inside of her tight, moist pussy.

"No, pleaseeee!" Candy sobbed.

"Shut up!" he grunted and back-handed her again.

Crook cocked her legs back and began to pump his dick in and out of her, hard. Candy cried and flailed, trying to get him off her. But Crook had blacked out, totally oblivious to her pleas. For him, she represented every woman that had tried to play him, always up in his face when he was on, but nowhere to be found when he fell off. Crook wasn't a bad looking cat, but he was seldom a choice woman's first look.

But tonight, that would change.

He was drunk out of his mind, and Nita's loud sounds of ecstasy in the other room drowned out the ones coming from beneath him. And then—she slapped him.

It wasn't a hard slap. It was merely the fact that she had the audacity to slap him.

"Bitch!" he barked and began choking her with both hands.

Candy's eyes got as big as plates as she tried to claw at the vise-like grip he had on her throat. The harder he choked her, the harder he fucked her, until her body betrayed her and she started to come all over his dick, just as the last breath of life left her body.

When her hand fell away and flopped on the floor, he knew she was dead. Her open eyes stared lifelessly at his sweaty face, but he kept fucking her dead body until the rumble built in his stomach and he came all over her.

Breathing hard, he struggled to his feet and pulled his pants up. He looked down at her, his cum oozing out of her.

"Damn!" he remarked, shaking his head.

A few minutes later, Shamar came out shirtless, wearing only his jeans and boots.

"Yo duke, let's switch! That bitch Nita is a freak!" Shamar exclaimed.

"I fucked up," Crook said, looking at him, wide-eyed and sweating.

"Fuck you talking about? What you looking so crazy for?"

"She dead," Crook replied, looking down at Candy.

"Dead?" Shamar echoed, then followed Crook's eyes to the floor.

At first, he hadn't noticed her down on the floor, but when he saw her, his eyes bucked.

"Oh shit! Yo, what the fuck happened?"

"I–I fucked up," Crook repeated, pacing the floor.

"How!" Shamar stressed, pacing with him. "Fam', we can't just leave this bitch . . . Goddamn, the fuck . . . ai'ight, hol' up." Shamar went back to the bedroom.

Fifteen seconds later, Crook heard Boc! Boc! and then a loud thump. Shamar came back out with the gun in his hand. They looked at each other, but no words passed between them because it was understood.

No witnesses.

"Now what?" Shamar questioned.

"Fuck it, let's just burn the shit down," Crook suggested.

Shamar shook his head. "Naw, too much attention. We need to get these bodies outta here and burn them somewhere."

"Where?"

"How the fuck I'm 'posed to know? Why the fuck you kill the bitch?" Shamar asked.

"She slapped me. Drank my shit up. Fuck that!" Crook mumbled.

Shamar went to the window and looked out. They were on the third floor of the apartment building, and right below the window was an alley that led to the parking lot.

"Yo, go get the car and drive it around to this side where the alley start," Shamar told him.

"For what?"

"'Cause we on the third fuckin floor! We can't carry 'em down!" Shamar scolded.

"Then just burn these bitches up," Crook reiterated.

"Just get the fuckin' car."

Once Crook had positioned the car, he came back upstairs. "Now what?"

"We toss these bitches out the window!"

They wrapped the two bodies tightly in sheets, then dragged them to the window. One after the other, they pushed the bodies out of the window for the three-story fall, ending in a bone crushing thud.

They then went downstairs, each one dragging a body to Crook's BMW. After they put Nita in the trunk, Crook remarked, "They ain't both gonna fit."

"Fuck it. Put her in the backseat."

Crook ran back upstairs for a few extra sheets and pocketed Nita's jewelry off the dresser. He went back downstairs and covered the backseat with the sheets before they laid Candy's body across it and drove off.

Thirty minutes later, they were still driving around aimlessly in circles.

"Let's take 'em to the County park," Crook suggested.

"Where the fuck is the County park?"

"How the fuck I'm 'posed to know?"

Shamar was getting frustrated, driving around and around with two dead bodies.

"Yo! I know what we can do," Crook exclaimed, as if he had just awakened.

"What?"

Crook grinned.

CHAPTER 30
- Disrespected -

Vanessa pulled up to Don Pooh's condo, after spending the night partying with her girlfriends in Philly. Don Pooh had forbidden her to come to the big party, which was cool with her, because she could do her dirt far from Don Pooh's watchful eyes.

She had a few ballers and got a few numbers, but truth be told, she couldn't stop thinking about GQ. She was definitely feeling him. First off, he was super fine, gangsta as fuck, and had a pretty dick that she couldn't wait to ride. She had called him a few times, asking him when he would be back.

"Gimme like a week," he repeatedly told her, because he was caught up in the scam he was running.

She unlocked the door and went inside. As soon as she entered, she smelled it . . .

Pussy, and it wasn't hers.

Vanessa had a keen sense of smell, especially when it came to what was hers. Not that she particularly cared about Don Pooh, but he was her deep-pocket sponsor, so she played it for all it was worth. But she wasn't about to be disrespected either. She started up the stairs, ready to spazz on his ass and the bitch too if she acted froggy. As she approached the bedroom door, all she heard was, "Goddamn, Angel, shit that feel good as fuck!" Don Pooh grunted lustfully.

Vanessa threw the door open so hard that the knob cracked the sheetrock wall. What she saw blew her mind. Some jet-black, shiny bitch wearing nothing but a big, black, strap-on dildo, fucking Don Pooh in the ass! She didn't know whether to be mad or disgusted. His eyes got wide, but the jet-black, shiny bitch just smirked and kept stroking.

"You nasty motherfucka! What kind of shit is you into!" Vanessa screamed.

"Vanessa!" he blurted out, getting up. He tried to grab her arm, but she jerked away and stormed down the stairs. "Wait, ma, I can explain!"

"Explain another bitch in my house, fuckin' you in the ass! Nigguh, I don't think so!"

She ran out of the house, but since Don Pooh was naked, he stopped and hid behind the front door, sticking his head out. "'Nessa! Come here, ma. Goddamn!"

"Fuck you, Pooh! I can't believe you disrespected me like that!" she said, jumping in her car.

She squealed tires as she pulled off. The first person she called was GQ. She was so hot (in more ways than one) that she was ready to drive to Newark. It rang five times, went to voice mail. It was four o'clock in the morning, so she figured GQ was asleep, but she was in no mood to not be heard. She dialed his number again.

"Yo," his voice cracked on the line.

Hearing his voice turned her rage into the tears of a little girl.

"I can't believe he played me like this!" she cried.

"Huh? Yo, who this?" GQ asked, hating to be awakened and highly aggravated.

"Vanessa! Pooh, he played me! Where are you? I need to see you!"

GQ picked up his watch from the dresser. "Ma, it's four in the morning! I'll hit you when I wake up."

"No! GQ, I need you," she sobbed.

He took a deep breath and ran his hand over his face. "Ma, calm down, okay? I'll be down there this week," he lied, "and we'll talk about it then."

Something inside of her clicked and made her play her hold card. Maybe it was the way he was treating her like his 'whateva chick' and she wanted to prove her worth, or like a whore leaving one pimp for another, she wanted to show her loyalty. Whatever it was, it made her blurt out, "He played you, too!"

"What?"

"The money, that's what. The cops pullin' me over wasn't an accident, baby! He set you up for the money!"

Now she had his undivided attention.

∞

"Yo, I had to sell the BM," Shamar announced, lying back in the driver's seat, smoking a blunt. He passed it to Crook.

They were in the parking lot of a small funeral home, waiting for it to open.

Crook took the blunt. "Word? What happened?"

"Nigguh, muhfuckin' broke happened!" Shamar chuckled, even though it was far from funny. "I ain't got but like fifty grand to my name!"

"When the dough get low, the jewels gotta go," Crook rapped, holding in his breath as he inhaled the exotic. When he exhaled, he added, "Finesse say he cakin' up in B-More. Won't you fuck wit' him on that heroin shit?"

Shamar shook his head. "Naw, heroin his thing. I got somethin' bubblin' wit' my white girl."

"Word? What's good? Break bread."

"As soon as—oh shit! What the fuck!" Shamar blurted, then jumped out of the car, like it was on fire.

"Wha—shit!" Crook barked when he saw it too. He jumped out and they both pulled their guns and aimed them at the car.

Candy had sat up in the backseat. The sheet was still over her, but she had risen and was sitting up. Both Shamar and Crook thought it was the weed.

"Yo, I thought the bitch was dead!" Shamar said, gun aimed, ready to blast off.

"How the fuck she ain't? I dropped her on her head from the third floor!"

"Yo, Candy! . . . Candy! Yo, you hear me?" Shamar called out.

No response.

"Yo, pull her out," Crook suggested.

"Nigguh, you pull her out!" Shamar shot back.

"Yo, Candy!" Crook called out, inching toward the back door. "Yo!"

When there was still no response, Crook leaned guardedly over and opened the back door and then jumped quickly back.

"Yo, Candy, quit playin', bitch!" Crook said, attempting to mask his nervousness.

With extreme cautiousness, he slowly reached in to snatch the sheet off her face. She was still wide-eyed and her skull was cracked open from the three-story fall, and she was definitely dead. All of a sudden, Shamar started laughing a laugh of relief.

"Fuck is so funny?" Crook wanted to know.

"Rigor mortis." Shamar cackled. "Motherfuckin' rigor mortis set in, yo. Sometimes dead bodies do that," he explained, remembering hearing that somewhere.

"Rigor–who?"

"Nigguh, you was shook as fuck. You thought the bitch was on some Jason shit!" Shamar cracked.

"Fuck outta here." Crook smirked, grabbing his dick. "You the one jumped like a white bitch in a scary movie!"

Each laughed at the other and at themselves as they met up in the front of the car. Crook sat on the hood and held up the blunt.

"Gimme a light."

Shamar handed him the lighter. As Crook puffed the blunt back to life, all the talk of dead bodies made him think of Black. He had dreamed about him a few times in the past few weeks. It wasn't guilt, because he felt none, but he knew the team deserved to know the truth. So, as the sun peeped over the trees, Crook shed his own light.

"Yo, Sha, let me ask you somethin'."

"What's good?"

Crook passed him the blunt. "You think Black snitched on Finesse?"

Shamar hit the blunt, inhaling the smoke, slow and long as he contemplated the question. "I don't know."

"I do. I know he did."

"How you know?"

"Finesse knew it, too. I could see it in his eyes that day I went to see him in the County. He ain't wanna push the button on his own baby brother, but he knew," Crook explained.

Shamar passed him the blunt, his mind disgusted with the thought that one of his brothers would tell on the other. At the time of Finesse's arrest, circumstances and the situation made him look at Black skeptically, but he had pushed it out of his mind. Now, Crook was making him confront it.

"I'm sayin', yo . . . we'll never know," Shamar remarked.

Crook pinched the roach of the blunt, hit it one more time, then thunked it away.

"If you had knew for sure, would you have pushed the button?" Crook asked, looking him directly in the eyes.

"I can't say," Shamar replied, really meaning no, he couldn't have.

Crook nodded with understanding. "Well, I did. I pushed the button."

At first, it didn't register with Shamar. "What?"

"I said I did it . . . I killed Black."

The admission almost staggered Shamar as he tried to wrap his mind around what Crook had said. His man, one of his best friends since grade school, had just told him he killed his brother. Of course, why he did it he understood, but that he did it was still hard to swallow.

"Naw, Crook . . . Black?" Shamar stressed, shaking his head.

It took eight minutes and twenty seconds for the sun to rise, and in that time, their relationship had changed forever. When Shamar looked at Crook, Crook could see the change in his eyes.

A car pulled into the parking lot from the end opposite of where Shamar and Crook were.

"Yo, it's on," Crook remarked, reminding Shamar why they were there.

Like a true soldier, Shamar blocked out everything else and concentrated on the task at hand.

An old black man with a short, gray afro got out of his Lincoln Town Car. He was the owner of the funeral home. He saw Crook and Shamar approaching, but he thought nothing of it.

"Good morning, sir," Shamar greeted.

"Good morning, young man. What can I do for you?"

"A friend of mine passed away. We want you to bury him for us."

"Glory, son. I'm sure this is a difficult time, but let's step inside and discuss it," the old man offered.

The three of them walked inside. The old man flipped on the lights.

"Let me make some coffee."

"Naw, yo, we good," Shamar replied.

The change in tone, with a more ominous edge, made the old man look back at them. He looked right into the black holes of twin barrels. He instantly threw up his hands.

"The embalming fluid is in there." He pointed, thinking they had come for the sherm.

"Naw, yo, this ain't a robbery. We need a favor," Shamar explained.

"O–okay," the old man readily agreed.

Once they explained the situation, Crook pulled the car closer to the back door. The old man wheeled a gurney to the door. He and Crook got Nita's body out of the trunk and then stacked Candy's body on top of hers.

"Where's the incinerator?" Crook asked.

The old man led the way. The incinerator looked like a gigantic oven, one designed to reach a temperature high enough to burn human bodies to ashes. When the old man lifted the steel handled door, the heat from the flames filled the room.

"We just toss 'em in?" Crook asked.

The old man was so scared, he just nodded.

Shamar and Crook wrestled Candy's body off the gurney and tossed it on the wheeled rack that was used to convey the bodies into the heat of the inferno. When they had put Nita's body on top of Candy's, the sheet fell away, revealing her nakedness. The old man looked away with grief and shame.

Crook shoved them in and slammed the door shut.

"That's that," he remarked.

It took a while, but both were burned completely. Crook kept checking, just to make sure. Once he was satisfied, he turned to the old man and put his gun to his head.

"Please don't kill me," the old man begged. "I ain't seen nothin'! Please, I have a grandson I haven't even held yet."

"Then you won't know what you're missing." Crook shrugged, then pulled the trigger.

Bloc!

The old man's gray afro flapped and turned crimson as his head opened up and ejected major parts of his brain. He slumped to the ground, twitching. Crook hit him twice more, and he became more still than deep water.

"Let's go," Shamar commented, turning for the door.

"Hol' up, he said. "The embalming fluid in there! We can make a killin'!" Crook exclaimed.

CHAPTER 31
- Be Careful What You Ask For -

The pussy felt so good to Don Pooh, the feeling made him go cross-eyed. All he was thinking with every stroke was: "I gotta wife this bitch; I gotta wife this bitch; I gotta wife this biiiiiiitch!" he grunted, squeezed her and came, body jerking like a numbed dog.

Meanwhile, beneath him, Chanel was staring at the ceiling, waiting for him to finish. She knew that once he had a taste of her juiciness, she would have him wrapped. And she was right!

"Real talk, ma, fuck all that beatin' around the bush. I want you to move in with me," Don Pooh remarked as he rolled off her and lay beside her.

Chanel giggled, turning on her side to face him and throwing her sexy, long leg over his hip. "Just like that, huh?"

"Yo, when a nigguh see somethin' he want, he do what it takes to get it," he replied, trying to sound arrogant instead of the pussy-whipped trick that he really was.

"Well, I really don't know if I'm staying in Wilmington. I've got something going on in Jersey," Chanel replied, throwing out words for him to run with.

"Oh, you from Jerz? I got people in Jerz! Matter of fact, that wild ass nigguh at the club from Newark."

225

"Is he?" Chanel found his mind easier to pick than a lock.

"Yeah yo. Crook, that's my man. But later for that. What's your thing? Dancin', right? Fuck that, I'll buy you a club!" He chuckled.

Chanel caressed his cheek like a mother would do to her retarded child. "That was sweet."

"Yeah, but I'm dead ass . . . Real talk, ma. I'm feelin' you—shit is serious. I want you in my life—right now!"

Chanel kissed him, then looked him in the eyes. He was too mesmerized to see the coldness.

"Be careful what you ask for," she replied.

∞

- ANGER AND ADMIRATION -

That's what GQ was feeling. Anger because Don Pooh had robbed the team of over two hundred grand, and admiration because as a fellow hustler and con man, the setup was so sweet that he couldn't wait to run it himself.

"So let me get this straight," he said, inching to the edge of his seat and resting his elbows on his knees, "the two cops, they were workin' with him the whole time?"

Vanessa nodded. She was sitting on the couch across from him, and her eyes were full of tears.

"I'm so sorry, baby." She sniffled, dabbing her eyes with a napkin. "But he–he made me do it! He's done that lots of time to different people."

"And what about the money he put in?"

"He just gets it back, plus his cut. He knows it looks like he lost too, so people wouldn't suspect anything," she explained.

"Motherfucka!" GQ cursed, punching his hand and jumping up to pace.

Startled, Vanessa jumped up and wrapped her arms around his neck, sobbing into his chest.

"Please forgive me, GQ. I love you."

Behind her back, he was smiling, his calculating mind wondering how he would use her, but when he pushed her away, he had on his poker face.

"Naw, yo, I can't fuck wit' you like that. How I'ma trust you? You broke my heart," he said, turning his back and dramatically going to look out the window, posing.

Vanessa gripped him from the back, gripping his dick in one hand and his waist with her other arm. "Don't be like that! I swear I'll make it up to you! I'll do anything!" she swore, tears streaming down her face.

"GQ turned back to her.

"Anything?"

"She looked him directly in the eyes and replied, "Anything!"

To GQ, that one word was better than her pussy.

∞

They call Baltimore 'Charm City,' and that was exactly what it was proving to be for Finesse, his lucky charm. Ever since he had hit town, he had been making money like water, thanks to his man, Fingers, so named because he had six fingers on his left hand.

He had met Fingers at the Feds the first year down. Fingers was on his way home and promised to stay in touch. Since the penitentiary was packed with promise-makers, Finesse didn't think about it until he received a card and some flicks from Fingers. For the next two years, Fingers held Finesse down and now, Finesse was returning the favor in spades.

Fingers had always told him, "All I need is the right connect, and I can take over B-More on some Stringer Bell type shit!"

Now that Finesse had come through, the two of them were doing just that. Fingers was seeing more money than he had ever seen, and he definitely needed it, because he had seven kids—that he claimed.

For his part, Finesse was on cloud nine, but truth be told, he was worried about Charisma. She hadn't been her usual self. They had a little condo out in Baltimore County, and she never left it. They had separate rooms, but lately he had been waking up to find her cuddled up in his bed with him. He could tell it wasn't sexual, so he didn't try to make it so. He had decided not to hustle on this weekend and to take her out. He even went to the supermarket and bought all the ingredients to make her a special meal.

"Yo, 'Riz!" he called out, as he came through the door, toting the plastic shopping bags.

He got no response. He put the bags down in the kitchen and went upstairs. He entered the bedroom and found her laid out across the bed.

"Yo, ma, get your lazy ass up. I'm 'bout to cook dinner, and why your phone off? I tried to call you from the supermarket 'cause I ain't know if you wanted turkey or beef sausage to go wit' the pasta, so I got 'em both," Finesse rattled off as he went about the business of taking his gun off his waist, putting it on the dresser, taking the large wads of money out of all four pockets and putting them on the dresser, along with his phone. When he turned back to her, she still hadn't moved.

"'Riz? Get up," he repeated, slapping her on the ass.

That's when he felt it.

Her ass wasn't the soft, jiggly cushion it usually was. It was harder, firmer—tense. He frowned.

"Charisma, wake up," he said loudly, shaking her shoulder.

The shaking caused an empty bottle of Excedrin PM sleeping pills to fall from her limp hand. Finesse's whole world caved in.

"Aisha! Aisha!" he frantically called to her, sitting on the bed and propping her up in his lap.

Her skin had a sickly pallor, and she was totally non-responsive, mouth slightly agape. He felt her neck and his heart leaped when he felt a slight pulse, but he knew there was no time to waste. He quickly scooped her up and carried her down the stairs, fighting a losing battle with the tears burning in the wells of his eyes.

"Please, baby, don't die on me," he ardently whispered as he half ran her to the car. He left the front door wide open, but didn't think twice about it as he gently laid her in the passenger seat then ran around the car, jumped behind the wheel and screeched off.

"Ma, why you—" He shook his head, the tears freely flowing down his cheeks. " It's gonna be all right, okay? Shit is gonna get better!"

Traffic lights, other cars, even opposite lanes, nothing was going to be an obstacle to getting her to the hospital. He would end up going to a hospital further away, because he wasn't aware that there was one a few blocks away.

The police saw him weave into the opposite lane, barely missing an oncoming car then swerving smoothly back into his lane and cutting all the way across traffic to make a right turn. The police made a U-turn and jumped dead on his tail.

Finesse glanced at the whirling lights in his rearview mirror, but there was no way he was pulling over.

"I know you hear me, girl," he remarked, glancing over at her. "This is bullshit and you know it! Why, ma! As soon as you wake up, I swear to God . . . I swear to God, I'ma slap the shit outta you. How you gonna leave me like this?"

Two more police cars joined the chase, and by the time he skidded into the parking lot of the hospital, there were several more, all converging on him from different directions. He skidded up to the Emergency Room entrance. Instead of getting out on the driver's side, he climbed over Charisma and emerged from the passenger side. By the time he stood up, he already had Charisma cradled in his arms.

"Freeze!" an officer yelled, gun aimed and quivering.

"She's dying!" Finesse yelled back then turned and headed inside the Emergency Room.

Several officers rushed to follow him inside. Seeing the teary-eyed man carrying the body of a woman, trailed by several police officers instantly got the attention of the Emergency Room staff. Finesse didn't stop at the reception desk. He headed straight back into the treatment area.

"Sir, you can't go back there!" the nurse cried.

Finesse was oblivious to her words. A white officer grasping the gravity of the situation held up his hand to the nurse.

Once Finesse saw a doctor, he laid Charisma on a gurney, looked the doctor in the face, his eyes filled with tears, pain, anger and conviction and said, "Save her!"

The doctor couldn't say no.

"What happened?"

"She overdosed on sleeping pills," Finesse replied.

The doctor took control and wheeled Charisma away, barking orders as he pushed her into an area screened off by a curtain. Finesse then turned to the police and stuck his hands straight out, wrists together, as if he anticipated being cuffed. A black officer started to do just that, but the white officer stopped him.

"You got some ID on you, son?"

Finesse shook his head. "All I got, they just took back there."

The officer nodded, with understanding. "That your girlfriend?"

Finesse nodded.

"If I lock you up, who can come sit with her?"

"Nobody."

"Then that settles it. You ever drive in my city again, I will lock you up, we clear?"

"Thank you, officer."

The officer nodded, and just before he turned away, he added, "I would've done the same thing."

The police left and Finesse began pacing the waiting room floor. Hours that seemed like days dragged by. Every nurse that passed, he asked for an update. Back and forth he paced, scared to sit down as if he thought motion meant life. Several times, he thought about praying, but each time he did, he brushed it aside. He refused to acknowledge any God, let alone one with the power over life and death, her life and death. The thought alone made him feel helpless. Finesse felt that his will by itself was sufficient to pull her through.

Finally, the doctor came out, looking firm but exhausted. They locked eyes as the doctor crossed the waiting room toward him, and by the look on his face, Finesse knew that he needed to be sitting down.

CHAPTER 32
- Animal Attraction -

"Yo Crook! We killin' 'em out here with this wet!" one of Crook's young goons named Quiz exclaimed.

Crook had just pulled up on the block. Business was booming. Not just because of the cocaine, but also because of what they called "wet," which was the embalming fluid that Crook had stolen from the funeral home. Cigarettes could be dipped in it, or weed or tea leaves could be soaked in it to result in a zombie-like high that made people see things, feel like they were floating, causing some to get naked and run down the street, and even jump off buildings.

Crook and Shamar had split all they had found, but Crook had given his part to his young goons to sell. He called his dealing with them "feeding the pups," because he really felt like he was training pit bulls.

Quiz jumped in the passenger seat and gave Crook dap. Of all his young goons, Quiz and Bleek were his favorites because they went the hardest, although they did not look it. Quiz was only seventeen, but was tall and lanky and looked like Derrick Rose.

"Yeah, yo, y'all killin' 'em, but where my muhfuckin' money, lil' nigguh?" Crook asked.

"You know I got you, big homie." Quiz smirked, handing Crook a McDonald's bag of rubber-banded wads.

233

"Yo, nigguhs ain't tryin' to flex or nothin', is they?"

Quiz sucked his teeth. "Man, them nigguhs know what it is. Ain't nobody tryin' to do the fire dance." He laughed, referring to the frantic movements K-Nut made when Crook set him afire.

They laughed.

"But still, shut the coke down at eight o'clock. Let them other nigguhs eat, too. Ain't no need to gorilla shit when it's yours already," Crook jeweled him.

"I hear you, big homie. Yo, what you about to do?"

Before Crook could answer, what he was about to do turned the corner.

Chanel.

She was driving an older model Nissan Altima, with her hair up in a ponytail, driving slowly and looking from side to side. Crook's heart dropped because he hoped she wasn't smoking. Then again, he thought, maybe she only smoked that wet.

He blew his horn and she looked. When she saw him, she smiled and waved him over.

"Damn, that bitch sexy as fuck," Quiz remarked, grabbing his crotch.

"Word, I bagged her the other night," he bragged, not knowing how true his words really were.

Crook hopped out, leaving the BMW double parked and running. He waited for a car to pass, then crossed the street. When he got to Chanel's car, he leaned on the driver's side window opening.

"Looking for me?" He grinned.

"Yeah, I am. Get in, this spot is too hot."

Crook rounded the car and hopped into the passenger seat. She pulled off.

"I never got your name."

"I know yours," she sang playfully.

"What is it?"

"Crook," she said, looking at him lustfully and glancing down at his crotch, "and I already know why."

He laughed, knowing that she was referring to the curve in his dick.

"Naw, that ain't why," he replied. When he saw that she wasn't just going around the block, he added, "You know I left my shit running."

"And?" she shot back with a mischievous smirk.

Crook chuckled. "Oh, so you just gonna kidnap me, huh?"

"Yep."

He got on his phone and called Quiz.

"What up, big homie?"

"Yo, go park my shit and hold the keys 'til I get back. I mean park my shit—don't be drivin' it!"

"I got you, yo. I'm parking it right now," Quiz lied.

Crook hung up. "So if you gonna kidnap me, at least tell me your name?"

She looked at him and replied, "Chanel."

"Like the perfume?"

"Just like the perfume."

But in Crook's mind, he didn't make the obvious connection.

Thirty minutes later, Chanel and Crook were back at her hotel suite.

"I'm just going to take a shower. I'll be right out," Chanel told him, and then headed for the bathroom.

Crook nodded, making his way over to the bar. He started to fix himself a drink when his phone rang.

Seeing that it was Finesse, he sent him to voice mail then cut the phone off. He heard the shower running in the bathroom, but focused on the task at hand. Crook took the top off the V.S.O.P. and started to pour it into a glass, but changed his mind and drank it straight out of the bottle. Curious, he looked toward the bathroom, picturing Chanel in the shower, butt naked and soaking wet. Crook could see the pinkness of her pussy peeping out from between her legs. In his mind, she was playing with herself with one hand and wiggling a finger on the other hand, telling him to "come here."

He hit the bottle once more. "Fuck it," he grunted, then headed for the bathroom.

The door was open a crack. He pushed it wide open and went in. He feasted on the ebony goddess in all of her splendor, looking wet and delicious, nipples erect and pinkness peeping, just as he pictured it.

"What took you so long?" She grinned.

Truth be told, Crook was a little intimidated by her beauty at first, but now seeing that she was as open as he was, the intimidation was replaced by a lustful hunger.

"Goddamn, you a sexy bitch," he said, standing there, simply admiring her.

That's when she knew.

There was no twitch, no intense aggravation when he called her a bitch. Chanel reached out and pulled him to her and, as she did, he poured the rest of the V.S.O.P. all over her pert titties and watched it travel down her stomach and into the V of her thighs.

He stepped into the shower, fully clothed. Neither one of them thought it was the least bit strange.

"Tell me you want this pussy," she gasped, her stomach quivering from the movement of his tongue over it.

"I want this pussy to be mine."

"It already is."

He cocked her foot on the side of the tub, then began fingering her and sucking her clit at the same time.

"Oh fuck!" she squealed, grabbing the back of his head to keep from falling.

He sucked her pussy until she was dizzy with lust and weak from the first of many orgasms.

"I want you to fuck me," she cooed.

Crook scooped her up and she wrapped her legs around his waist, tonguing him down ferociously, all the way to the bed. He dropped her on the bed, and she bounced with a giggle, then sat up, anxious to get him out of every stitch of his soaked clothes.

"Hurry up so you can really get wet," she urged.

By the time she got the words out of her mouth, he was butt naked and pushing her back on the bed.

"No, I wanna ride you."

"Bend yo' ass over," he growled lustfully, and the timbre in his voice made her pussy twitch.

Chanel hurriedly bent over, putting her ass in the air and face on the bed, looking back at him with the 'fuck me' face. "Like this, daddy?"

He answered with a grunt and 8 curved inches of hard dick that made her scream his name as soon as he hit bottom.

"Crooookkk!' she moaned, as if he was killing her.

Crook grabbed her around the waist and began long-dicking her pussy, slowly but forcefully, making sure that she felt every inch.

"Oh yeah, you hittin' my spot, my spot!"

The pussy felt so good to Crook that he had to fight to hold back his nut, but she didn't even try to hold back hers, cumming for the second time and coating his dick.

"I can't stop cummmminnnn'," she moaned.

Smack! Her ass jiggled on contact.

"Whose pussy is this?"

"Yours, daddy."

Smack!

"Yours!"

Crook grabbed her by the thigh and roughly flipped her over on her back, cocking her legs in front of his arm and over his shoulders. When he thrust forward, his dick slid straight in her pussy like it was a heat-seeking missile.

"You drive me crazy, you know that?" Chanel purred, caught up in the throes of frantic lust.

She dug her nails in his back, to mix pleasure with pain and marking what she considered hers. The deep, burning sensation triggered a memory in Crook's mind.

The memory of Candy.

Crook vividly remembered the way that she thrashed and fought, her body slowly submitting to the pounds of his lust. He saw the way she gasped as he choked the life out of her, the whole time her body fucking him back. Before he realized it, he was choking Chanel. The familiar sound of "pssssst!" brought him back to reality.

Chanel had spit out her razor.

GAME OF GWOP

When Crook first started choking her, it turned her on even more. Chanel was an animal, primarily attracted to other animals, and Crook was definitely an animal. She couldn't care less about a timid man, so she naturally responded to Crook. But once the pressure continued, increased, intensified, she responded as an animal and went into survival mode. She grabbed the razor and aimed for the jugular, knowing the human body so well. The only reason she missed was that Crook opened his eyes at the sound of her spitting the razor out and leaned away just in time. The razor slit him from the base of his earlobe to the edge of his jaw line. Blood spurted profusely.

"Bitch!" he barked and lunged at Chanel.

As he lunged, she rolled off the bed and onto the floor. Crook started to go after her, but she was holding a .45 caliber pistol with both hands. Clearly, she knew what she was doing.

Boc! Boc!

She fired two shots. One caught Crook in the shoulder, whereas the other missed. He shot out the door and headed for the front room.

Boc!

She blew a hole in the door where his head had been a millisecond earlier. She ran out behind him.

Crook remembered the patio behind the bar. Below it was the pool. He quickly calculated his chances of getting out the door and down the hall as slim to none. But he saw his chances of running out on the balcony, hopping the rail, and surviving the fall into the pool as fifty-fifty.

He went with the odds.

Boc! Boc! Boc!

Chanel came into the room just as Crook's naked body barreled through the flimsy Plexiglas door, then he bunny-hopped the rail. One of the shots caught him in the hip.

"Aaarrggghhh!" he screamed all the way down. The second shot seared his flesh as he began his thirteen-story plunge.

Chanel ran to the balcony and dumped two more shots before the clip was empty.

Boooooosh!

Crook hit the water, feet first, and the water felt as if he were breaking through glass. It damn near broke his ankle on contact. He was moving on pure adrenaline. Once he got his bearings, he dragged himself up the short porch steps leading from the pool and headed for the parking lot. He caught a white woman about to get in her Chevy Impala.

"Get the fuck out!" Crook bellowed, punching the woman dead in the face and knocking her unconscious.

He pulled her limp body out of the way, got in the car, and pulled off. He was losing a lot of blood. The adrenaline had begun to wear off, and now all he could feel was pain. He felt listless, sleepy.

The Chevy crashed into a fire hydrant, not hard enough to make the air bags deploy, but hard enough for Crook to crack a rib against the steering wheel. He slumped in the seat.

"I'm done," he mumbled, thinking he heard the sounds of approaching sirens.

All of a sudden, the driver's side door opened. He looked. It was Chanel. He thought he was dreaming.

"You know I love you, right?" he slurred, but he was straight sincere.

She looked at him for a moment, then replied, "I love you, too," just as sincerely.

Then he saw a big, bald figure reach into the car. That was all he saw before he passed out.

CHAPTER 33
- Bad News Comes in Threes -

As soon as they got the word, Shamar and GQ headed straight to Baltimore. Shamar came from Wilmington and GQ from Newark. Finesse tried to get Crook, but got his voice mail. He texted him: Call me ASAP. Riz in the hospital.

When he got no immediate response, Finesse thought it strange, but didn't press. He had more important things on his mind. He had to take care of Charisma.

The moment the doctor came out to him was a moment he would never forget. He saw the look in his eyes and knew the doctor was coming to tell him that Charisma had pulled through, but the sense of relief that washed over him weakened his knees and made him want to sit down.

"She's alive," the doctor announced.

"I know," Finesse replied, his tone exhausted but relieved.

The doctor nodded. "Then I take it you know that she's a very strong woman."

Finesse smiled for the first time all night. "I definitely know that."

"It must've taken a lot to push her to this point," the doctor surmised, looking at Finesse as if he thought Finesse was probably the 'pusher.'

Finesse just dropped his head. "Yeah."

"We're going to keep her for a few days for mental evaluation," the doctor announced.

"I understand." Finesse nodded, then looked at the doctor. "Can I see her?"

"Can you?" the doctor retorted, but it was as if he was asking, "Can you face her?"

"Yeah, I can, but first I need to go home and close my front door."

The moment he got back to the hospital, he headed straight to her room. He entered to find her sleeping, her face, the face of an angel. A chill ran up his spine, thinking he had almost lost her. He sat down by her and took her hand and squeezed it. She squeezed his. They spent the rest of the night in silence.

∞

GQ walked into Charisma's room, to find Shamar and Finesse already there.

Charisma was in bed watching the Home and Garden channel. GQ gave Shamar and Finesse gangsta hugs, then leaned over, kissed Charisma on the cheek and gave her a warm hug.

"How you, mama?"

"I don't know," she answered truthfully, not knowing how she truly felt to still be alive.

GQ reached in his pocket. "I started to get you some flowers, but instead I brought you this," he said, handing her a Zero candy bar because he knew it was her favorite.

She took it and smiled. "Thanks, G."

"You already know."

"Ay G, you holla at the lil' nigguh?" Finesse questioned, referring to Crook.

"Naw why? What up?"

Finesse shook his head. "Somethin' ain't right. I texted that nigguh a thousand times and he ain't hit back."

GQ propped up on the edge of Charisma's bed. "Well, they say it comes in threes."

"What?"

"Bad news. I gotta tell y'all somethin'," GQ announced.

Shamar could tell by his expression that it was serious. "What is it, G?" he questioned.

"Don Pooh . . . he set us up."

The room got tense and quiet.

Finally, Charisma broke the silence. "What do you mean, 'set us up?'"

"When the police pulled you and 'Nessa over. Those two cops wasn't only dirty—they were working with Pooh! They didn't rob us. He did!" GQ exclaimed.

"I knew somethin' funny was up!" Shamar said, punching his hand. "I'ma fuckin' kill that bitch ass nigguh!"

"Not before we get our paper," GQ added.

"Fuck it. Rob and kill his fuckin'—" Shamar started to reply, but Charisma cut him off.

"No!" she yelled sharply, loudly, and deep down. "No! Do you hear me! No more robbin', no more killin', no more!" She shook her head. "—just no," she finished softly.

The three of them looked from one to another, not knowing what to say or do.

"Yo, 'Riz, I know he your family, but yo . . . he violated," Shamar reminded her. But as soon as the words were out of his mouth, he thought about his brother Black and his violation.

Charisma's expression softened as she looked at Shamar and replied, "It's not because of that, Sha. I'm just sayin' let it go, okay? For me."

Shamar shook his head. "'Riz, I lost damn near seventy grand in—"

"Please, Sha, for me," she pleaded, head cocked innocently to the side.

Shamar took one look at her face and of her lying in the hospital bed and knowing why she was there and he couldn't say no. "Yeah, ma."

"Gimme your word, Sha."

Their eyes met. She knew he was only appeasing her, so she wanted to lock him in.

His jaw fixed with aggravation. "My word, yo."

She turned to GQ. "G?"

"Yeah, yo, my word."

Finally, she looked at Finesse.

"I ain't the one you gotta worry 'bout. When Crook find out—"

"Then don't tell him," Charisma cut him off. "Let me tell him. Just give me your word, DeAngelo."

"You already got my word, ma."

She nodded and went back to watching TV.

Shamar turned to Finesse. "Ay yo, God, lemme holla at you."

Finesse and Shamar left the room. They went out the exit that led to a back stairwell and stopped on the landing between floors. "Yo, what happened to her?" Shamar asked.

"I don't know. We ain't talk about it yet. I think she still feeling guilty about Sonja. She think it shoulda been her," Finesse answered.

Shamar nodded as he paced, having a lot on his mind. "I get that, God, but on some real shit, Don Pooh can't get away like that. Fuck that! I lost a fuckin' grip, yo, and my pockets fucked up. Hell no!" Shamar huffed.

"I know, I know—just give her a minute. But if you need somethin', let me know," Finesse replied.

"Naw, you know I don't fuck with the 'Ron like that. I'm good, I got somethin' bubblin wit' my white girl."

"That's what's up."

"But that ain't what I need to holla at you about."

"Speak on it, God."

Shamar looked Finesse in the eyes and said, "Tell me about Black."

∞

GQ had lain down beside Charisma. She placed her head on his shoulder, as they both watched TV.

"You wanna talk about it?" GQ asked.

"No."

He nodded. They fell silent for a few moments, then he said, "I do, real talk, 'Riz. You can't bottle shit up. I mean, I know Finesse love you to death, but I've known you longest. Shit, I introduced you to the team," he reasoned.

"I remember."

"Ai'ight then, I got seniority in this muhfucka," he joked.

She laughed. "You stupid."

"It's Sonja, ain't it?"

Charisma didn't respond for a moment, but then replied, "It was a lot of things, G. Don't you ever get tired of livin' like this?"

"Hell yeah, every day," he admitted. "But you know why nigguhs hustle today?"

"Why?"

"So they ain't gotta hustle tomorrow."

She grasped it instantly. "But what if tomorrow never comes? What if today is like a fuckin' treadmill?" she asked.

"Then we walk faster, run faster, fuckin' jump, anything to beat the machine," he answered.

She shook her head. "I ain't got it in me no more, G."

"Yes you do. You just don't want it to be in you no more."

She paused. A tear rolled down her cheek. "You're right," she admitted.

He put his arm around her and pulled her close. "Just don't give up, baby girl, not when we about to win."

"I don't want to win, G. I just want to live."

∞

"What you mean, 'tell me about Black?'" Finesse returned.

"You think he snitched on you?"

Finesse leaned against the wall, looked away, then back at his brother and replied, "Yeah, I do."

247

"Is that what you told Crook when he went to see you in the County?" Shamar probed.

"Sha, what you gettin' at?"

"Just answer my question."

Seeing the intensity of his younger twin's eyes, Finesse relented. "I didn't tell him shit. I'm sayin', it came up, but we didn't talk about it."

"What you do when it came up?"

"I just looked at him," Finesse replied, knowing what Shamar was getting at.

Shamar shook his head, because now he understood. Crook really didn't move on his own. Finesse had pushed the button. He just did it with a look instead of a word.

"So then you already know."

"Know what?"

"That Crook killed Black," Shamar answered.

Finesse pinched the bridge of his nose, dropped his head, and then looked at Shamar.

"When Charisma told me how it went down, I knew. Just like she did . . . she knew. And from how GQ move, I know he know too. Everybody know, lil' brah, except you, because you refused to see it," Finesse explained.

"That's only 'cause you don't wanna know," Shamar remembered Crook saying that night at the club, and now Shamar could see that Crook had been right.

Shamar sat down on the steps. He felt like a man who had a secret, only to find out that the only thing secret was that he didn't have one.

"So what if it was me?" Shamar asked.

"You what?" Finesse countered, although he knew exactly what he was talking about.

Shamar looked at him. "What if it was me that snitched?"

"Come on, Sha. You buggin' the fuck out now," Finesse replied.

Shamar stood up and approached Finesse. "Naw, I'm dead ass. What if it would've been me? Would you have pushed the button?"

"You my brother, yo."

"And Black wasn't?"

"Half-brother. Product of our sorry ass father."

"Blood is blood!" Shamar roared in his face. "Would you have?"

"Would you have!" Finesse roared right back. "You talk this family shit, but what would you do if you stood in front of that goddamn judge and he said life? You never seein' the streets again, and the reason—the only reason—is a muhfucka that claimed to be your brother! Then what! It was fuck me, so now it's fuck him!" Finesse was raging by the time he finished, having finally gotten all of that off his chest.

Shamar remained calm throughout the whole outburst. When Finesse finished, he said, "You just answered my question." Then he turned and began walking down the stairs.

"Yo, Sha! Sha! Why the fuck is you buggin'! You never woulda snitched! You're a soldier, nigguh. What the fuck is the problem!" Finesse bellowed, his voice filling and echoing in the hollow concrete stairwell. When Shamar didn't answer, Finesse yelled out, "I love you, nigguh."

The only reply was the sound of a slamming door.

CHAPTER 34
- Cherry Hill -

When Crook came to, he was laid up, clad only in his boxer shorts, under the 500 count sheets of a bed that looked like it was made for Shaq. The sunlight coming in through the blinds made him turn his head.

He sat up slowly, still sore and saw a brace wrapped around his midsection because of his cracked ribs. He looked around. The bedroom was huge and laced like MTV cribs. The 50-inch HD sat inside a mahogany cabinet, with several shelves containing a state-of-the-art sound system.

"Whose shit is this?" he said to himself, though his words were audible.

"My husband's," Chanel answered, walking into the room accompanied by a girl in a maid uniform, carrying his breakfast on a tray. She set the tray on its legs across his lap. When he got a look at the girl's face, she was definitely pretty, but her skin looked pale and Crook could tell she was on something. Her movements were slow and deliberate. He also recognized her face, but couldn't place her. If he had given it more thought, he would have remembered her as the drunk girl that the bald, dyke-looking female toted out of the club—the same one that had purposely spilled her drink on Chanel.

Crook saw something else in her eyes . . .

Fear.

She looked like a trapped animal that had been defanged, declawed, and broken. She looked like the slave she was in the process of becoming.

As soon as she put the tray down, Chanel instructed her, "You've done well. As soon as you clean up, get ready. You'll be leaving tonight."

"Please don't do this. I—"

"Now, now," Chanel cut her off firmly, then softened it with a smile. "Just do as you're told, and maybe we'll talk about it later."

The girl nodded sheepishly, then left out, closing the door quietly behind her.

Crook watched the whole episode, thinking to himself, "Goddamn, shorty cold-blooded."

Chanel turned to him smiling, sat on the edge of the bed, and said, "Good help is so hard to find."

"Yo, you Haitian," he remarked.

The thought just popped in his mind because he vaguely remembered drifting in and out of consciousness and hearing Chanel speak a language that he remembered from his childhood, a language in which his mother used to speak to him, sing him to sleep and scold him before she was killed. Chanel had been speaking to the doctor that had stitched Crook up.

"You're very observant." She nodded.

"Naw, you was speaking Creole. My mother was Haitian," he explained.

She put a grape in his mouth. "I knew it was something about you I liked."

He chuckled. "That ain't all you like," he quipped, referring to the other memories he had from his delirium.

Crook thought he was dreaming when Chanel wrapped her full, sexy lips around his dick until it stood up, attentive as a soldier, and she rode him until he was limp.

Chanel threw her head back, laughing. "You were the one who was unconscious, not me."

"I know that's right. Where this husband of yours? I ain't in no shape for Papa Bear to find me in his bed," he said.

She traced her lips with her fingers, then kissed him. "Don't worry about him. Besides, I think he'll like you." She smirked.

Crook shot her a sinister look. "Don't fuckin' play wit' me. I ain't into no freaky shit."

She giggled, then fed him another grape. "Tough talk turns me on. You already know I like it rough." She winked, referring to the fact that she tried to kill him.

"One number's been blowing you up and texting you like crazy."

"Good look," he replied, scrolling through his phone.

"If I thought it was a female, I would've answered it," she remarked, her tone was playful but her eyes weren't.

Crook saw all the ASAP entries from Finesse and hit him back instantly. "What up, yo?" Crook asked as he drank some orange juice.

"Yo, Crook, where the fuck you been? Locked up? Where you at!" Finesse questioned, relieved to hear his voice.

"I don't know." Crook chuckled.

"You don't know!"

"Yo, ma, where I'm at?"

"Cherry Hill."

"Cherry Hill, my nigguh," Crook repeated into the phone.

"You need to come to B-More."

"Why? What up? Beef? Money?"

"Charisma tried to kill herself."

"What! I'm on my way!" Crook said, lurching forward, forgetting about his ribs and other injuries, but being starkly reminded when experiencing sharp pains.

"One!"

They hung up. Crook looked at Chanel. "We goin' to B-More."

CHAPTER 35
- Sweet Setup -

"How you gonna stop me, huh! How? Look at that pass!"

"Goddamn, nigguh, run!"

"Touchdown!"

GQ and Shamar sat on the couch in Crystal's apartment on the outskirts of Wilmington, playing Madden 13. Vanessa sat curled up in the love seat, while Crystal sat next to Shamar, smoking a blunt.

"Like two big ass kids." Vanessa giggled, shaking her head and accepting the blunt from Crystal.

"Naw, ma, this shit like taking candy from a baby," GQ bragged, jerking the controller.

"Interception!" Shamar cackled as he watched his man scamper down the field for a touchdown.

"My thumb slipped," GQ tried to protest.

Shamar cackled. "Nigguh, that's your thumb!"

When the game ended, Shamar had won 35 – 30. He picked up the money off the table and started counting it.

"Ay yo, G. Why the fuck you always gotta be so goddamn slick? This eight hundred! Gimme the other two!"

"You sure?" GQ asked with a straight face. "Count it again."

"Fuck that. You know this shit short."

GQ handed over the two hundred dollar bills.

"Slick ass nigguh." Shamar chuckled.

GQ shrugged. "You slow, you blow. You know the game don't stop. But check it, 'member the thing I told you about?"

"Yeah."

"This shit is definitely a go. Walk wit' me, talk wit' me," GQ urged, as he got up from the couch.

"I take it we're not going to the movies," Crystal remarked sourly.

"Naw, we goin'. I'll be right back," Shamar assured her.

"GQ and Shamar walked outside. The air still felt damp from the rain, and the twilight sky was still overcast.

"Ai'ight, so I got Simmons ready to kick hardbody," GQ announced.

"How hardbody?"

"He 'bout to cop ten bricks from me at thirty a brick!" GQ laughed, then gave Shamar dap.

Shamar couldn't believe he had really gotten this far. Who knew the police were that stupid?

"How the fuck you pull that off?"

"Check it, when I went at him askin' for buy money, I knew he was gonna turn me down. But I played the cracka like I had just thought up the scheme, but in reality it was the con the whole time."

"Yeah."

"I asked him, what if I cop and you reimburse me? When he paused, I knew I had his ass!" GQ laughed. "I'm tellin' him, yo, the only way I can get close to Coco Chanel is if I spend dough."

"And he just bought that?"

GQ nodded devilishly. "That cracker thirsty as fuck! I think he thinks he gonna be fuckin' Chief of Police off this shit!"

They both laughed.

GQ continued. "So boom, I might sell him a couple of ounces here, a couple there, but each time I buy a little more. The last I sold him was a brick."

"A whole brick?"

"Goddamn right, a whole brick! But for this ten-brick lick, I'ma need your help," GQ explained.

Shamar frowned, but before he could protest, GQ continued, talking fast.

"I'm sayin', I'm sayin, fam', the setup is so fuckin' sweet, yo. It's like a fuckin' movie out this bitch! I'm tellin' you, fam'. You ain't even gotta be there, and I'ma kick you twenty-five stacks!"

He had Shamar's attention. "I ain't gotta be there?"

"Fam', I'm tellin' you, if this shit was a song, it'd be a symphony," GQ boasted.

Shamar nodded, rubbing his chin. "Gimme fifty and I'm down."

GQ threw his arms up and stomped through a rain puddle. "Fifty! Goddamn, Sha, you killin' me!"

"Nigguh, cut the drama wit' your Jew ass. You lickin' three hundred large and kickin' me down crack head change. Besides, nigguh, you was already ready to offer me fifty. You just wanted to see if you could Jew a nigguh." Shamar smirked.

GQ couldn't help but laugh. "Yo, I'm teachin' you too goddamn much. Ai'ight, fifty."

They shook hands and half-hugged to seal the deal.

"Now, what we need to do? And where these five bricks coming from?" Shamar questioned.

GQ blinged a big smile. "That's the best part."

∞

"No, Finesse . . . stop," Charisma said reluctantly, because the sensation he was giving her felt almost too good to resist. But she knew that she had to—her life depended on it.

Everything had started off innocently enough as those type of moments usually do. Finesse had been trying to play the streets less and spend more time with Charisma. They had been watching one of Charisma's favorite movies, Love Jones and Finesse had fallen asleep, head back, mouth open, snoring. She mushed his leg with her foot.

"You could at least not snore," she huffed.

He popped right up. "I wasn't sleep."

"Oh for real? So what was that sounding like a train comin' through?"

"I was clearing my throat."

She laughed and mushed his leg with her foot again. "Stupid self."

"And how about you keep your paws off me," he cracked.

She mushed him again. "Or what?"

"Ai'ight now."

When she tried to do it again, he grabbed her foot and started tickling it. Charisma went crazy. The remote went in one direction, the soda in another, and popcorn flew everywhere.

"Finesse, stop!" I'ma pee on myself!" she scream-laughed, kicking and flailing.

"Naw, gangsta, talk that shit now!"

"I'm sorry!"

"Say I'm the man and you a punk!"

"Fuck that! I'd rather peeee!" she squealed, eyes full of tickle tears.

He grabbed both feet and tickled them both. Her whole body arched.

"Okaaay!"

"Say it!"

"You–you the man and-and–stop! Stop!"

"Say it!"

"I'm a punk!"

He stopped and let her feet go. "Exactly."

"I peed on myself, dumb ass."

"Let me see." He chuckled, reaching for her cut-off sweatpants.

She tried to squirm away, but he pulled her to him and stuck his finger between her legs and then licked her thigh.

"I don't taste no pee, but I do taste candy," he hummed, pulling the sweatpants down further and licking up the side of her thigh.

"Finesse." She squirmed.

He ran his tongue along the silk of her panties then began to pull them aside. He took her clit in his mouth and felt her whole body melt around his tongue.

"Oh please," she whispered, temperature rising, her wetness increasing. She felt herself slipping into that erotic temple of the familiar, succumbing to the passion.

And then it hit her.

Hit her like a burst of light, telling her that it was now or never. That's when she said, "No, Finesse, stop."

He looked at her.

"Why?"

"You know why."

Slowly, reluctantly, he sat up with a sigh. "Ma, listen . . . me and you, we like magnetized to one another. I had you since you was in pigtails. We inevitable," Finesse said.

"That's just it, baby," Charisma replied, folding her legs under her. "How do you expect me to move on with my life if you keep this up?"

"Why you gotta move on?" He scowled.

Charisma smiled and caressed his cheek. "Baby, you know I love you. You really made me into the woman that I am and I thank you for the good and the bad," she remarked with a slight chuckle to mitigate the pain. "But—and I'm not sayin' it's your fault, but part of why I did what I did is because I can't let go of the past."

Finesse dropped his head and remembered the doctor's words: It must've taken a lot to push her to this point.

Finesse reached out and took her hand.

"Aisha, you my heart, ma. You know that and I ain't tryin' to lose you. Whateva I gotta do to make it right, I will. Just me and you. I wanna marry you, yo. That's my word. I'ma do right by you," he vowed on bended knee.

Charisma laughed. "No you ain't and you know it. Yeah, you'll be cool for a few months, but once shit is sweet, you'll fuck up again."

"Naw, yo, I—"

She put her finger to his lips. "But that's who you are. Some people aren't cut out for monogamy, and you're one of those people. I mean, shit, look at your name. Any chick fall in love with a nigguh named Finesse is askin' for it in the first place!" She laughed, and he couldn't help but laugh with her.

"Then I'll change my name."

She gave him one last kiss, then looked him directly in the eyes and said, "Don't change a thing."

He nodded.

"Now," she said, pushing her hair out of her face and starting anew, "I wanna show you something. You wanna see it?"

"That's how we got into this conversation," he quipped.

She gave him the finger, then popped off the couch. "Get your mind out the gutter," she replied, grabbing a notebook off the table and handed it to him. "I want you to read this."

He looked at it. "What is it?"

"My book."

"Your book."

She nodded apprehensively, like he was holding her baby, and she was afraid that he would drop it.

Finesse thumbed over the pages, watching them fan in his hand. "What's it about?"

"Us, the crew, life—just read it," she urged.

"Okay," he replied, then started to put it down.

"Now."

"Now?"

She gave him a look like a spoiled child—the one that had always worked and always would. He sighed, opened the notebook, and began to read.

The whole time, Charisma watched him anxiously. She paced, gnawed at her fingertips, played with her hair, read over his shoulder.

"Ma! Sit your ass down. Damn!"

He read and read . . . and read. He read for five hours, read until the sun came up. There were parts that made him grunt, parts that made him laugh, and even some parts that made him misty-eyed.

"Yo ma, why you put that in there?"

"It's my life." She shrugged.

Finally exhausted, he put the notebook down and stretched.

"Well?" she asked, anxiously.

"I'm sleepy. I'll tell you when I wake up."

She punched him in the chest and he laughed.

"Naw yo, it's platinum. I love it."

"For real?"

"Yeah, ma, dead ass. I ain't know you could write," he remarked, sincerely impressed.

"Me neither," she admitted.

"So what you gonna do with it?"

"I went online and found this chick named DC Book Diva. I e-mailed her. We're supposed to meet up, and she wants to publish the book."

"So that's what's up. I'm proud of you, ma," he said.

Charisma's face beamed. "Thank you. I am too."

Finesse's phone rang. He answered, "Yo Crook, where the fuck you been? Locked up? Where you at? . . . You don't know? . . . You need to come to B-More

. . ." Finesse looked at Charisma with a questioning look. She nodded. "Charisma tried to kill herself . . . one!" He hung up the phone and looked at her. "The lil' nigguh on his way."

∞

Three hours later, Crook was knocking on their door. Finesse answered it, letting Crook and Chanel in.

"What up, fam'? How you?" Finesse greeted, giving Crook a gangsta hug.

"I'm good, I'm good. Yo fam', I want you to meet my lady. Chanel, this Finesse. Finesse, this Chanel."

Finesse hadn't noticed her right away, but when Crook introduced them, and he got a good look, he had to do a double take.

"Goddamn, Crook, word up? Yo, you wit' him?" Finesse only half-joked.

Chanel giggled.

He looked at Crook. "Yo, what you tell her, you know me?"

Finesse and Crook laughed as Crook threw a playful jab at him.

"Watch your mouth, nigguh." Crook chuckled. "Where she at?"

"Upstairs."

Crook turned to Chanel.

"You make yourself comfortable. I'll be right back.

"Okay, baby."

He took the short flight of stairs to the second floor, only then realizing that he didn't know which door. He peeped in one room then knocked on a closed door.

"Come in," Charisma called out.

He entered as she was getting up. He crossed the room and gave her a big hug, lifting her off her feet and making her laugh.

"Nigguh, put me down." She snickered.

"I just wanted you to know I'll still go to that ass." He chuckled, putting her down. "Now, what up wit' you?"

They sat down on the bed.

"Shit was crazy," she replied.

"Well, look, I know all them soft ass nigguhs brought you flowers and candy and shit. Holdin' your hand, talkin' 'bout 'Charisma, we love you.'"

Charisma laughed.

"I'm right, right? Well, I'm tellin' you, if you ever kill yourself, I'ma kill myself, come to hell and beat yo' fuckin' ass for the rest of your life!" Crook snarled, only half-joking.

She threw her arms around his neck. "Awwww, I love you too, Snookie," she sang and gave him a wet kiss on the cheek.

He wiped his face. "Goddamn, what are you, a fuckin' puppy?"

Charisma exploded with laughter. "That's why I love your stupid ass."

"On the real, ma. We all we got, you know?"

She nodded. "I know."

He bumped his body against hers. "Then act like it," he retorted, then stood up. "Now come on, I got somebody I want you to meet."

"Who?"

"My girl," Crook replied proudly.

"Dammmn," Charisma cracked, covering her mouth. "She must got you open!"

"How you figure?"

"'Cause you ain't say 'my bitch' like you usually do."

"Oh yeah, yeah, yeah, I call her that when I'm blowin' her back out," he stated, demonstrating his point.

Charisma hated to sour the mood, but she knew that she had to. She stood up.

"Crook, hold up before we go down. I need to tell you somethin'."

He turned back to her. "What's good?"

She looked at him a moment, and then said, "Don Pooh set us up."

Crook's whole expression changed from smile to stone.

"The police that pulled us over were workin' with him," she added. "I know that's some bullshit, and I already know what you thinkin'. I just . . . I need you to give him a pass. I'll make sure he pay the money back."

"And if he don't?" Crook probed, his tone low and menacing.

She didn't even want to think of that scenario. "He will."

Crook shook his head and tried to digest her words.

"Please, Crook. For me."

"Ma, that's my word. I don't give a fuck if the nigguh gotta sell ass to get that gwop. If he come up short, we fuckin'—"

"He won't," she assured him with a smile. Relieved, she added, "Now, let me meet the chick that got you so fucked up."

CHAPTER 36
- A Pretty Good Informant -

Vanessa was becoming addicted to GQ.

She just couldn't get enough of his dick. No man could make her cum as many times as GQ, and she especially loved the way he fucked her pussy from the back.

"I love you, daddy. I love you. Oh! How I love you," she shivered, speaking in the rapid-fire fashion of a woman speaking in tongues.

GQ slid his thumb in and out of her asshole. At the same time, the pussy seemed wetter, and she threw it back harder.

"Take this dick, bitch!"

"Oh, I am daddy, I ammmm!" she cooed.

Her ass was so fat that it rolled with every stroke of his dick, turning him on even more, and making him fuck her harder.

GQ dropped his hips low, like a man with a stick shift, down shifting, and he began to grind her pussy harder.

"Oh. My. God. My . . . sp-sp-spot!" she squealed, trembling all over.

GQ was ready to cum, Vanessa could feel it in the urgency of his thrusts.

"Oh, daddy, wait! Cum in my mouth, I want you to cum in my mouth!"

"You wanna swallow this nut, bitch?"

"Yes, daddy, yes!"

He pulled his dick out of her pussy as she flipped around, taking his dick in her mouth just as he exploded. Vanessa swallowed every drop.

GQ collapsed on the bed with Vanessa beside him.

"I love you, baby," she sang, wanting to cuddle.

GQ wiggled away. "Yeah, I know, but you know I hate that snuggle shit," he replied, aggravated.

"I'm sorry, baby. I just want to be close to you," she pouted.

This bitch gets too clingy, he thought, but took a deep breath and kept it all in, because he knew it wouldn't be long before she served her purpose, and then . . .

He caressed her nipple with his thumb to take the sting out of the rejection. "Naw, ma, I just got a lot on my mind. Once this thing get done, then we can relax, feel me?" GQ smiled.

"All over," she cooed, stroking his chest. "What about Pooh?"

"Oh trust me, I got somethin' real nice in mind for him."

"But I thought you gave Charisma your word you wouldn't do nothin' to him?" Vanessa questioned.

Bitch, you just worry about your own ass, but I got somethin' for you too, he thought, but said, "I ain't gonna kill 'im, but he damn sure gonna wish he was dead."

There was a knock at the door. GQ put his finger to his lips. "Get in the closet," he whispered as he got up and put on his pants and stepped into his sneakers.

Vanessa got in the closet.

GQ walked up the short hallway to the door and opened it. It was Detective Simmons.

"Hello, Quincy. I—" Simmons began, then stopped, sniffed and said, "either you just got some pussy or you just grew one."

"Yeah, you got jokes huh, Detective? What are you, part hound?"

"Close. I have a wife who likes to fuck less than a nun, so I'm very sensitive in this area," Simmons retorted as he walked to the back of the apartment. He opened the bathroom door and the bedroom door, then walked back up front. When he returned, he found GQ on the couch, lighting a blunt.

"You shoulda told me you were comin'. I woulda told her to wait for a few seconds," GQ said as he puffed.

"I'll remember that. I'm still a cop, you know?" Simmons remarked as he sat down.

"What's this? It's medicinal," GQ concluded.

"What you got for me?"

"What you got for me?" GQ shot right back.

Simmons glared at him.

"Didn't I tell you I'd handle it? And listen, I had to fight like hell to keep the Feds from hogging my investigation. I mentioned Coco Chanel, and they practically salivated," Simmons said with glee.

GQ could see the greed in his eyes. He definitely thought this was going to make his career. GQ leaned forward, resting his elbows on his knees.

"Listen, yo, this shit is real serious. Coco is going to be there, so I don't need any fuckin' mistakes, and the money better not be short," GQ warned.

Simmons waved him off, dismissively. "It'll all be there, and you better watch that money like a hawk. You walk it in, get her committed, and then give the signal. We'll take it from there," he instructed.

"Don't worry, I got my end. You just have yours."

"You know, Quincy, you make a pretty good informant."

"Go fuck yourself, Simmons. What happens to me after this?" GQ asked.

"Take care of me and I'll take care of you," Simmons answered.

"Oh, don't worry." GQ winked. "I got you."

∞

That night, it all went down . . .

Simmons and his team of cops were ready to swarm the small, storefront building where GQ's deal was supposed to go down. They were parked in a surveillance van, halfway up the block, with two more vans filled with officers further up the block, just waiting for the signal.

GQ, Simmons, and three engineers were in the van, monitoring the equipment. GQ had his shirt off while one of the engineers taped the wire to his chest.

"Yo, make sure you tape that shit good. If it fuck around and fall off, then I'm a fuckin' dead man," GQ griped, feigning nervousness.

"I've done this a thousand times," the engineer assured him, smugly.

"Well then, you due a mistake," GQ shot back.

"Ay, Quincy, relax, okay? Everything'll be fine. We'll be right here," Simmons said.

"That's easy for you, yo. You ain't gotta be in the room with the bitch. You heard what she did to her own family?"

"No."

"Muhfuckas told me that back in Haiti she was some kind of rebel leader, right? The government troops decided to capture her family and used them as bait. When she caught them, she didn't just kill the soldiers—she killed her own fuckin' family! They said she did it because she'd rather know her family was in heaven than to go through hell on earth," GQ said, recounting a street tale, not knowing that it was actually true.

He saw the look on Simmons' face when he looked at his engineer. GQ thought, Look at this muhfucka. He really think he 'bout to catch a ghetto Bin Laden!

"Well, all that ends tonight," Simmons remarked. "You ready?"

"Where's the money?"

The other engineer dragged out a duffle bag and slid it over to GQ. He unzipped it and peered inside. Stacks and stacks of new, multicolored Benjamins smirked up at him. His dick almost got hard. He reached in and pulled out a stack, fanning through it.

"I told you, it's all there," Simmons said.

"Just makin' sure."

Simmons took the money out of his hand, tossed it back into the duffle bag, then zipped it up.

"You just concentrate on bagging Chanel. Remember, she has to admit to selling you the coke on tape."

"I know. I know. And when I say the password, y'all gonna come runnin'," GQ added.

"Exactly," Simmons confirmed.

GQ looked at his watch. "I betta get inside. I definitely don't want the bitch seeing me get out the van."

Simmons patted him on the back. "Good luck."

GQ hopped out of the van, carrying the duffle bag. He could hardly control his excitement. This was the easiest money that he had ever made. Already, he had come up with a scam on how to take his show on the road, but first he had to finish the job at hand.

He disappeared inside the building.

"He's in, Detective," engineer one reported.

"I can see that," Simmons replied, then got on his walkie talkie and said, "All units stay off frequency until I give the word to move in." Simmons' whole body was tense. He saw this as the biggest bust of his career. He could hear himself conducting his press conference, bouquets of microphones in front of him, cameras rolling and flashing everywhere.

"The reign of the infamous Coco Chanel is over. Tonight, we apprehended—"

"Detective, a car just pulled up!"

Simmons was pulled out of his fantasy as a pair of headlights burned through the fog-misted street. A man got out waving a small box. The only thing visible was a bleeping red light that pulsated like a heartbeat as the man scanned the street.

"Scanning for frequency," Simmons surmised, glad that he had instructed his team correctly.

The man then walked around the car and opened the passenger door. A woman stepped out.

"Can you get a close up?" Simmons questioned anxiously, his eyes glued to the monitor.

"It's dark, but I'll try," the second engineer replied.

Simmons had heard that she was beautiful. He wasn't into black women as a fetish, but the things he had heard about Chanel made his fantasies run wild. Bedroom eyes, skin so smooth and chocolaty, it was like she was poured from a heavenly spout. But in the dark, he could only see a profile of her face.

The man and woman disappeared inside the building.

"Here we go." Simmons said, rubbing his hands together.

The monitor filled with voices coming directly from GQ's wire.

"Yo, GQ, how you?"

"You already know, Sha. I'm tryin to eat."

"Shit, you come to the right place. Let me introduce you to Coco Chanel."

"How you, ma?"

"I don't shake hands. Do you have money?"

"That's a cold bitch," Simmons remarked. "Get her to commit, GQ."

"No doubt, right here."

The sound of the duffle bag being unzipped filled the engineers' headphones.

"The cocaine is in the car. I trust all the money is here, or I'll kill you as sure as my name is Coco Chanel."

"Bingo! We got her!" Simmons cried, high-fiving his engineers.

"No need for that, Miss Chanel. It's all there."

"If so, you can do business with me directly from now on."

"Word. Ay you, either one of you have a pen?"

"That's the password! Go! Go! Go!" Simmons barked into his walkie talkie, ripping open the sliding door of the van.

He pulled his gun, as the street lit up like it was New Year's Eve. Police came from both directions, cherries flashing. The two vans full of officers accelerated, then came to a halt in front of the store front.

Simmons was right behind the slew of Robocop-looking officers, outfitted like a SWAT team. Automatic weapons locked and loaded, they pushed ahead, already barking orders.

"Freeze!"

"Don't move!"

"Lay down!"

"What the hell!"

They had expected to find three people involved in a drug deal. They had expected them to shout it out. They had expected to find a room full of drugs, but they didn't expect to find what they found.

A radio.

A simple Radio Shack boom box-styled radio was placed in the room. Next to it was GQ's wire. The radio was on and voices were still coming from the tape that had been playing throughout the episode, one of the voices which Simmons assumed was Coco Chanel's.

"How much more cocaine can I get?"

"As much as you want."

"I need more, much more."

"I have all—"

Simmons couldn't take it anymore, so he aggressively kicked the radio over, sending sparks flying. Once the voices stopped, the room was stone silent. The officers looked at Simmons. He had never been so humiliated in all his life. Instead of making his career, this debacle could break it.

"Detective, should we put out an APB?" one of the officers asked carefully.

Simmons eyed him. "For what?"

He tried to appear calm, but he was red in the face. He looked at a table by the back door, the door in which he knew GQ had used to get away, and he saw a bottle.

A bottle of Coco Chanel perfume.

He walked over and picked it up. His temperature finally exploded.

"That black son of a bitch! I'll kill 'im, I'll fuckin' kill 'im, I'll fuckin' kill him!" he ranted, cocking his arm back, about to launch the bottle against the wall.

But then he looked at the bottle and smiled.

"Yeah, for what?"

∞

GQ couldn't stop laughing. The plan had gone off without a hitch. He sat in the backseat while Bam drove and Vanessa sat in the passenger seat.

"Yo fam', I don't know what the fuck you just did, but cops is all over!" Bam remarked, seeing all the sirens on the block that they just left.

"Believe me, my nigguh, you don't wanna know. Just take this five grand." GQ handed him a stack of bills.

"Damn, baby, you a genius," Vanessa sang, turning in the seat to look at him.

"I am, ain't I?" he replied, cockily.

But he had earned the compliment. He had made the tape at Crystal's place when he made the deal with Shamar. He had it scripted down to exactly what every person would say. Vanessa played Coco Chanel.

"Yo, this shit will never work." Shamar had laughed, reading his lines.

"And that's exactly why it will," GQ had answered. "The police don't expect a muhfucka to play 'em so short. As long as they hear voices, they'll think we in the room. By the time they find out, I'll be long gone," he explained.

And he was.

Bam dropped GQ and Vanessa off by the rental that he had waiting. He gave GQ dap. "Yo, G, the way you got the city swarming, I don't expect to see you for a while."

"You already know, fam'. I love the Brick but I'm 'bout to be in exile."

They laughed. GQ threw the duffle bag in the backseat, while Vanessa curved up shotgun.

"Where you goin', daddy?"

"First, back to Wilmington to get the fam', and then we hittin' Vegas! I'm feelin' lucky!"

CHAPTER 37
- The Game of Gwop -

Phwokk! Phwokk! Phhhhhwokk!

Crook, GQ, and Shamar all popped bottles of Moet and let the champagne fizz down the sides, while they took the bottles straight to their faces.

They were at Crystal's apartment, along with Crystal, Vanessa, and Chanel. GQ had ordered the works: lobster, pounds of shrimp and lamb, as well as buckets of champagne.

"Whose birthday is it?" Chanel giggled.

"Mine!" GQ laughed. "Sorta."

"Well, sorta happy birthday," she replied.

He looked at her curiously, a slight smirk on his face. "You said your name is Chanel, right?"

"Yes, why?"

"Nothin'. Crazy coincidence." GQ chuckled.

"I'm sure." Chanel smirked, sipping her drink.

Crook walked over. "Nigguh, how you gonna hit a lick and you ain't come get me?" Crook bassed, throwing a playful punch that GQ suavely blocked.

"You wasn't in place, but you know I got the family's cut," GQ replied.

He reached over and grabbed a book bag off the floor and handed it to Crook.

"That's fifty grand. Twenty go to Charisma, fifteen each for you and Finesse."

"Why come she get more? 'Cause she tried to kill herself?" Crook asked, then pulled out his gun and put it to his own head. "I'ma kill myself. Now gimme five grand."

"Nigguh, pull the trigger and I'll give you ten." GQ laughed.

Crook and Chanel laughed too.

"Ay yo, Sha! Sha! This nigguh like Obamacare over here," Crook joked.

Shamar cracked a smile, but didn't engage with Crook like he usually did, so Crook knew he was still in his feelings.

"Ay yo, we gotta take a flick, yo! Who ain't got a cheap ass phone?" GQ called out.

"No, no, no, I've got a really good camera. Wait a minute," Crystal replied and padded off to get it. She came back with it directly, programming it as she walked.

"This is really cool, because you can set the timer," she explained.

"Come on, Sha. We gotta flick it up. You know how we do," GQ urged.

Reluctantly, Shamar got off the couch.

The whole team stood against the far wall of the room. GQ and Vanessa were in the middle, Shamar and Crystal were on the left, while Crook and Chanel were on the right.

"Ay yo, why we takin' this shit like it's a goddamn prom picture?" Crook grumbled, hugging Chanel from behind.

They were basically the same height, but in her heels she was taller. "Ma, why you had to wear them fuckin' heels? They make you taller," Crook complained.

A beat passed.

"You want to wear them?" she replied, hiding a smirk behind her straight face.

Crook cracked a smile, but he had a malicious glint in his eyes.

"You got a slick ass mouth."

"And wet too." She winked, reaching behind her and giving his dick a squeeze.

"Five seconds, everybody," Crystal chimed. "Four–three–two . . ."

Click!

As soon as the picture snapped, Shamar turned to Crook. "Lemme holla at you," he said, heading for the door.

Crook followed behind as they both stepped outside, taking in the night air.

"Ay yo, you heard Shifty got knocked?" Crook asked.

"Naw, when?"

"I don't know. My young boys told me he got pulled, but he had a warrant in Trenton for murder. I think it's the thing I told you about," Crook explained.

Shamar looked at him with concern. "You good?"

Crook shrugged. "I'm sayin', I feel like he solid, but regardless, I'm 'bout to be on some gingerbread man shit. Chanel said she knew some heavy hitters in Miami, so we on our way down there."

"That's what's up, yo." Shamar nodded.

They stood in silence for a few moments before Shamar resumed conversation.

"Yo, fam' . . . I thought about what you told me, and in the muscle I can't say you did the wrong thing, but that don't make it easier to stomach."

"Yo, I feel you," Crook remarked solemnly.

"You can't though, fam', really you can't. I ain't got no doubt in my mind, if it was your brother, you would've done the same thing, but that's still you, not me," Shamar explained.

"True."

"So I'm sayin', right now, I just need some time to deal with this shit, yo. Too much goin' on. So I'ma fall back and just chill."

"Then come down to Miami wit' me. Shit 'bout to be official! We fuck around and get a sweet ass connect," Crook suggested.

"Naw, yo, I can't do that 'cause I can't fuck with you," Shamar emphasized.

They looked at each other.

"What you mean, dog?" Crook questioned, with concern in his eyes.

Shamar shook his head and looked away. "Just what I said . . . When I see you, I see him, and as much as I love you—" Shamar shook his head "Right now, I don't need to be around you."

Crook understood, but he didn't want to understand. "I did it for the good of the team."

"Yeah, but it wasn't your call." Shamar started to walk back inside.

Crook wanted to call him back, but he knew that what Shamar had said was for the best. They were friends, family, brothers, but they were also both killers. A situation with that much emotion could turn lethal at any time.

As Shamar closed the door behind him, Crook reassured himself that time would heal the rift. He hoped . . .

∞

As soon as Charisma saw her, she liked her style. Her name was Juatiah Short, and she was the CEO of a boutique publishing company named DC Book Diva. The title fit her well. With her long, shapely legs, short, sassy cut and butter-toned complexion, her look, style and strut screamed "Diva!"

Charisma and Juatiah met at a sidewalk café in DC.

"Charisma? Sorry I'm late, but there were last minute details that I had to handle," Juatiah apologized after shaking Charisma's hand and sitting down.

"Cost of being the boss," Charisma quipped.

"Exactly." Juatiah snickered.

The waiter floated over and Juatiah ordered a coffee. Charisma was already sipping a latte.

"So let me get right to the point. I love the book, my team loves the book, and I know my readers will love the book," she remarked.

Charisma beamed. "Really? Wow! I was expecting you to say, 'Sorry chick, maybe next time.'"

They both laughed.

"Hell to the naw! Girl, your shit is fire! I mean it's so real, you know? Like, you definitely don't pull any punches. I mean . . . and I'm just being honest, sometimes it feels too real." Juatiah looked Charisma in the eyes.

Charisma nodded and sipped her latte. "I know what you mean. Like the rape?"

"Among other things."

"Oh that. Believe me, names have been changed and I switched cities around, so we good."

"Okay. I just ain't want the Feds knockin' on my door like, 'who told you all this?'" she joked.

And they laughed again.

"So what do we do now?" Charisma asked.

"Well, now we put together a contract, get the book's cover done, marketing, you know, the works. So are you saying you want to sign with DC Book Diva?" Juatiah asked.

"I'm a diva, ain't I?" Charisma asked, and they high-fived.

"Oh! You didn't give it a name."

Charisma smiled.

"That's easy. I'm making it what me and my team call life, The Game of Gwop."

CHAPTER 38
- What Were the Odds? -

"Baby, wake up. We here."

GQ came out of his slouch in the passenger seat of the rented Escalade and squinted into the sun. Vanessa had driven the last leg of the trip while he and Shamar slept.

"Where we stayin', baby?" Vanessa questioned.

"The Bellagio," GQ yawned, stretching his limbs.

He reached back and shook Shamar. "Yo, Sha, Sha, we here, yo. Wake up."

Shamar sat up and looked around. "I gotta piss like a muhfucka."

"We 'bout to get the room."

"Yeah, nigguh, and you payin' for mine too," Shamar said with a snarl, "'cause you know that was some bullshit."

GQ chuckled. "Man, I told you, the fuckin' police got me! I shoulda known 'cause he got nervous when I reached in the bag. But I said 'fuck it.' Goddamn cracka beat me out of seventy-five grand."

He was referring to the duffle bag. When he finally dumped it out, the whole bottom row of what was supposed to be money was telephone pages cut to the size of money. So, instead of three hundred, GQ only got two and a quarter.

"Fuck it, yo, charge it to the game." He had laughed when he thumbed through the telephone paper.

They arrived at the hotel and booked two rooms, right across from one another. They all went into one of the rooms, looking around at the beautiful décor.

"This is beautiful," Vanessa marveled, having never been to Vegas.

"This how my fuckin' apartment gonna be laced yo, watch," GQ vowed, adding, "Gimme a year and it's over."

"I know that's right." Shamar chuckled, giving him dap.

GQ turned to Vanessa.

"Oh yeah, ma, I forgot to tell you. It's Sha's birthday."

"Oh, happy birthday, Sha," she sang cheerfully.

Shamar looked at GQ strangely. "Nigguh, it ain't my birthday."

GQ shrugged. "Well, consider this an early present," he remarked then slapped Vanessa on the ass. "Handle that. I'ma take a shower."

She shot GQ an incredulous look. He shot her one back. Hers wilted, as his gaze asserted his dominance. It was time to turn her into pussy for the next phase of his plan.

Vanessa looked at Shamar, then slowly advanced toward him. When she got close enough, he could see the tears well in her eyes. But he was as heartless as GQ, so why turn down lips as pretty as hers? He placed a hand on her shoulder and guided her down to get her eagle on, while he pulled out his fat dick. The tears had begun to fall, so as he cupped her chin, he wiped the tears away with the head of his dick, then slid it between her slightly parted lips. He grabbed a handful of her hair and began to fuck her mouth vigorously.

The tears continued to fall as Shamar fucked her face until he shoved himself deep down her throat and burst all over her tonsils. His body shuddered as he withdrew from her mouth.

"Happy birthday," Vanessa remarked with bitter sarcasm, as she stood up, wiping away her tears.

GQ came out of the bathroom with a towel wrapped around his waist.

"Why did you do that to me?" she questioned.

He shrugged. "Because I can, right?" he retorted, his look boring into the core of her resistance and tearing it away.

She went into the bathroom while he went back up front.

"She got a mean head, don't she?" GQ smirked.

"No doubt, but it damn sure ain't worth fifteen grand!" Shamar quipped, referring to the fact that he only got thirty-five grand for his cut, instead of the fifty they agreed upon.

∞

Later that night, the casino at Bellagio was abuzz, a circus of activity. Casinos are designed to get the adrenaline flowing, your hopes high, and your money low, flooding your senses with the bells and whistles of the great money illusion.

GQ knew the game well. He knew that slot machines were for suckers, the roulette wheels were mathematically rigged and the crap tables had the greatest house odds. His game was black jack, and he planned on hitting big.

"Okay, you remember how this go, right?" He checked as he glanced around the room.

"No doubt, baby," Vanessa assured him.

They had spent the afternoon going over the simple art of counting cards.

"Give it to me one more time," he insisted.

"Every numbered card is 1+, every ace, ten and face card is 1-. When the dealer deals, keep the count. So if he deals, say, a three of hearts, a nine of diamonds and a deuce of spades, that would be +3; if he then deals an ace, it drops to +2."

"When do you signal me?"

"If the count hits +8 or 1+9."

GQ smiled and nodded. Vanessa was definitely no slow leak.

"Exactly, now we got the upper hand because they don't expect blacks to be card counters. So keep it ghetto as fuck," he joked.

"I gotcha, daddy. Now watch mama." She winked then wiggled down, heading for the black jack table.

∞

Shamar was the exact opposite of GQ. He wasn't a true gambler. The only game he knew how to play was craps, so that's where he headed, holding in his hands five thousand dollars' worth of chips. He told himself that was the limit.

He squeezed up to the side of the crap table, as a big, redneck Texan shook the dice. He looked like a rich, oil cowboy who had a little too much to drink, but he was on a roll.

"Go 'head, JR, show them dicey thangs who's boss," the platinum blonde beside him drawled in her syrupy Texas slang.

"Seven!" cried the Croupier.

"Again!" the big Texan added with a guffaw.

Unlike the Texan though, Shamar couldn't catch a break. His first four bets went the other way. He finally won one bet, but it didn't set the tone, as his luck wavered on and off. Once he was down to a grand in chips, he turned away from the table and ran smack into her.

"You know, you got some nerve," she said, looking Shamar in the eyes.

Shamar looked her up and down. The woman was beautiful. He couldn't tell whether she was Latin or Asian, but his mind finally settled on mixed. The way her hips and ass was filling out her jeans and the pretty peek of her toes in her stilettos made Shamar determined to see the whole package.

"Excuse me." He smirked.

"Oh, now you don't know me? You know what . . ." she huffed, as if she was fed up and began to turn away.

Shamar reached out and took her arm while furiously searching his mental data bank for, if not a name, at least an event or place to connect her with. Was it 40/40? Naw, she wasn't Spanish. The All Star game! Naw . . . he thought.

What were the odds? she thought as she turned back, eyes full of flame and full of tears. "Let go of me, DeAngelo!"

She thinks I'm my brother! His mind lit up. Now he understood why he didn't know her. But she was too sexy not to get to know, so he replied, "My bad, for real. Will you forgive me and at least hear me out?"

She stopped and folded her arms, looking at him, her expression saying, "I'm waiting . . ."

"Shit just be real hectic, yo. One of my best friends tried to kill herself—it's been crazy."

"For months, DeAngelo? When you left, you said it would be a couple of days! I was ready to move to New York for you," she shot back, a tear tracing her cheek.

Damn, brah, you musta put it down, Shamar mused, not knowing how real the situation was.

He pulled her close and gave her a hug. After a moment, she hesitatingly gave in and hugged him back. Once he broke the hug, he said, "I'm sorry, okay? I live a crazy life, but that's no excuse to treat you like that. I lost my phone, so I had no way to call you," Shamar lied, not knowing it was really the truth. "But here . . . put your number in my phone and I'll never lose it again."

She searched his eyes for a moment, then took the phone and put in her name and number.

Marissa, he thought with a smile, happy that his play to find out her name worked. "So what's up? I'm losin' . . . but now that we back together, I feel like my luck's turning around." He grinned.

She giggled subtly. "Oh yeah? So you think you're going to get lucky?"

"Shit, finding you again, I already am," he charmed.

She smiled with a blush.

"My room's upstairs," he suggested.

"No."

"No?"

Marissa smirked. "I want you in my bed."

"Then why we still standin' here?"

GAME OF GWOP

CHAPTER 39
- That's My Brother -

As soon as they got to Marissa's room at the Monte Carlo, they were all over each other.

"I missed you so much," she cooed as he picked her up and carried her over to the bed.

He laid her down and pulled her out of her jeans, while she squirmed on the bed. He could tell she worked out because her legs were shapely and toned.

Marissa looped her thumbs inside her purple panties and slid them down to her ankles. Shamar pulled them the rest of the way off, kissing along her ankle.

"Don't taste me, Finesse. You know what I want," she whispered lustfully while playing with her clit.

She didn't have to tell Shamar twice. He dropped his pants around his ankles and his dick sprang out like a tiger being released from its cage. He spread her legs, cocking them back and using her thighs to drop her back and position her at the edge of the bed. Her pussy lips sat out, fat and juicy, just waiting to be filled and fucked.

Shamar grabbed his dick and pushed deep inside her tight wetness.

"Ohhhh!" Marissa cried out, arching her whole body as his dick went deeper and deeper. "Fu-fuck me good, baby! Oh, I missed you!"

To Shamar, Marissa had the wettest pussy he had ever felt. The first few strokes had him ready to bust, but he clenched his teeth and concentrated on long-dicking her hard.

"You like that, huh? You like it?" he gritted.

"Ohh, yes! Yes! I love it! Don't stop, Finesse. Oh, I love you!"

He watched every expression his dick was causing her. The sexy contortions, the lip-biting moans, the mouth agape, the fuck-me face. He cocked her legs back and began licking and sucking her pretty toes while he beat her pussy relentlessly. When he saw the tears roll down her face, he knew he was doing his job.

"Oh Fi–Fi—" she gasped, her body twerking. "I'm about to—"

And she did, all over his dick, thick and creamy. Shamar couldn't hold it anymore and released his load, deep in her pussy.

"Oh baby!" she cried out. Feeling his hot cum made her cum again.

Shamar lay down beside her, catching his breath. Marissa rolled over onto him. She looked into his eyes, while fingering his lips.

"Thanks."

"Believe me, it's more where that came from," he replied.

She smiled, but it didn't reach her reddened eyes.

"What's wrong, ma?"

"Why'd you have to lie to me?" she asked, shaking her head. "All you had to do was to tell me the truth. I would've still helped you."

He caressed her cheek. "Marissa, I swear I didn't lie. Shit just got hectic. But I'm here now, right?"

Again, she shook her head. "It's too late, Finesse. It's too—" she began to say, but her voice caught in her throat.

The scar . . .

She looked at the side of his neck. There was no scar—the long, thin scar along the side of his neck, the one that, as a nurse she surmised must have taken eight stitches.

"I got it when I was in the youth house when I was fourteen," Finesse had told her.

Her mind seized up. Something was wrong. She frantically pulled up his shirt. There were no stab wounds, no 'Finesse' tattooed across his stomach. Her mind flipped.

She jumped away from Shamar and stood on the other side of the bed.

"Wh–who are you?" she questioned, breathlessly.

Shamar sat up. "Ma, relax, okay?"

"Who are you!"

"I'm Sha, Finesse's twin brother."

Marissa covered her mouth, shocked. She felt she had made a mistake when she first spotted Shamar. It was like the eyes of a woman scorned. She had come to see her cousin Sophia, the boxer, fight. Jorge and his entourage had come too. But she saw Shamar, and her blackened, charred heart seized the opportunity to see him hurt like he had hurt her.

"You've got some nerve," she had said to him, her heart full of malice. She had loved Finesse hard. He had left her cold. Now she hated him just as hard as she had loved him. But looking into his eyes, being close to him again, the love that she kept hidden—even from herself—refused to be ignored. She had to have him one more time. But she would have her revenge.

As they had ridden in the cab to her hotel, she texted Jorge: He's here. I'm taking him to my room.

"Your boyfriend, huh? Tell him you'll be home real late." Shamar chuckled.

"Something like that."

Once he was inside of her, something felt . . . different, but she was too caught up in her own lust to pay attention. She wanted Finesse too badly, so she looked on whom she thought was him. That is why the tears ran down her face; she knew this would be the last time. She just knew it was him, until she didn't see the scar. Now her fear and guilt had all but extinguished her rage and scorn.

"You have to get out of here!" Marissa yelled.

Shamar thought she was spazzing because she had fucked the wrong dude. "Yo, ma, don't flip out on me. You a sexy muh–"

"No! No! You don't understand. You have to go quickly! Now!"

Shamar pulled up his pants. "Cool, yo, I'm gone."

When he opened the door, his whole face exploded with pain, and all he could see was stars as he hit the floor. When he looked up, he saw four Spanish dudes leering down on him.

"What up, homes? Remember me?" Jorge screwfaced him with a wicked grin.

"No, Jorge, no! That's not him. That's not Finesse."

Shamar kicked out, kicked the closest dude in the stomach, and tried to scramble to his feet. As soon as he got halfway up, the biggest dude upper cut him then rammed his head into the wall, face first. He left a large blot of blood on the wall, as he slumped back down to the floor.

"Please, Jorge! I made a mistake! It's not him," she sobbed. "It's his brother!"

Jorge gently pushed her away. "Marissa, go now. If it ain't him, he'll get the message," Jorge sneered.

"Jorge!"

"Go!" he barked.

She knew she had better listen. She looked down at Shamar's crumpled body and hurried back into the room. One of Jorge's goons closed the door.

Jorge squatted beside Shamar and rolled him over, so he could look into his face.

"I'm only gonna ask you once. Where is your brother?"

Shamar mustered every ounce of strength that he had left to hawk and spit a wad of blood and mucus into Jorge's face. Jorge fell back as his goons administered a massive beat down to Shamar.

Jorge wiped his face and stood up.

"If you would've gave him up, I would've killed you anyway for being a fuckin' puta!" Jorge snickered. "Now, what I have for him, I'll give to you. You ever seen Training Day, homes? Take him in the bathroom. He tried to resist, but he had been beaten too badly to put up a fight. When they got him in the bathroom, they dumped him in the tub.

"So the blood don't get everywhere." Jorge chuckled, then he gave his men the nod.

Out the corner of his eye, Shamar saw the gleam of the straight razor, and he knew that it was over. The only comforting thought he had was that at least Finesse would live. He would die for his brother. Shamar felt a hand grab him around the forehead, and then a stinging, cool sensation came across his throat. In seconds, he was choking on his own blood. It was spewing out of him rapidly, his life energy seeping out of him with it. It didn't hurt like he always thought death would. In fact, he felt nothing at all . . . nothing.

He was simply conscious of becoming sleepier . . . and sleepier and . . .

"What you wanna do with the body?" one of the goons asked Jorge.

"Clean up and throw him off the balcony," Jorge replied as he walked out, checking his watch, hoping he could catch Sophia's fight.

∞

"Oh my God, baby! Look! We won! We won!" Vanessa exclaimed as they walked away from the table.

GQ couldn't believe she had done well. After cruising the tables, she finally found a hot table. Vanessa sat down with her drink and played a few black jack hands. She wasn't concentrating on winning or losing. Her concern was on the cards coming out of the card shoe. At first, she thought it would be hard to keep count, but she took to it like a pro. When the count hit +5, she began to get excited, but held her composure. When it hit +7, she was so anxious that her pussy got wet. When it hit +8, she signaled GQ just as he had told her. Vanessa sipped her drink with her left hand instead of her right. GQ moved in and took over from there. Before the hour was up, they walked away with close to twenty grand.

"We won! Let's do it again!" Vanessa squealed.

"Naw ma, fall back. It's time to hit another casino," GQ replied.

The next spot they hit was the same hotel where Marissa was staying. Police were everywhere. A big crowd gathered, all gawking at the body that had hit the pavement and splattered.

"He must've jumped!"

"Probably lost all his money!"

"What a shame!"

The crowd collectively ranted.

Out of curiosity, GQ moved to the edge of the crowd. He was about to keep moving when something caught his eye—the original Timberland boots on the feet of the body.

His eyes searched the rest of the body. As he took in detail after detail, a sense of dread and foreboding was building within. Everything on the body matched the clothes Shamar was wearing when he last saw him. GQ didn't know what he was looking at—his mind went blurry.

Sha . . .

Before he realized it, he had ducked under the yellow police tape.

"Hey you!" an officer yelled, but GQ was oblivious.

He ran up to the body, mangled and broken. The face beaten and swollen, but it was clear, unmistakable, and unacceptable to his senses.

The police officer grabbed his arm. "Sir, you must step back behind the tape."

"That's my brother, yo, my brother!" GQ screamed at the cop. His eyes watered with the closest thing to tears that he had felt in years.

"I understand, but you must step back!" the officer repeated.

Another officer came to assist the first.

GQ tried to break loose from them both. "That's my brother! That's my fuckin' brother!" he continued to scream like a mantra, and no one in the crowd would ever forget those words.

Fade . . . to . . . black

CHAPTER 40
- New York State of Mind -

The Starbucks' latte seemed to tumble from her hand in slow motion. Charisma had just gotten into Wilmington and decided to stop at Starbucks because she was becoming a latte junkie. She had come back to the city for one thing.

To talk to Don Pooh.

She knew that despite the crew's promises, Don Pooh was living on borrowed time, unless he paid them back. So she came to lay it on the line to him.

Charisma stepped to the counter and placed her order. "Can I have a small green tea, with two sugars please?" she requested.

"That'll be $2.18," the barista replied.

Before she could extend her hand that held her bill, a hand, a very masculine hand, smoothly reached over her and handed the barista a crisp, new fifty dollar bill.

"Make that two," said a deep, rich baritone voice from behind her.

The timbre of his voice titillated her senses and made her turn in his direction. She looked directly into an inviting, Colgate smile, and further down at the conservative but dapper suit. It was a nice understatement, one that Charisma appreciated.

297

"Thank you," she remarked.

"You're welcome, Miss Lady. Or would you rather I call you Beautiful?" he charmed.

Charisma smiled.

"No, Charis—I mean—Aisha will be fine."

They shook hands.

"I'm Gavin and it's very nice to meet you."

"Same here," she replied, making no attempt to hide the fact that she was checking him out as much as he was checking her out.

The barista handed them their orders.

"Do you have to be some place or do you have time for a chat?" Gavin asked.

Reluctantly, Charisma replied, "No, I'm sorry. I really need to take care of something, so I'm kinda in a New York state of mind right now."

He chuckled.

"Midtown or Uptown?"

"Just a figure of speech," Charisma answered, adding, "but if you'll give me your number, I'll let you know when we can have that chat."

"Hold up. I thought I was kickin' it to you?" He smirked.

Charisma smiled flirtatiously. "I'm aggressive, too."

They both laughed.

"555-8311."

She put it in her phone.

"Can I have yours?"

"I gotta check you out first." She winked.

"Well, I'll be looking forward to your call."

She nodded, started to walk away, then stopped.

"Anybody ever tell you, you look like Denzel Washington?"

"I get that a lot." Gavin smiled.

"I bet you do . . . Bye, Gavin."

"Bye, Aisha."

Charisma walked to the car and couldn't stop smiling. It wasn't just his looks, but he had an energy that she easily connected with. It was like a breath of fresh air.

As she opened her car door, her phone rang. She looked at the caller ID.

Crook.

"What up, big head?" she answered, and was greeted with something that she had never heard before.

The sound of Crook crying.

"Crook?" she called out more urgently.

He was almost incoherent. "Why I ain't tell him, man? I shoulda—I can't believe it," he sobbed.

A feeling of dread formed in her stomach because she knew it was bad. "Crook, what are you talking about!"

"Sha, yo, Sha! I'm talkin'—"

"Sha, what? What's wrong with Sha?"

"He's dead, Charisma. He's fuckin' . . . dead."

Everything seemed to go silent except the sound of her own heartbeat pulsating in her ears. She felt sick, like she wanted to vomit a scream. The green tea seemed to tumble from her hand in slow motion.

CHAPTER 41
- Coco Chanel -

It was a small funeral. Shamar and Finesse's mother had died of AIDS when they were teenagers, and their father had been dead to them for almost as long. They buried him in Las Vegas because no one wanted to put their name on the paperwork needed to ship his body, and even if they could, there was really nowhere to ship him. They couldn't go back to Jersey, and Wilmington was quickly becoming a memory for everyone except Crook (and soon, Charisma). It was a hustler's life that culminated in a hustler's death. They even buried him under an alias: Shallah Masters.

Besides the team, the only people who came were Crystal, Vanessa, Crook's young goons, Quiz and Bleek, and Chanel. For Finesse, he hadn't only come to attend the funeral—he came to be the cause of one. Even behind the shades, he couldn't hide his pain. Shamar was more than just a brother. He was his other half. The three years that he was incarcerated was the only time they had been apart. The night Shamar was killed, Finesse had a dream he would never forget.

During the dream he was flying, but he felt like he was drowning. He couldn't breathe or talk, but he was zooming through the air, until he realized . . . He wasn't flying—he was falling, faster and faster, until he crashed into the ground.

Finesse jumped up out of his sleep, startling the woman sleeping next to him.

"Baby, you okay?" she had asked, still half asleep.

"Yeah," he mumbled, lying back down.

The dream had him fucked up because he had always thought that if you hit the ground in your dream, you died for real. When he got the call from GQ, he knew exactly what the dream meant.

As he stood there watching them lower a part of him into the ground, the worst thing he felt was the lack of closure—not knowing who, not knowing why. They had murdered so many, robbed so many, and terrorized in so many different places, he didn't know who had finally caught up with them. Las Vegas was a place where you could run into anybody, so Finesse had no idea where to begin to look.

"Baby, I'm here," Charisma said, bringing him out of his zone.

He looked at her, then gave her a big hug.

"I know, mama, I know."

"No . . . I mean . . . I'm here," she repeated, looking him in the eyes.

Now he truly understood. The old Charisma was looking at him, the one that could be as cold as a soldier.

Finesse nodded and felt someone walk up on his other side. When he looked, he saw that it was Chanel.

"May I speak to you alone for a moment?" she asked, looking at Charisma.

Charisma kissed him on the cheek and walked away. When she was out of earshot, Chanel said, "I'm sorry for your loss."

"Yeah, me too," he replied dejectedly.

"I know who did it," she remarked, watching the casket disappear into the ground.

Finesse looked at her with eyes of stone.

"How?"

"That's not important. What is important is that I know, and so do you, DeAngelo," she replied, looking at him for the first time.

He knew there was no way Crook would have told her his real name, so her knowing hadn't been easy to come by. Before he could question her further, she explained. "It was the Guatemalans, your Guatemalans. They felt that you had forgotten them, so they wanted to remind you. So they did . . . this," she concluded, nodding toward the burial site.

Finesse couldn't believe what he was hearing, let alone who he was hearing it from. He had looked at Chanel as just another pretty face. Crook's girlfriend. He saw what she wanted him to see—now he would see the truth.

He grabbed her by the arm and turned her body to him.

"How the fuck do you know that?" he seethed, grilling her hard.

"If I were the enemy, would I have told you all this? Now, let go of me before we cause a scene," she warned.

The tone she said it in didn't scare Finesse, but something told him he would definitely have his hands full, so he let her go. Besides, his mind was on the

Guatemalans. His guilt would ravish him later. For the time being, his anger had him boiling.

"I still want an answer to my question," he demanded.

A subtle smirk played across her lips. "I know more than you think and I'm closer than you know. We met because of . . . let's just say . . . adverse circumstances, but since then I've changed my mind, an eventuality that a woman is entitled to," she stated. "Now, I'm here to help."

"Help me?" he echoed, looking her up and down. "What makes you think you can help me?"

"What makes you think I can't?" she shot back smoothly.

Finesse looked at Chanel. Then he knew she definitely wasn't just another pretty face.

"Yo, ma, who are you?"

She smiled slightly, looked him in the eyes, and replied, "I'm Coco Chanel."

GAME OF GWOP
Reading Group Discussion Questions

1. Did Game of Gwop capture your attention immediately, or gradually? Please explain.

2. Who was your favorite character? Least favorite? Please explain their qualities and motivations.

3. Was Crook justified by his actions concerning Black?

4. Did any of the characters remind you of someone you know? Please explain.

5. Finesse had the choice to sue the government for millions while remaining in prison and fighting for an appeal or he could be released from prison immediately if he signed an agreement not to sue. Would you have chosen the money or your freedom? Explain.

6. Which chapter(s) resonated strongly with you? Why?

7. Should Charisma and her crew have gone to Delaware? Did it make things better or worse?

8. What surprised you most about the book?

9. What are your thoughts about the character Coco Chanel? Does she seem capable of loving Crook? Why or why not?

10. If Game of Gwop were made into a movie, who would make up your cast?

11.   If you could give a well-deserved beat down to any character, who would it be and why?

12.   Did you enjoy the ending? Why or why not? If you could change it, how would you rewrite it?

13.   Should Charisma have given Finesse a second chance? Why or why not?

14.   Would you have made the same choice as Marissa regarding Finesse and her brother Jorge?

15.   What do you think will happen next to the main characters?

WAHIDA CLARK PRESENTS PUBLISHING
#TEAM WCP

CPSIA information can be obtained at www.ICGtesting.com
Printed in the USA
BVOW06s1335221015

423475BV00010B/182/P